THE BOOK OF MARY

D1602777

THE BOOK OF Mary

by

Gail Sidonie Sobat

SUMACH PRESS

Library and Archives Canada Cataloguing in Publication

Sobat, Gail Sidonie, date
The book of Mary : a novel / Gail Sidonie Sobat.

ISBN-13: 978-1-894549-54-7
ISBN-10: 1-894549-54-6

I. Title.

PS8587.O23B66 2006 C813'.6 C2006-900350-5

Copyright © 2006 Gail Sidonie Sobat

Edited by Charis Wahl
Copy-edited by Jennifer Day
Designed by Liz Martin
Cover art by Laurie Lafrance

Sumach Press acknowledges the support of the Canada Council for the Arts and the Ontario Arts Council for our publishing program. We acknowledge the financial support of the Government of Canada through the Book Publishing Industry Development Program (BPIDP) for our publishing activities.

ONTARIO ARTS COUNCIL
CONSEIL DES ARTS DE L'ONTARIO

Printed and bound in Canada

Published by

SUMACH PRESS
1415 Bathurst Street #202
Toronto ON Canada M5R 3H8

sumachpress@on.aibn.com

www.sumachpress.com

For Carolyn Pogue

ACKNOWLEDGEMENTS

There are so many to thank for their part in this novel:

To the women who help to make the house of Gail well. For their examples, and for their inspirational and spiritual guidance: Carolyn Pogue, Karen Hamdon, Patti Hartnagel, Joanne Reinbold, Shirley Serviss, Criselda Mierau, and my mother, Jeannie Sobat. To Rebecca Luce-Kapler who urged me on to the path forbidden. For their guidance, expertise and advice: Cheryl Dyck, Rivvy Meloff, Suzanne Davis, Patricia Clements. To the late Joanne Kellock for believing in this novel and in the character of Mary. To Loren McMaster for her great story. To my careful and patient editors, Charis Wahl and Jennifer Day. To my dear friends who read or listened, cajoled and urged me onwards: Carol McDonald, Christine Wiesenthal, Kelly Thomas, Kelly Spilchak. To the Women in Black for showing me that sorority can be a lived, not just a fictional experience.

To Duane Stewart, beloved mentor and friend. To kind readers and dear friends Mark Haroun, Vern Thiessen, Wally Diefenthaler. To the Very Reverend Bill Phipps for guidance and encouragement and for allowing an unbeliever into the manse. To Geoff McMaster who believes in Mary and in me.

Part One

Magnificat

August 1

I got these scrolls for my birthday from Mama, so I spose I should use them. Nothing ever happens in my life, so I don't know what I'm sposed to write in here anyways. My life is the same day in and day out. I help my mother in the market. She's a spiceseller. My father, Joachim the merchant, gets to do all the important stuff. Bartering with the growers, travelling, drinking with the dealers. My mother, Anna, works all day in the square. Roosts over the house in the evening. I follow her around taking orders. Doing her bidding.

The only relief I get is when I hang around the temple doors waiting for the boys after shul. Oh, and I get to dance. My sister Deborah and me take lessons. From Judith who teaches all the nice young Jewish girls to dance.

There is another kind of dancing I do. Not for nice young Jewish girls. At Jezebel's. On weekends, if I can slip out. Jez taught me and my best friend, Adi. I'd never tell my mother. She'd kill me. So would my father. Literally.

So I'm crafty. And careful. Always. You have to be to survive in this world.

I live in Nazareth. Nothing ever happens here. Nothing good ever came out of Nazareth. And I don't have a boyfriend even. Everybody has a boyfriend except me. Even Martha. And she has a droopy left eye.

But I do have a father casting his shrewd eye around for a husband for me. Please. I'm fourteen. But as my mother loves to remind me, she was already long married at my age. So far, thank Elohim, no one is good enough for his daughter Mary.

I'd just like a boyfriend. A handsome one of my own choosing.

As if. As if I ever get a say in anything.

Oh, and rich would be nice.

Shit, I sound like a bad song. That familiar one everyone's always singing.

My looks are alright, I guess. I like my hair the best. It's black. Blue-black. It falls to the middle of my back when my mother lets me wear it down, which is never. She says I'm vain. My eyes are almond shaped and hazel. I like them. My lips are full. I don't have a lot of colour in my cheeks, though. Guess you can't have everything. My body's nice enough. Not too skinny. Wish my legs were longer, but my breasts are pretty big. And they might even get bigger, who knows. After all, I'm only fourteen-going-on-fifteen. My birthday's in May. I'm a Gemini.

I've gotta go now. It's my turn to haul water from the well. Lucky lucky me.

August 9

I haven't written for a week because my life is so booorrrring. I can't stand that Martha. She's throwing it in all our faces that she has a boyfriend. Ebediah is ugly anyways. I don't know why she's bragging, really.

Adi and I think she's so stuck up. She used to be our friend. I mean, we'd let her tag along with us and everything. But then she met Ebe and now all they do is snog every chance they get. It makes me and Adi sick.

We went to a party at Jez's last weekend, but it was a drag. Though the boys were kind of cute. I like Jeremiah, but he doesn't know I exist. I put on my sexiest scent too. My father brought it back from his last trip east. But it was lost on Jeremiah. He didn't even look at me, never mind ask me to dance for him.

To make matters worse, Adi got drunk and started crying about how her father is going to marry her off to some old geezer who's been sniffing around their door looking for a bride. I said, "Adi, you've got seven sisters. He'll pick one of them. Relax."

But the wine had gone to her head and she was a snivelling mess. So I took her home. Another wonderful night.

Since then not much has happened. We're going to hang around the doors after shul and see what we can see. Until then, I've got about a zillion chores. We've got a pregnant goat due anytime. She's always getting knocked up by the neighbour's billy. Ha ha! This is her third time.

Sabbath evening, August 12

Well, well. Shul was actually interesting tonight. The boys were hot! Adi met some guy named Aaron and I talked to Jeremiah briefly. He actually responded. When I said I'll see you at the party at Jez's, he actually looked right at me and said, "yeah." I even told him my name again for about the third time. My mother would kill me, but I don't care. I need to be resourceful if I don't want to get married off to some old fart.

But that's not the best part! The best part is that he got talking with some buddies a few feet away, still within earshot, when this old nerdy-looking guy, Joseph, stopped to talk to me. He's a neighbour of ours, and I've known him all my life. I pretended to be real interested in everything Joseph said. He told me he was planning to visit some relative in Bethlehem. King David's sposed to be some great-great-ancestor of his. Like I care. Anyways, I chatted him up quite a bit. I mean I flirted with him. Loud enough to catch you-know-who's attention. Asked Joseph about Jez's party like I'd asked Jeremiah. Then Jeremiah did a double take. I could see it out of the corner of my eye. I knew he'd heard. When I walked away from Joseph, I could feel Jeremiah's eyes all over me. I was all hot. Hurray! I can't wait for tomorrow night!

August 14

Last night was too perfect! Everything worked. I wore my white shift, which looks great with my tan, makes my skin even darker than usual, and I put my scent on *all* the right places. I slipped out the window and tore off to Jez's. Adi was already there. She beats me every time. It's easier for her. Her parents are heavy sleepers.

The music was great and the incense inviting. Jez throws the best parties, even if she is looking for girls for the trade. Well, it is part of her business. But she sure knows how to mix business with pleasure and I'm just grateful to even be invited to her place. And to dance there.

Anyways, Adi met up with that Aaron guy, and I hung around drinking wine and waiting for Jeremiah. The only damper on my evening was that annoying gnat, Joseph. Finally, I sent him for another cup and while he was gone, in walks Jeremiah.

God is he beautiful! He has curly dark brown hair and grey-green eyes. They see right through you in an unnerving way — when he finally looks at you. His camel-coloured shirt was open at the neck to show his chest and tufts of curly hair. What a body. He's about six feet tall and broad-shouldered. I can't believe how much I like him.

Joseph buzzed back and whined something in my ear, but I shooed him away as soon as Jeremiah noticed me. Which was almost right away! I couldn't believe my luck. After all these months.

He got himself a drink and sauntered over. I tried to act casual. He was very close when he spoke.

"What's your name again?"

"Mary."

"Oh yeah, right."

"We were introduced in the summer."

"Oh yeah?"

"And I told you again yesterday."

"Right."

"And once before at another party."

"Really?"

"I guess you don't remember."

"Not really."

"Did you come with friends?"

"Yeah."

"Oh."

It went pretty much like that for a while. Then the music changed tempo.

"Uh, Sarah?"

"Mary."

"Oh yeah, Mary. You dance?"

"Well, not just for anyone …"

"How about for me?"

Like only a thousand thousand times in my dreams. "Uh huh. But I'm just a *dancer*, see?"

He nodded.

"And I have to change into my costume. Come upstairs in five minutes."

I went to the little storage room where Adi and I stash our dancing skirts and veils. There's no way I could ever hide them at home, so Jez lets us keep them at her establishment. Which is the only place we would ever dance like that anyways.

The room for dancing — and negotiations with Jez for her various girls — is strewn with pillows. Certain select customers are invited upstairs for a private audience. Lights are low. Three musicians play tabula, oud and ney on the corner stage. No one does much chatting, if you know what I mean. Down the hall are the *rooms*. Adi and I have only ever danced for Jez, who knows we're nice Jewish girls who would never venture down that hall. I mean, you have to be pretty desperate to turn whore.

So this was my first time dancing for a man. I was pretty nervous.

When I appeared at the beaded doorway in my many colours bedecked with jingling coins, Jez raised an eyebrow of surprise. She signalled the musicians. I took my cue.

And writhed into the room. Losing myself in the music. I know how to move. To follow the drum. I raised my arms above my head, twisting my wrists, my fingers beckoning, inviting. I found Jeremiah's eyes. And I showed him exactly what I know.

How my hips are meant for gyrating. My stomach for undulating. I flashed him dark eyes as I moved away from his reaching hand. A flick of my thick hair. A roll of my shoulders. I bent forwards to show him the tops of my breasts, melon ripe and rosy in the flickering candlelight. He watched the floating of scarves about my body, their fluttering in purple and scarlet deliberately, tantalizingly across my curves. Heard the seductive tinkle of my coins, my anklet. Caught a flash of my leg. Sway of my head. Shake of my shoulders.

Jeremiah was mesmerized.

The tabula reached a crescendo. I turned my back to him and shimmied the length of my body. Bent backwards and looked into his perspiring face.

As I had so often practised, I dropped just as the music stopped. A collapse of silk. I could feel the pulse at my neck. I stood to acknowledge the applause. And though there were several men in the room, there was only one. Jeremiah. My breasts were heaving from the exertion of my performance. I felt a surge of power.

I have never felt so sure, so certain of myself. It was intoxicating.

As Jeremiah was intoxicated. I came over to him. "That was … you are … beautiful."

"Thanks."

He looked at me with those eyes, and he must've been able to read my expression. It was getting hard to breathe. So I darted off to change back into my white shift.

I saw Jez saunter over to talk with him.

When I returned, Jeremiah led me outdoors behind the building. We looked at the stars for a bit and then he took my face in his hands and kissed me. Okay, it wasn't my first kiss. But it was my first kiss from a *man*. He kissed me gently at first, just brushing my lips and then harder and then he slipped the tip of his tongue in my mouth. I couldn't believe it!

I pulled away, and he kind of grinned at me. He leaned into my neck, put his lips to my ear. "You smell so good, Mary. Too good."

All kinds of sensations danced up and down my body. I whispered back. "You too, Jeremiah."

I kissed him then. I was getting the hang of it. And he was pressing me against the wall and kissing me deeply and then he put his hand on my breast and I thought I'd die right then and there. We stopped suddenly because someone was coming down the street.

Jeremiah and I went back inside and sat very close together in the downstairs lounge. He got me a drink. Whenever he looked into my eyes I got wet between my legs.

At the end of the evening, well actually, it was almost morning, I told him I had to get going. He walked me part way home. He kissed me again and this time rubbed his hands along my body. All you could hear was the sound of us both breathing hard. I had trouble getting to sleep thinking about him and wanting him in my bed.

I'm going to have to burn this scroll.

I am dead meat if my mother finds this.

Or worse yet, my father.

They would call me the whore of Nazareth.

I don't care.

I'm in love.

August 20

Not much to write today. Just waiting for sundown to end the Sabbath. I realized I don't even know where Jeremiah works or who his family is. I'm going to have to do some digging, aren't I? If I want to be the future Mrs. Jeremiah.

Today a woman was stoned to death in the market square. Adultery.

August 21

What a wonderful night!

I just got in. It's dawn. I'll never sleep again. And I'll never wash my body. I'll never wash him from my body. I can smell his scent on my skin, on my hair. I feel beautiful.

He loves me.

He said so.

I got to Jez's just after my parents went to bed. Adi was upstairs dancing for Aaron. Joseph was standing near the entranceway, but I ignored him and went straight over to Jeremiah. He was in fine spirits, waiting for me, he said. At least I think that's what he said; the music was loud.

Jeremiah bought me wine all night. I drank it slowly, though. That's all I'd need is to puke in front of the guy of my dreams. So when he wasn't looking, or when he went to take a piss, which he does a lot for a guy, I poured half of my wine into the nearest decorative palm plant. When Jeremiah told me I could sure hold my liquor, I just smiled.

Anyways, I was just standing around, waiting for him to get back, when Joseph slithered over.

"Hi Mary."

"Oh, hi."

"You look lovely tonight."

"Thanks." I added quickly. "I'm waiting for my *boyfriend*, Jeremiah."

"Your boyfriend?"

"That's right."

"Jeremiah?"

"Yeah." God, is Joseph daft. He stood there, looking at me funny, with a stupid sad little smile.

"Do you know Jeremiah very well, Mary?"

"That's none of your business and for your information, I do!"

"I meant no offense. It's just … well, Jeremiah has a bit of a reputation. He's a …"

"I'm a what?" Jeremiah sounded none-too-friendly. "Buzz off, pal." And Joseph scurried away. But I could tell he was watching me all night. What a sorry schlump.

"Who's that?"

"Joseph. A neighbour. I have to be nice to him or he'll tell my parents …" I almost died. Here I was talking like I was some ditzy girl! But Jeremiah didn't seem to have heard.

"Well, he better beat it. You're my girl, now." He pulled me to him and he felt warm and hard.

I could barely breathe. My heart was beating like crazy.

Still, Joseph's words had aroused my curiosity. So I asked Jeremiah what he did for a living.

"Oh, a bit of this, a bit of that."

"I don't know your parents."

"Amos and Rebecca of Capernaum."

"How old are you, Jeremiah?"

"Twenty-one. Enough questions. Let's go somewhere."

He led me outside, wondering how a twenty-one-year-old gorgeous man could still be single, and gulping to think what would happen if my mother knew I was out with an older guy. Or out with any guy period.

Behind Jez's we started kissing again. God, is he hot. Such a sexy kisser. I felt myself melting when his tongue entered my mouth. I felt his hand on my breast and his lips on my neck and I was kissing him back and then his fingers were pressing my shift between my legs and I kind of gasped.

"You're beautiful." His voice was throaty and sexy.

"You are." My voice didn't sound like mine either.

"I know a place."

"Oh."

We walked for what seemed like miles. Every chance he got, Jeremiah pulled me into the shadows and kissed and felt me. I was learning what to do to him. I moved my hands over his broad shoulders and his chest and then ran my hands over his bum. It felt tensed and firm. Then I gingerly touched him between his legs. He felt hard and urgent. Jeremiah groaned.

"Come on!"

We ran to a stable on the edge of the neighbourhood. Jeremiah pushed open the door, found a lantern and lit it.

"Come here, baby."

Jeremiah pulled me to him and we fell back into the hay. He was kissing me all over and fumbling with my shift. I helped him by slipping my shoulders out. I was naked to my waist. I always thought that when the time came I'd be embarrassed by my body, but I wasn't. I felt beautiful. Then Jeremiah had my breast in his mouth and our hands were all over each other, pulling off his clothes and my clothes, and then we were naked and out of breath. Jeremiah looked into my eyes and stretched on top of me. I opened myself to him like we'd done this a thousand times and somehow he found the opening I've never been able to find and he pushed. He must've seen me flinch.

"How you doin'?"

"Oh."

"Relax baby."

I was all wet and when he thrust inside, I wasn't scared. We kind of sighed together and kept looking into each other's eyes. He started to move and the hurting went away and I couldn't believe how incredible and how big he felt and I was making noises in my throat and he was groaning and it all went faster and he put his mouth on my nipple and then I arched my back and I kind of sobbed and he came and came and I came and came and came. Oh, my God!

Then we were holding onto each other and I said, "Jeremiah, I love you."

And he said, "I love you, too," and he kissed me softly and it was everything I'd dreamed the first time would be. We lay in the straw and explored each other's bodies. He is very good with his hands. I was feeling that pulse between my legs and he was getting big again. Then he was teasing my nipples with his lips and his tongue until they were rosy brown erect and then he slid down my body and down and down and spread my legs and held me open with his fingers and licked me, a little bit at first and then he buried his whole face and seemed to eat me and I came in his mouth.

Then he entered me again and we moved together slowly. He is so passionate and hot.

We made love three times.

Then I heard the cock crow.

I had to scramble to get dressed. He pulled some pieces of straw from my hair and kissed me. We could barely pull ourselves apart. He told me he loved me again and I said I loved him.

"When can I see you again?"

"I don't know. Next weekend."

"Too long. Tomorrow. Where do you live?"

"On Moses and 5th, but you can't come to my house! My parents ..."

"Mary, I've gotta see you." He reached inside my shift for my breast. I caught my breath.

"I'll try. Where can I send word?"

"I stay at the Galilean Motel."

"Oh."

"Mary ..."

"I — I work at the market. Come by and I'll see. But I can't promise anything."

I kissed him goodbye and ran all the way home. I just snuck in now and I can hardly breathe. I'm sore and exhausted and delirious and I'm sposed to be up in an hour. I'd better get some sleep if I can. I've found the perfect hiding place for my secret scrolls behind a loose stone of the wall of my bedroom.

I close my eyes and all I can see is Jeremiah.

August 22

I saw Jeremiah for a few minutes this afternoon. He walked past my mother's stall several times. I hope my mother didn't notice the hungry look in his eyes. Or in mine. I snuck away to meet him in the alleyway.

"When, Mary?"

"I'll try for tonight, but I've never slipped out during the week, Jeremiah."

"I'll wait by your corner."

He kissed me hurriedly, pressing his hard self against me. I was dizzy when I got back to the stall. My mother noticed, I'm sure. She had that look. You know the one. The "I know you're up to something" look. Anyways, she got me a glass of water. As if that would cool this fever!

I'm in love.

Did I say that already?

August 29, early August 30

The week has flown by. I met Jeremiah that night and every night this week. We go right to the stable. No stopping. Why wait? There's nothing I want but him anyways. And he wants me.

And there's no man I will dance for but him. Ever.

He tells me he loves me all the time. I tell him back. I've learned what gives him pleasure, what to do with my lips and my tongue. It doesn't take much. And he loves to see me naked and wanting him. Which is pretty easy.

I asked him about meeting my parents. He said someday soon. And would he offer a dowry? He was a little vague about that.

I tried not to press him. But I am nervous. My father was talking to Chava the matchmaker in the market last week.

Jeremiah is going out of town this week, so we stayed together 'til the last minute. It's a good thing he's going. It's my fertile time. I don't know how I'd keep him away from me and I don't know how I'd resist him.

Oh yeah. Our goat had her kid.

September 3

I miss Jeremiah.

September 7

I'm so bored without Jeremiah. I called on Adi, but her and that Aaron guy are … you know. Adi lost her virginity a year ago to a guy she met one night at a Sukkot party. She doesn't even remember his name. But I couldn't do that. So she wasn't really interested when I told her about Jeremiah and me. It was no big deal to her.

"Did it hurt?"

"Yeah. A little at first. And then …"

"Ha! You liked it, didn't you? I told you so. Do you think this lip colour is right for me?"

That was it. The most exciting moment of my life and all she can think about is her makeup. Oh, and Aaron. She goes on and on about *him*.

So I have to keep my thoughts to myself. I don't even have a sister old enough to talk to. Joanna's mouth is the size of the Sea of Galilee. I'm currently not even speaking to Ruth because she wrecked my hairbrush. And Deborah has to be bribed into keeping anything secret.

The only other relative close to my age is my stupid cousin. Not Elizabeth, she's too old and full of herself. Mary. But she is such a goody-two-shoes. And I hate that we share the same name. Why in God's name did our mothers name us both Mary? Don't they know any other stupid names? What about Delilah? Or something exotic, Shakira. Nope. I get stuck, like a million other girls, with *Mary*. If anyone ever reads this it'll be so confusing. Hey! What if someone thinks this diary is written by my cousin? GAWD! Over my dead body is anyone ever going to ever read this!!!

Another stoning in the square today. Adultery, what else?

So how come I've never heard of a man stoned for adultery, no matter what the Torah says? Doesn't happen in my village. Only women and girls. Unmarried girls like me who lose their virginity. Women like Jez, paid for their services. I wonder how many of us there are. Bad girls and women, that is. Probably quite a few. Hiding. Hiding from men and their stupid laws.

I miss Jeremiah.

September 9

I can't believe it! The gall of some people! That rodent Joseph came to talk to my father just before shul today. I don't know what they said, but if he told Papa anything about Jeremiah I will slit Joseph's throat. I swear I will.

Anyways, they both left for shul together, so I'll have to wait to find out.

I feel sick to my stomach.

I wish Jeremiah would come and take me away from all of this. We'd just steal out of town. Maybe go to his people. I don't care. I just can't stand this waiting. I can't stand that I have no say over my life. I am no better than a slave.

September 17

I barely slept! Still no word from my father about what Joseph said. I threw up. From the anxiety.

I'm going to sneak out to Jez's tonight, see if I can find that worm Joseph.

Mary of Nazareth. Reduced to a creeping spy.

September 17, near midnight

Damn it! I waited for three hours at Jez's. Men kept coming up to me. I sat at the bar by myself like Jez does. They thought I was working.

I'll skin him alive, that Joseph. I'd go over to his house and do it, but I can't. Girls don't call on men neighbours.

Shit, I hate all these stupid rules! If I had my way, I'd grab Jeremiah and fly to Egypt!

September 18

I've cried so many hours my face is swollen.

Joseph came to supper tonight. Mama and I prepared all day as if some great sultan were dining with us.

He and my father took wine together. I tried to hear their words, but my mother kept shooing me from the doorway.

Finally, we all sat together to eat. My brother and sisters were at Bubeh's for supper, so I should have seen it coming. Papa cleared his throat importantly.

"Joseph wants you for his wife, Mary. He has offered three cows and three sheep, five of his finest hens and a cock. He is a good man, a carpenter. Honest men work with their hands. I pronounce you betrothed."

My mother gasped in delight and set about pouring us all wine. I could not touch my food. My father and Joseph carried the conversation. I looked at my hands for the entire supper. Everything was blurry. Finally, supper was over and my parents left us alone briefly after the meal. I drank my wine in one gulp and glared at the locust seated across from me.

"How could you?"

"Mary, I have been alone these many years. Waiting." Joseph's face was red. "For you. To come of age. It's only that … I love you. Perhaps have always loved you."

"You love me. You *love* me! You don't know the meaning of the word.

You know I care for Jeremiah!" I hissed.

"I don't think Jeremiah is right for you. He will hurt you, I think ..."

"As if you have anything to say about Jeremiah! You know nothing, Joseph. About me. About Jeremiah. About anything!"

He looked at me sharply then. His eyes betrayed that he knew about us. Our secrets.

"Yes. I followed the two of you," he seemed to read my thoughts, "and I sensed the danger for you so I had to act ... I will be a kind husband, Mary. A good provider. I will take care of you ..."

"You will take care of me! The way my father has taken care of me tonight! The way men always take care of women."

"And, God willing, you will come to love me ... in time."

I spat, "I could never love you!"

"In time. Perhaps you will."

"I will never love you the way I love Jeremiah. I will never give myself to you."

Joseph paused and looked a little sad. I almost pitied him. But I hardened my heart.

"I am Jeremiah's!"

"So you say. That may be, Mary," he said quietly, "but where is Jeremiah tonight?"

"Out of town. On business."

"I see. You still don't know about him."

"I know what I need to know and that is that he loves me."

"And will he offer to be your husband?"

"I don't ... why, yes, I think he will!"

"I think he will not and cannot, Mary."

"Wh-what do you mean?"

"That is all I will say. Your father and I have an agreement. You will come to your senses. And I will be a good husband, Mary. That is my promise to you." He rose to go. I had a thousand questions to ask him about Jeremiah, but I stopped myself. I didn't want to give him the satisfaction.

He said good night to my parents, who were sickeningly happy. I went to my room and that's where I am now, sick to my stomach and sick in my heart.

Oh Jeremiah, please come soon.

September 19

Still no sign of Jeremiah. I ran to Jez's last night before she opened shop and asked her if she'd seen him and she said no. She was pinning up her hair and so I thought I'd ask her a few more questions about him. After all, she knows her customers.

"Where does he live, Jez?"

"In Capernaum."

"Yeah, that's what he told me. Do you know about his business? Or when he'll be back?"

"He's in sales, and no honey, sorry I don't."

"Thanks Jez."

"You got it bad, don't ya, kiddo?"

"I guess I have."

"I'll keep a lookout for him. Letcha know."

I've got my eye out, too. I even dared to go to the Galilean Motel. Dressed myself in veils. The manager said he'd checked out with no forwarding address. Said he often stayed there, so he'll likely be back. Likely??

I know Jeremiah will come back for me.

In the meantime, I'm thinking asp's poison is too good for that Joseph.

September 23

No Jeremiah.

Joseph the nebish brought over the first of the dowry. Three cows.

We have no room for them. But my parents are going on and on like there's no tomorrow. They want to set a wedding date.

I tried to talk to Mama.

"Mama, don't you think I'm a little young?"

"What? I was married at eleven and pregnant with Sam at twelve." Trust my mother. "Besides, you've known Joseph all your life."

"He's a lot older than me."

"So? Look at your cousin Elizabeth. She married a man twenty years older. She's happy. He's a rich man."

"Joseph's a carpenter."

"A good carpenter."

"But he's not rich."

"For not a rich man he offered a rich brideprice."

"But I don't love Joseph."

"So who says marriage is about love? You think I loved your father when I married him? No. I learned to love him. That's what marriage is. You should be so lucky to have a nice man like Joseph. Some girls aren't lucky. Look at that poor Adi. Such an unfortunate nose."

It's no use talking to her when she gets like that. She always has my best interests at heart. And now three cows to boot.

I'm getting my cramps. Gawd! Cursed at every turn!

September 24

No Jeremiah.

No curse, yet. Just wretched cramps.

It's Rosh Hashanah.

Joseph is coming for supper.

Maybe I'll vomit all over his chopped liver.

September 25

The date is set: a week after Hanukkah I'll be a blushing bride.

Jeremiah, where are you?

Jez still hasn't seen him.

Adi never comes over anymore; she's always busy with Aaron. She thinks he's going to talk to her parents soon, despite her nose. Can you believe it?

October 3–4

Yom Kippur. No time to write much. I have to atone.

Fasting today, but that's alright. The sight of food turns my stomach.

I hope Jeremiah's doing some atoning!

October 7

Sukkot. I couldn't wait for the evening festivities to be over. *Finally,* after midnight, everyone went to bed and I snuck out.

Adi met me in the street and we flew off to Jez's. Well, well, who should show up at long last? I thought I'd die with longing, but I made myself seem cold. He's been gone two weeks without a word! Every time he came up to me I turned away. I finished my wine and left with Adi. I think he followed me home. Now I'm in my room writing this.

I just heard a noise in the street. It had better be him.

early October 8

It was. I slipped out and we walked towards you-know-where. But I didn't let him touch me, at first.

"What's the matter with you?"

I just kept walking.

"Mary, what's up? Why're you sore at me?"

"As if you don't know."

"I don't know." We'd reached the stable and my back was pressed to the door. He leaned against it very close to my face.

"I'm sorry I was away so long, Mary. It's just business and all. And family obligations. I thought of you every day. Swear to God. I missed you."

It was the longest speech he'd ever made, and I believed him. We slipped inside the stable and into each other. I'm sure they could hear us yowling down the street.

I guess I'll tell him about Joseph tonight.

October 8

Damn that Joseph! He's coming to dinner again! He'll probably bring his bleeping sheep this time. I can't stand his stupid crooked smile and his eyes on me!

And most of all, I can't stand waiting to see Jeremiah. My parents' bedtime is delayed at least an hour when we have dinner guests.

later

I'm so scared. I don't know what to do.

I was an hour and a half late to see Jeremiah because my father and Joseph kept yukking it up after dinner. I almost crawled out of my skin.

I ran to the stable. We devoured each other. Afterwards, I lay back in the straw and stroked his head the way I know he likes.

"I've got something terrible to tell you, Jeremiah."

"Um hum."

"You know my neighbour Joseph who was hanging around, talking to me at Jez's that night? Well, he's approached my parents and asked to marry me."

"What?" Jeremiah sat up.

"And it gets worse. They've agreed!"

"What?"

"We're to be married two weeks after Hanukkah."

"No way!"

I began to cry. "You've got to help me, Jeremiah! You've got to approach my parents and ask them for me and maybe, just maybe, they'll reconsider … if you offer them a larger dowry …"

"I can't."

"Why not? You have to! Or we'll have to steal away, Jeremiah. Please, please take me away from here and from him. I'll die if they make me go through with this. It's you I want for my husband. I can't sleep with him … not after you!"

He looked right at me then. "I don't want him to ever touch you … But I can't …"

"What can't you?"

"I can't marry you."

"Why not? You're Jewish, aren't you? I mean, I saw … and I assumed …"

"Yes. It's not that."

"Then for God's sake, why can't you marry me?"

"I already have a wife."

"What?"

"In Capernaum. We've been married for six years. Since I was fifteen."

"Six years?"

"Yeah."

"Six years! Married! And you've been sleeping with me? Leading me on? What's wrong with you?"

"She — me and her were betrothed, like … like you are now. I never wanted her. I don't want her now."

"You've been using me."

"No, not … maybe at first … but after that first night we did it, when I saw you and how beautiful you are I thought what an awful trick God has played, trapping me with her and giving me you. Now, of all times."

"What is her name?"

"Mary."

I laughed then. "It figures." But this was hardly a time for laughing. "What will I do?"

He didn't answer right away. "Like you said. Come away with me. To another city. We'll set up a home. I'll come whenever I can. I make a good living. I love you."

I didn't know how to reply. I thought of my parents; I'd never see them again. They'd disown a girl like me. I thought of the women stoned in the square. I thought of life with Joseph, without Jeremiah. "I need to think," I said, then kissed him, gathered up my clothes and left.

It was a long walk home.

October 9

I was so distracted today. I'd be churning the butter and then I'd forget what I was sposed to be doing. I even broke one of Mama's best bowls. She screamed at me and I burst into tears. I ran into my room and slammed the door.

But she came in after me. It's one of those mother things. She just has to know everything.

"I already told you what's wrong!"

"What did you tell?"

"I told you! I don't want to marry Joseph!"

"Are you having your period?"

"God no, Mama! How many times do I have to say it?"

She must've listened though because she let me off doing chores that afternoon, which is good because I felt sick to my stomach from all the crying.

"I asked Papa if maybe we could postpone the wedding a little while. Until he gets back from his next trip. How would that be? That way you could get used to the idea and we'd all get to know Joseph better." She positively beamed.

Still, postponing the marriage buys me time, at least six months. It's the first glint of hope I've had. I stopped crying and managed a smile. My mother did the best she could.

Mama always says I'm a clever girl. Half a year is a lot of time to figure out a plan.

I kind of wish I could tell my mother, though. The truth. About Jeremiah.

But I can't. She wouldn't understand.

My mother never talks about sex. My mother's never even had sex.

Eeww. Anna and Joachim doing it. That's a creepy thought.

When I first got my period Mama was all glad and everything, but it was immediately hush hush. A big rush to stop the flow and stop up my mouth.

Of course, soon after, the Marriageable Mary talk began between my parents.

I didn't know that the curse meant I could make a baby until I talked to Adi. And later, Jez was the one who filled me in on the details. Which were pretty scary at the time.

But not anymore. Funny how that changed. With Jeremiah.

With Jeremiah. Is that so much to ask? That I could be with Jeremiah?

Six months, Mary. Start thinking!

October 10

I slept through the whole night. Tired from crying, I guess.

My little brat sister Deborah said some guy was throwing pebbles at the house last night. She almost woke Papa up to chase him away, but when she looked out the window the guy ran off. I grabbed her by the shoulders and made her swear on our great-bubeh's grave *not* to tell Mama and Papa. I promised she could wear my khaki shift this week. She swore she wouldn't tell, but plied me with endless questions. I told her it was probably the rabbi's son who has a crush on me. I think I convinced her. She ran off to help my mother.

I threw up.

I must have the flu or something.

All day — between the cramps and nausea that is — I could only think about Jeremiah and his body next to mine and how he can never *be* mine. Not as a husband anyways. Mama told me to stay home and prepare the meals because I looked pale; little does she know that the smell of food makes me want to hurl. She kissed my forehead and looked so concerned that I wished again I could tell her everything about Jeremiah and me.

But of course, I can't. She'd throw me out into the gutter. If my stupid brother Samuel slept with a girl, she wouldn't think twice about it. She'd think the girl was a slut. That's how it goes. Sam and the boys get all the breaks. I wonder if it's different anywhere else.

Well, I think it's stupid.

All you have to do is read Song of Songs to know that God wants us to celebrate each other. I don't feel dirty when I'm with Jeremiah. I feel beautiful. And I'm not ashamed of anything we do.

Sleeping with someone I don't love, now that would shame me.

If ever I have a daughter, I'll bring her up differently.

I think a lot about these things.

Thoughts like mine can get you killed.

I think I'm going to be sick.

October 11

Last night Jeremiah came to our house and threw pebbles again. I snuck out the window and he caught me up in his arms. We clung to each other. Right there in our street across from Joseph's stupid house. I didn't care who saw. Of course, no one did. It was one in the morning.

We walked hand in hand through the shadows. Inside the stable, I undressed slowly. Then I undressed him. Slowly. I'm getting quite good at this, if I do say so myself.

Jeremiah lay back upon his cloak, watching me as I poured scented oil into my hands to anoint his feet and wipe them with my hair. I massaged what was left of the oil over his body and over my breasts and then I lay beside him. He traced my body with his hands and I opened my legs to his warm lips. I watched him taste me and when I was gasping and could barely control myself, he knelt up before me and spread me wide and pulled me onto him. I felt him enter me and the flutter began in my stomach and spread downwards and I arched up to him. Afterwards, we lay drenched in the straw, stroking each other and drifting in and out of sleep and then I reached for him again. I put him in my mouth, just the tip, and moved him in and out until he was making sounds deep in his throat. I climbed on top of him and rocked and rocked until I gushed all over and around him.

I love to learn about my body through his body.

I don't believe that such knowledge is wicked.

October 12

Joseph Schmoseph brought over his five hens and rooster this afternoon.

My parents almost crapped themselves with gratitude.

If you ask me, they look pretty scraggly.

And guess who's in charge of all the lively livestock???

Joseph beamed, watching me sweep up manure. Finally, the smell got to me and I upchucked. He left in a hurry.

I made love to Jeremiah three times tonight. Each time a miracle.

October 16

Shit. I'm pregnant.

Can't lie to myself anymore. I'm three weeks late.

Shit. I just checked my calendar and my scrolls. I counted wrong all right. And guess when it happened? The first time Jeremiah and I did it.

Shit!

All the nausea. The puking. Who was I kidding? I've got to see Jeremiah tomorrow. I couldn't see him tonight because guess who came to dinner.

Besides, I felt like …

Shit!

October 17

Well, I told him.

"Pregnant? You sure?"

"No, Jeremiah. I'm making it up."

"Shit."

"Great. Now you're going to run off on me. Here's where I get dumped, right?"

"No. It's just …"

"What? For God's sake what?"

"Shit."

"Shit what??"

"I … Mary and me, I mean my wife and me, we've been trying for six years and now …"

"Don't talk to me about her!"

"I mean. I know you for like a month and budda boom, budda bing!"

"Pardon me?"

"You know. You're so hot and all *and* you give me a son."

"A son?"

"Or whatever."

Which pissed me off. Why is it that the only people who count are guys? And by the way, why is it only girls who get auctioned off for some stupid cows and sheep, some wheezy chickens?

"So?"

"Ah, Mary. Don't get mad. I love you and I wanna be with you and take care of you and the baby and all. We'll figure something out. C'mere."

And that pretty much ended the talk. At least now he knows. I don't think he'll bolt.

October 18

This afternoon I got to stay home again because Mama thought I looked peaked. I sat in the backyard upwind of the menagerie and caught some rays.

Joseph stopped by. Even though there was no chaperone. He's got a lot of nerve.

"Hello Mary."

"Hi."

"I just have a minute. And wanted to talk to you."

"Yup."

"I thought you should know that I know."

"Know what?"

"That you're still seeing Jeremiah."

"Piss off."

"Even though you're betrothed to me. And I wanted to ask you to please stop seeing him."

"Are you going to tell my parents?"

"No. I'm asking for your own sake. And mine, too, to be honest."

"You think you have a right to barge into my life. Well, you don't, Joseph!"

He got that sad look again. "You're wrong, Mary. I do have that right. But I'm not trying to control you. I'm not threatening to tell on you. I ask only that you stop seeing Jeremiah. He is … not good for you."

"And you are."

"Well." He smiled and turned to go.

"Why don't you just leave me alone, Joseph?" I was suddenly very weary.

"Because I can't, Mary. I don't know how." He sat down on the bench beside me. I noticed that he didn't come too near. "I have known you since you were a little girl on this street. And I've always liked you — your spirit."

"You watched me. As a little kid. That's just gross, Joseph."

"It's not what you think. I'd look up from my workbench and see you and your sisters at play. You the leader. Always so … sure of yourself."

Joseph paused. I looked at his hands. Rough-hewn like the wood he works.

"Why me? Why not some other woman? Older? Why aren't you already married anyways?"

He shrugged. "God has not seen fit to bring me a wife." And he got all sheepish sounding and pink around the ears again. "Since you became a woman there has been no other woman." Then Joseph rose abruptly and said goodbye. Leaving me exasperated in the afternoon sun.

He's so weird. And old. He must be about forty.

So I got right to the point with Jeremiah tonight. Well, we did it. But only once. Then I got to the point.

"Jeremiah, what are we going to do?"

"I've been thinking about our plan."

"Tell me." I rolled over and put my thigh over his.

"I know a place in a suburb of Capernaum. Far enough from our families. We could make like we're married and live there. Raise the kid. Go to the sea on vacation. You know."

I did know.

"What about your wife?"

"Yeah. Her."

"Well?"

"I'd have to support her."

"How?"

"Well, I have to … you know … take care of her and visit her."

"Visit her?"

"Okay. Stay with her sometimes."

"How often?"

"Shit, I don't know. Sometimes."

"Once a year? Once a month? At Yom Kippur? When?"

"Every two weeks or so. Like I do now."

"And sleep with her?"

"Yeah. I guess."

"What? Did you sleep with her this last time? When you went away?"

"Mary, she's my wife. What was I supposed to do? But I was thinking of you …"

I turned away and wouldn't talk to him for half an hour. I made him work long and hard.

"Goddammit Mary! I'm married to her. If I could change it I would. But I can't. We can't. And we're just gonna have to make the best of it."

"Is she pretty?"

"She's plain."

"You're just saying that."

"No. I mean it. She doesn't compare to … she isn't you." And he kissed me and we were off again.

Afterwards, while he slept in my arms I thought about moving to Capernaum. And about losing my family forever. My sisters Deborah, Joanna and Ruth. My brother Samuel. My father. My bubeh. Zaydeh. My mother. Everything and everyone I've ever known. Even Adi. Even Martha. No aunts. No uncles. No cousins. No one in those times when Jeremiah would be lying like this in his wife's arms.

And then I thought about the baby growing inside me. The miracle from our miracle of lovemaking. A heart beating just under mine. Our child. Beloved. I thought about how good Jeremiah and I are together. I thought about making love to him the rest of my life. About more children. About living a lie.

I thought about living a different lie with Joseph. Kind and patient and old. Joseph the schlemiel.

I looked into Jeremiah's beautiful face and there was my answer.

October 19

It's settled. I'm leaving with Jeremiah in two weeks. He was so excited and made all kinds of promises about how happy we'll be and how much he loves me.

Then we made love, what else?

If this keeps going, I'll have ten kids before I'm twenty.

I hope I like Capernaum.

I feel such relief. My nausea even seems better.

Earlier today I looked at baby clothes in the market with Adi. She doesn't know anything yet, but I still have a few days to tell her. I will miss her, and I will miss not going to her wedding this fall. Oh God, now I'm going to start bawling and everything.

I wish there was another way out.

October 20

Joseph's coming to Sabbath dinner tonight. Hurrah.

Jeremiah's gone to Capernaum so it'll be a dull, dull weekend. I don't go to Jez's anymore. I've got enough trouble. So I guess I'll try to be polite to Joseph.

Maybe afterwards we can go out back and play with the herd my parents inherited on my behalf.

October 21

Boorring!

The nausea's back.

I wonder if my mother suspects anything. Lately I've been catching her looking at me funny. I'm probably imagining things.

October 25

Four days to go. Jeremiah should be back tonight or tomorrow.

October 26

Nope. No Jeremiah.

I've started to pack some things on the sly.

October 27

This is beginning to pick my butt. Where in Sheol is he?

Finished packing. I'll tell Adi tomorrow.

Jeremiah had better be back.

October 28

Oh my God! Adi came over this morning to tell me the awful news! Jeremiah's been arrested!

Aaron works at the jail and saw him being brought in for questioning. I can't go out to ask about him, even on the quiet, until sundown after Havdalah, and I'm going crazy with worry.

I threw up twice.

October 29

Fuck me.

Well, now I know the truth.

After a sleepless night of puke and misery, I snuck out before dawn and ran over to Jez's. She knew everything by now. I guess as a business woman and harlot, it's her job to keep an ear to the ground about these underworld things.

So now I know why Jeremiah was always going to the can at Jez's.

Jeremiah is an opium and hashish dealer.

That's how he makes enough money to support two households.

Fuck him.

It turns out he double-crossed a customer. At least that's what El-Shariz of Acco says anyways. He's very rich and powerful and had him arrested.

Jeremiah's trial begins in a week.

I might as well drink hemlock.

Jez says she thought I knew what kind of salesman Jeremiah is.

Please. I'm fourteen. What do I know?

Here's what I know. I am fourteen-going-on-fifteen with a bun in the oven and a nebish for a fiancé and my parents would sooner have me killed than return their fucking barnyard friends. And the man I love is locked up and maybe he's going to die, and he doesn't deal in perfumes or spices or herbs like any self-respecting merchant, he sells opium and hashish and not only that Jez tells me he uses it and not only that but he knocks me up and not only that but he's already married to another woman whose name for fuck's sake just happens to be Mary.

Ha ha ha. Very, very funny, God. Just what do you have in store for me, Mary, your handmaid?

October 30

Sunday afternoon I managed to sneak back to Jez's. I hate having to wear veils, but I can't get caught hanging out in that part of town. It's bad enough I'm pregnant. You know what they assume about anyone consorting with harlots.

But I like Jez a lot. She's Persian, not Jewish, and she reeks of perfume, but I don't care. Whenever she sees me she smiles that big toothy grin. And she's wise in many ways.

"Heya, M. Weren't you just here this morning? Place doesn't open up until after sundown."

"I know, Jez. Can I talk to you more about some … stuff?"

"Sure honey. You look a little pale though. Can I getcha something? Some water?"

"No thanks."

"Some of the hard stuff?" I must've looked green. She chuckled. "So it's that way with you, is it?"

"Wh-what?"

"Let me see. You're about ten weeks along."

"How could you know that, Jez?"

"It's my trade. Part of my mission, ya see. Fact, I've even incorporated. Secretly, of course. We call ourselves Sisters of the Eastern Star. You know I come from the East. That's where I learned all the tricks of my profession."

"I don't get it. I thought you were a … I mean … "

"A whore. Sure, hon. I am. But that's not all. I help out, see. Women, girls come to me. You think you're the only one's been in trouble? Through the years I've built up some contacts. I figure the Sisterhood's saved the lives of hundreds. Hell, who knows? Maybe thousands."

She lit up one of those obnoxious cigarettes. I kind of gagged, so she laughed and put it out. "Sorry. So what for you can I do?"

"I don't know …"

"Jeremiah's the father?"

I nodded.

"He knows?"

"He knows. We were going to leave yesterday for Capernaum."

"But he's in a hot place now, ain't he?" She began to pace. "If he's freed that's one thing. Might not be for months. And if he's not …"

"Please, Jez. Don't say it!!"

"Do you know his people?"

"We weren't planning to actually marry. He already has a wife."

Jez eyed me. "You can sure pick 'em, Mary. Didn't your ma teach ya about counting your days?"

"You did. Me and Adi."

"I did? That was good of me. Hey, how's she doin'?"

"She's marrying Aaron this fall."

"Lucky girl. But Mary. Not so lucky. You kinda slipped up on the numbers, hey?"

"Yeah." I sighed. "And that's not all. I'm betrothed to Joseph the carpenter." I told her about everything: my parents, the bride price, the excrement that is my life.

Jez was quiet for a bit. "You're a smart girl, M. You can read and write, can'tcha? Me, I can read. Barely. So we could use your smarts, hon. If I can fix this problem of yours, would you consider joining the Sisterhood?"

"What would I do?"

"You'd learn the ways. Join the profession. Or not. We need midwives and healers, too. Teachers. Women to help women. Wherever you go, you dedicate your life to helping your Sisters."

"What can you do for me?"

"I can help you to get rid of the kid."

I thought carefully about her offer. If circumstances were somehow reversed, if the child were Joseph's, I'd agree.

But only twelve nights past Jeremiah was asleep in my arms. His heart, mine, the baby's, beating in rhythm. There is something sacred about this conception. My child is Jeremiah's, my only link with him. Maybe forever. I will not sever this cord.

"I am certain. I want this child."

"Okay, then."

"What I don't want is Joseph. Abort him!"

Jez laughed from her belly. "No can do, kiddo. Sorry. Not in my particular line of work. Listen, I know he's no great shakes in the looks department. Or in the sack." I gulped and she laughed again. She laughs a lot for a harlot. "Yeah, it's true. I've known him a few times. But look." She suddenly got serious. "You want the kid, you *need* Joe. Otherwise, you and the baby end up bleeding to death in the town square. Get it?"

I got it.

"So use that smart head of yours, M. Convince him he's the father."

"H-how?"

"Shit. How else? Sleep with him. Marry him. Raise the child with him. Use your wits, Sister."

"I c-can't."

"Then die, Mary."

Well, that's it. If I don't pretend the baby's Joseph's and he finds out I'm pregnant by Jeremiah, the betrothal will be off. My parents will disown me. Jez would offer me sanctuary, but I'd have to earn my keep. And I know what that means.

Maybe I'd be arrested and Jeremiah and I could spend our last days together …

I don't want to die.

Jez is right. I have to spread my legs for the schlemiel. And soon. But it pisses me right off. Either way I prostitute myself.

God damn!

Where are you God? Damn you! When I most need you.

Yahweh!

There, I've said your name. Aloud. I've written it. And no thunderclap has come to claim me.

You cannot and will not stop my tongue. Or my stylus. I've got things to say. Lots of things. Lots of questions, too.

Beginning with — why did you put love in my heart if I'm not meant to be with the one I love?

Why give me passion if I'm to quell it?

Why give me a mind if I'm not to use it?

Why did you make women if we matter so little in this, your world?

Yahweh? Are you listening? Can you hear me?

November 1

Joseph came for supper tonight, but I was too nauseated to eat. I sat in the yard, sipping tea. Joseph came out, looked at me funny. Just like Mama's been doing lately. It gave me the creeps.

"Mary, you are ill?"

"Just the flu, Joseph. Better not get too close." How am I ever going to sleep with this moron?

"I brought you a get well gift."

"You didn't need to do that. What is it?" I opened the small narrow box. Inside were sheets of writing parchment and a new stylus. I couldn't believe my eyes.

"I know you are schooled in writing and reading. I thought perhaps … I am not a man to deny one knowledge, even a woman."

"Th-this is a thoughtful gift." I swallowed some of my high and mighty Mary pride. "Very thoughtful. I will write you a letter to thank you."

Joseph smiled. "Then you will have to read it to me. I was never taught."

He left me then. He puzzles me, my schlemiel.

I sat for a long time, thinking. Stroking the fine paper. Then I took the stylus and began to compose. The stars were out and the air was chilly before I finished.

I know I am breaking some great law again …

Yahweh help me, it may just work.

November 2

Dear Joseph,
As my future husband, you should be the first to know.

I saw a vision last night. It was no dream. I know because I pinched myself.

A soft glow at my window awakened me. The angel Gabriel appeared and introduced himself to me.

I was very afraid at first, but he said, "Mary, you are blessed among women. Adonai is with you."

Of course, I didn't believe him and thought perhaps this was some prank, but he continued with some authority, "You have found favour with Adonai. Behold!" Then on my wall appeared a vision of me holding a small babe and of you standing nearby.

"You shall conceive a son and you shall call his name Jesus. He shall be great and Adonai will give to him the throne of his father, David. And he shall reign over the house of Jacob forever and there will be no ending to his kingdom."

Then I asked, "How is this possible? I have never known a man and Joseph and I are not yet married."

Gabriel pronounced, "A holy spirit will visit you, and come upon you and make you quick with child."

"But when? How will this be?"

"It has already begun!" Then the most amazing thing happened. Suddenly the room was filled with great light and I felt the world spinning. Then the light seemed to enter my very being, my very soul, lifting me upwards and upwards.

When I came to my senses, day was dawning. I felt something move within me!

It is just as Gabriel said. I am with child! Oh, Joseph, is this not a miracle??

> *My soul is gracious to Adonai*
> *My spirit rejoices in him*
> *He has seen the lowly state of me, his handmaiden*
> *He has given me a great gift*
> *I am truly blessed among women*
> *Holy is his name*
> *Merciful is he*

He shows great strength
He humbles the proud
He deposes the corrupt
He exalts the meek
He feeds the hungry
He denies the greedy
He helps his Israel
In remembrance of the covenant
As he spoke to our fathers
So does he speak to me.

I am thrilled to be chosen, and I want to share my joy with you, Joseph, my future husband. I have yet to tell my parents. Will you be present when I do?

Your future wife,
Mary

P.S. Thank you so much for the writing paper. It has truly inspired me.

Pretty good, huh? Angels are all the rage these days. I used my best grammar and most artistic calligraphy. I'll send it over to Joseph's this afternoon. Maybe he'll come over to have me read it to him tonight. For the first time, I can't wait to see him! I'm sending a copy to Jez, too. She'll split a gut.

November 3

Everyone has gone to sleep, so I have some time to write my thoughts. It's been a long day.

My mother came into my room early this morning.

"Get up, Mary. Your father has left for the day. Before we go to market, I think we should have a little talk."

I sat up, my heart in my throat. I'd been dreading this conversation.

"Mary, are you pregnant?"

The suddenness of her question brought my stomach to my mouth. I reached for the bowl that is always by my pallet these days. As I was retching my guts out, she said, "I thought so."

She waited for me to finish and brought a wet cloth for me to wipe my face. Afterwards, I lay back on my pillow.

"Well?"

"Well?"

"So tell me."

I started with the angel story. "An angel appeared in a great light. And he said, 'Mary you are blessed among women and you will conceive a child this night. And his name shall be called Jesus. And he shall reign over the house of Jacob and there will be no ending to …'" It didn't sound as good as the letter. I knew she wasn't buying it.

"May God strike me dead for such a daughter!!!" And she beat her breast, which she likes to do when she's really upset.

"Mama, I swear it's true."

She slapped my face. Hard.

"What do you take me for? A fool? Now the truth. Or I will take you to your father."

Through my tears, I managed, "I am pregnant. The usual way."

"Hmmph. The usual way is after smart girls get married. When? When did this happen?"

Mentally, I tried to think back to the time of Joseph's proposal. How many weeks? Before Rosh Hashanah. "Ten or so weeks ago."

"So Joseph is the father?"

I looked down at the sheets. "Yes."

"I didn't hear you, I think."

"Yes."

"Look at me, Mary."

She knew the father was not Joseph. But she said nothing. Just looked at me.

"I sent him a letter."

"Who?"

"Joseph, of course." And I rummaged through the package of paper for the rough draft of the letter.

"Where did you get this parchment?"

"A gift from Joseph."

"From Joseph?" She sounded incredulous. But she began to read. My mother came from a very wealthy, enlightened family. Her parents insisted that she learn to read and write like her brothers. And Mama insisted that all of her children learn, too. My father protested, but she stood firm. Eventually, he came to see her point of view, even grew proud of us girls, taught us himself. I owe her a lot for that. And Papa, too.

I watched her face. It went from frowning to raised eyebrows to pursed lips. My mother has a myriad of expressions. Finally, she finished. And burst into laughter.

My mother doesn't often laugh.

"Oh, Mary. Angels. Such an imagination!"

"Angels are in vogue, Mama."

"You sent this? Already? And you think Joseph so gullible that he will swallow this make-believe?"

But I didn't get a chance to answer. There was a knock at our door. It was Joseph, come before work to have his letter read to him.

It was the performance of a lifetime. My mother ushered him in while I dressed. Then we three sat together in the front room and Mama served coffee.

I read the letter. Shaky voice and all. I lifted my face up to heaven and fell to my knees. I even cried.

But my mother! She was the best.

As I knelt, she leapt to my side, embraced me and began weeping with me.

"Truly this is a miracle! A blessing upon our houses! Wise and powerful is God." And then we prayed, two weeping, kneeling, wailing women.

What else could he do? Joseph bent his creaky knees and prayed with us.

My mother embraced him, too. "My son, my son! Great and mysterious are the works of our God!"

Joseph said nothing the whole time. His mouth opened and closed as though to speak, but our zeal and passionate prayers were overwhelming.

Finally, we broke apart. My mother kissed him. "I have always liked the name Jesus. My daughter is twice blessed with such a husband and such a child. Your wedding will be my joy."

He nodded dumbly.

She kissed him again.

My mother is very powerful.

I showed Joseph to the door.

"Have a blessed day, Joseph." I was still sniffling.

"And you, Mary …" His eyes met mine and he smiled that sad Joseph smile. "Blessed among women." Was there the barest hint of something in his tone?

I came back into the parlour and hugged my mother for a long time. Then she said, "Get the water gourd. Put on your shawl. We're late for market."

"But Mama …" I saw the look in her eyes and stopped. "I'll throw up all day." I knew I was whining.

"So? Bring a pail."

It wasn't so bad working with Mama at our stall in the market. Business was brisk and it kept my mind off Jeremiah, even though I'm worried sick about him. I felt protected there under the canopy with my mother. I admired her ample hips, her sure arms, her quick bartering tongue. She smiled over at me from time to time. And I only threw up twice.

That afternoon my mother made the Sabbath meal to end all Sabbath meals. I helped her, realizing I would soon have to do this in my own home.

We walked to shul together and prayed fervently together and walked back home together.

It was the first Sabbath meal I can remember appreciating in a long time. I was full of love for my family. I said a blessing for Deborah, Joanna and Ruth. Even for Samuel. For my parents. Bubeh and Zaydeh. But especially for my mother, who plied my father with enough wine to convince him of my "miraculous" pregnancy.

And even for Joseph. I realize I have to marry him, but having my mother know almost the truth, to know that she's there, to know I can keep my baby and that I will live to see it born is calming me.

But the thought of sleeping with Joseph, I mean "knowing" him, makes me need to take a sudden and lengthy bowel movement.

Tonight my mother saved me.

Who'd have thought?
Maybe she's a secret member of Jez's Eastern Star?

So, Jeremiah. You are beyond my help. Beyond my reach. I will say a prayer for you every night. I will dream about you with me, beside me, inside me. But you are lost to me.

Thank you for my son.

Holy shit!!! What if it's a girl??

Part Two

Matrimony

May 5, the desert

I have a pain in the ass from riding one and being married to another.

I could just kill the schlemiel.

Here we are camping (and I *told* him how I hate camping) in the middle of the fucking desert. If we're lost I'll kill him.

If the buzzards don't get us first.

Meandering through the heat of the day on the Sabbath, Yahweh forgive him, a bloody wandering Jew!

And do we take a camel like other pilgrims and travellers??? No! Rent-a-camel is too expensive, he says! So we borrow his stupid cousin Maury's ass.

And why? For some stupid census in Bethlehem. I said, "Let's wait until the baby is born," but Joseph refused. He is in such a hurry. Men and their ridiculous patrilineal lines. Joseph claims he's begotten of David. David Schmavid!!! Do I need this??? I'm nine months pregnant, but does he give a sacred shit? A kid and a handmaiden blessed by you, Yahweh (well, that's what Joseph thinks anyway), and this is the treatment we get!!!

Every ten minutes I have to pee. Do you think it's easy to ride with a full bladder on an ass?? Every few miles Joseph stops the beast and I roll off, lift my layers, bare my arse in the desert sun to take a whiz. You try squatting to pee at nine months pregnant. I've stopped caring how I aim. I've pissed all down my legs and over my sandals.

I think I'll give Joseph the pleasure of bathing my feet tonight.

I'm exhausted. We'd better hit civilization tomorrow, that's all I can say. I'm due any moment. I can barely sleep at night. God, my back aches. And Joseph's snoring!!! It's driving me crazy. I could just throttle him in his sleep! I'm telling him to sleep outside the tent tonight, if he can't shut up.

Every night I say a prayer for Jeremiah. He was still in jail when we left. I know his trial is sometime in the next two weeks. Of course, we'd have to leave Nazareth before I learned the outcome.

I fear for the worst. It makes me sick to think about it, even though I haven't been nauseated for about four months now.

Jez has friends among the prison guards and sent word to Jeremiah from me and about me.

He heard about the wedding.

It was a nice enough wedding as weddings go. Rabbi Elijah married us. Under the canopy. On the eighth of December. Joseph quickly set a date after the visit from Gabriel. I talked it over with Jez and with my mother, separately, of course, but they are two women of one mind. It was best to wed before people started talking. I mean, what if someone convinced Joseph that he was a gullible old fool? Then where would I be?

So I married him when I was barely showing.

I wore white, what else?

It was all very fine, except that I married the wrong man.

We got lots of presents: mortar and pestle, some knives, bowls, cups, candlesticks. The usual loot. Though I'm grateful, none of it really matters.

Adi and Aaron were there. They were married three weeks before we were. At their wedding, Adi positively glowed. While I was glad for her, it was also hard to bear witness. They've moved away now and are living in Safad. I've lost my confidante. So much has changed in my life.

My father is satisfied that I've married well, or so he thinks. I'm glad I don't have to take care of the dowry beasts any longer. That special chore has fallen to Deborah. My mother looked lovely and passed me knowing glances, but mainly she was relieved, I think, as if she'd been afraid that Joseph would catch on to our scam and back out at the last minute.

I don't think anything would have deterred the man.

The wedding night. It passed. Joseph groped me a bit, but I told him not until the baby's born. He accepted that. He's decent enough, I guess.

Anyway, like I said, Jeremiah heard about my marriage. Jez told me that he was very upset, according to one of her Eastern Star sources. And he sent me a message two or three weeks after the wedding.

It was a difficult afternoon. I had been arranging my things in Joseph's home, trying to make it feel like mine, when the tinker came to the door. He tried to sell me something, knives or cheap perfume, I don't remember. I tried to close the door on him, but he clutched my hand.

"From the Eastern Star," he muttered. Then turned to his cart and rolled away from the house.

When I opened my hand, I found a dirty piece of linen with writing scrawled across it. I had never seen Jeremiah's handwriting before, didn't even know if he could write, but I knew before reading that these words were from him. The baby moved just then. I had to sit down.

Mary I wish you joy   think of you always   always love

Jeremiah

I had a good, long cry, me and the baby. Then I burned the message into my soul and the linen in the oven.

I've not heard from him since, only word from Jez that he is alive. I asked her to send to me in Bethlehem as soon as she knows anything about his trial.

Damn him! He had to get himself arrested and foil our plans. I was prepared to go anywhere with him. But not to jail. And not to my death.

So here I am in May in the bloody desert as near to my time as I can possibly be without anyone but Mr. Begotten-of-David. Far from friends and family. And a clean chamber pot.

While Joseph is tending to the ass, I'd better put this scroll away before we break bread for supper.

Break wind is more like it.

I've been passing gas like a she-devil. Good luck to Joseph in this tent tonight.

May 17, Hebron

Well, Jez said it would be a boy. I thought her crafts were just so many old wives' tales. I didn't believe her and made myself almost sick with fear. But after all my worry and prayers, he is a boychild.

Conceived in one barn and born in another. May the seventh. A Taurus.

"No vacancy!" signs everywhere in Bethlehem when we finally arrived. A carpet sellers' convention. Trust a carpenter not to check out this rather important little detail! We wandered all over that city. Not a room to be had. No compassion for an old man and a pregnant woman. People in Bethlehem have bad manners.

I was the one who spotted the stable. I lurched over and opened the doors, just as my water broke. I'd been having pains throughout the torturous day. Now the contractions were only minutes apart, so I didn't care where I had the child.

Joseph was absolutely useless, so what else is new? With neither my mother nor Jez there to help, I grabbed onto an iron ring in the wall and hung on for dear life as I squatted in the straw. Panted and grunted for the better part of an hour. Finally, push came to shove.

"Joseph," I screamed, "for God's sake! Hold the baby's head! Catch the child!" The man was hovering around, looking pale and stupid. He dove between my legs just as I gave my final push and we were all three of us covered with blood and I was shaking and so was Joseph and the baby was wailing.

I knew from Jez's last-minute birthing instructions to drum my stomach to loosen the afterbirth. When it came out, Joseph was fit to faint. Jez once told me that afterbirth is so ugly all newborns look beautiful by comparison. She and I had a good yuk at the time. Now Joseph was seeing the truth of her joke. I took the baby from him and cut the umbilical cord with a string tied taut. Exhausted, we lay on clean hay together. Joseph left the barn for almost an hour.

Good riddance.

My baby is beautiful, what can I say? He is dark and clear-skinned, not purple and ugly like my little sister when she was born. I have kept my word to my spirit and muse and named him Jesus.

When Joseph came back, we were drowsing together, me with my son at my breast, asleep on the hay. I smiled dreamily. He reached out tentatively to stroke the soft, dark down on the baby's head. Joseph's look of wonder was really quite tender. He lay beside us.

"I … am without words, Mary. Such a thing has happened here. I … love you and the child. My wife. My son."

Then gingerly he drew a blanket over us and put his arm carefully around me.

The barn wavered in and out of focus. There was quite a menagerie around us. It was all somehow comforting. Then I slipped into sleep alongside my snoring husband.

The banging awoke us sometime in the earliest hours of the morning. My first thought in sleepy delirium was that I was somehow trapped with Joseph's dowry animals as though eternally condemned to some horrible, bestial Sheol.

Joseph turned up the stable lantern and answered the door. There were a few moments of conversation that I couldn't hear. He returned, bewildered.

"Mary, we have company!"

"What? Are you kidding me? Look at us!" And he did. Traces of my labour were about my body, the baby, the barn. "I'm not seeing anyone until I've bathed and done my hair!"

"They seem important men, Mary."

"I don't care who they are! I've just given birth! To a descendant of King David ..."

"They seem to know this, Mary."

"What?"

"They ... know. I ..."

"Go tell them to return in a quarter of an hour!"

"But they insist ..."

"*I* insist, Joseph. *Go!*"

He scuttled off and I wondered what kind of meshuggeners would come to the door in the middle of the night! Then I wondered how they knew to find us in a barn, how they knew it was us they were looking for, and as I plaited my hair, I got to thinking about the angel story and how it had spread through our neighbourhood, thanks to my mother and Jez and my dopey sister Deborah.

I peered at the men through a crack in the stable wall. Three of them. They rode camels (Joseph should take a lesson), but otherwise I couldn't see much in the starlight.

I washed myself and the baby as best I could in the trough water, wrapped him in swaddling, cleaned up the blood and had Joseph scatter clean straw. While changing into something clean, I lamented that my stomach was not immediately flat again after the birth. Shit!

Finally, I told Joseph to usher the men in.

Apparently, outside the stable a small crowd had gathered.

But only the three came in together, at first.

They were well-dressed, darkly handsome men. Turbaned. Rich, flashy garments compared to our homespun travel clothes.

The first man spoke, "We follow the Star of the East and have at last come to the place of the child."

His words sounded rehearsed. Of course, it made sense to me now. The Eastern Star! Jez knew Joseph and I had been bound for Bethlehem.

"Welcome," I said.

Then a second said, "We's soiched the city for yous, but da whole joint's full."

"Yeah," said the third.

"So ah, at last we came here. And here yous is."

What strange accents they had. "Who are you?"

The first man piped up, "I'm Mel, this here's Kaz and that over there is Balt."

"Where are you travelling?" asked Joseph.

"Oh y'know, here and there."

"We's on a mission," Kaz spoke up.

"Yeah." Balt grinned.

"And your business?" Joseph queried.

"Oh, we's in sales," Kaz volunteered.

"Rugs?"

"Ha! Yeah, rugs! And, ah, other exotic moichendise. In fact, if yous ah like, I could bring in —"

Mel interrupted Kaz. "Shaddup. We's here for da kid!"

"Yeah," said Balt, a real conversationalist.

"We come bearing gifts for the boychild." Mel went back to his rehearsed speech.

"Gold," offered Kaz, setting down a small trunk and opening it.

"Frankincense," said Balt, opening a small, brightly coloured box.

"And myrrh," finished Mel, producing a beautiful jar. "From da East. Where we came from. Ya get it?"

"Got it," I said and thanked them heartily. These were rich gifts indeed. Who could afford them? Certainly not Jez, even though she runs a good profit. She'd already given me a present: a bronze lamp.

"Who gives us such gifts?" Joseph was completely baffled.

"Oh, a silent benefactor, a freeman, who wishes ta remain anonymous, but who knows da whole story of da miraculous kid, if yous gets my drift," Mel spoke quickly.

"Ha! Yeah."

Mel handed me a scroll. "This is his message. Ya know, wishing yous goodwill. Oh yeah. And da mister, too."

I unrolled it and read it rapidly, careful not to reveal the effect of the words upon my heart.

"Thank you. Give our benefactor, whoever he is, our thanks."

"Will do. Well, we's gotta shove off. Miles to go t'night. Nice kid. Mazeltov. See yous." And off all three of them went, leaving the barn door and Joseph's mouth agape.

I pondered how to explain the letter to him, but thankfully the people outside began to pour in, saving my breath.

What a crowd! Shepherds, street people, beggars and urchins. They saw me and the baby. Knelt down muttering, "Thanks be to Abba," "Mazeltov," on and on. It seems the three men following the Eastern star had told the people about a son of David being born to a woman "visited" by God and that we were in the stable. Just what I need.

"It's the Messiah!" an ancient shepherd rasped.

"The Messiah! The Messiah!" the others repeated breathlessly.

Fuck! What could I do? I couldn't tell them I made it all up. That it was just a story! Joseph was right there! I tried to explain that Jesus was a descendant of David, and that's all, but the people would have none of it.

"Our Messiah! Elohim has seen fit to finally grant us a Messiah!"

"Can I touch your hair?" a beggar woman asked me.

"No!"

"Mary," Joseph remonstrated.

I sighed. "Fine. Touch. Touch." And she and seven others reached over their gnarled and dirty hands to stroke my hair. This! This is what comes of a simple lie! "Alright, already." I shooed them off and they fell to fawning over the baby. That woke him up and he began a steady scream.

"Feeding time. Everybody out!"

Respectfully, the people backed slowly out of the barn, bowing and whispering. I quieted Jesus and nursed him asleep.

They camped all around the barn.

In fact, crowds kept coming for three days and nights.

Finally, I told Joseph that was it. No more visitors. "We're checking into a motel." The convention was over. The Masada Inn had to have vacancies.

We tried to give the people the slip on the way to our new lodgings, but they followed us, chanting, dancing and singing. I was really getting annoyed.

Joseph was awed and humbled by the experience. "Mary, this is indeed a miracle," he repeated endlessly, so that I could kick him.

That evening at supper with Joseph, I broached the subject of the scroll from the three men. Well, not all of it. This is what it said:

Dear Mary,

I paid a scribe to write this letter to you. The wise guys who come to you are business associates of mine. Jez told us where you'd be. You can probably guess that I am free. Aranius, a friend, bribed my way out of jail. Nazareth guards are easily paid off. I am running to Sidon, where I'll be far enough away from El-Shariz, who maybe won't be living so long anyway.

I'll send word when I can. In the meantime, here are some gifts for you and the baby.

Keep in touch with the Eastern Star, Mary. It's my only way to reach you. I heard from Jez the wild story you made up. But listen, the word's spread and you are in danger. It's reached even Herod's ears, and he's a madman. He thinks a new king will try to depose him and so he's put an order out to kill any kids under the age of two. Jez told me to tell you that there are members of her organization throughout Galilee, Samaria, Judea, Perea, Egypt. But Herod controls all these places, except Egypt. Save yourself and the child, Mary.

I am yours. Even though we are apart.

Love, Jeremiah

I told Joseph only that the letter was a warning about Herod and his demented plan.

"We must go to Tanis in Egypt," I told Joseph, "to save our child."

He nodded. No argument. "After the eighth day we will leave."

"By camel, Joseph. You must get camels."

The carpenter saw the wisdom of the merchant daughter's words. "Camels."

In the central market of Bethlehem, we bought camels and saddles with some of the gold the wise guys gave us. I came with Joseph to make the purchase. I am, after all, better at bartering. I know a good bargain when I see one, and I never buy retail. So I haggled while Joseph just stood there. Such a deal! Eighteen shekels for two dun-coloured beasts with good teeth.

On the eighth day, after we returned from the synagogue for Jesus' circumcision and naming ceremony, we had to wade our way through the people to get back to the inn. I was weeping because my family wasn't there for the festivities. However, the crowd had brought gifts of wine and bread and sweets. For the first time, I was glad of their presence. I miss them as I write this, now that we've left everything familiar so far behind.

The next morning we set out, two camels and supplies, an eight-day-old baby, a young mother, and an old man. The retinue of believers followed us for many miles, wishing us well. Poor misguided fools.

I worry that their stories will add to mine and follow us for years to come.

Sometimes I'm just too clever for my own good.

June 2, Tanis, Egypt

At last we are settled in Tanis. My scrolls were buried at the bottom of some pack and I've just now found them.

Where to begin to tell about our journey? My head still reels.

After Hebron, where we remained for Sabbath, we took a wrong turn. Joseph missed the road entirely, what else? And there we were: lost in the wilderness of Judea, miles off track, playing right into Herod's hands.

The night in the desert was wretched. A nasty windstorm blew up and our tent was poor shelter from the writhing sands. To make matters worse, Jesus fretted, then screamed and kicked and wailed. My nipples were very sore and red. I was not very adept at breastfeeding. I rocked the baby and tried re-wrapping his swaddling, while Joseph looked on miserably from the shadows of our oil lamp.

In the morning, the camels were indistinguishable from the sand. I scanned the map, trying to make out where we might go, but the mountains and hills of sand of western Judea were not recorded. Near despair, I glanced up at the shimmering horizon and saw first one, then a second, then another camel appear. A caravan of Bedouins!

"Joseph, run! Get directions!" But the stubborn nebish wouldn't budge.

"I can find our way," he said obstinately.

"For the love of God!" I thrust the baby in his arms, and Jesus began to cry. Off I stormed towards the caravan, waving my arms and shouting.

The camels slowed as I approached. One knelt down and its rider dismounted. I cast my eyes down demurely and began to explain our predicament. He did not understand my words. But then a woman dismounted. A beautiful young woman, dark-eyed and in an elaborate black and red headdress jingling with coins. She held up her left palm — a gesture of peace or greeting? On it was tattooed a five-pointed star, a large open eye staring from its centre.

"I know your tongue." And she translated my request for directions.

The man listened solemnly and spoke rapidly.

His daughter smiled at me. "My father insists that we accompany you. We too are Egypt-bound. My own son is but eighteen months and we would flee Herod. Ride with us. We are nomads of these parts and many beyond besides. My family understands the tricks and fortunes of the desert."

I ran the news back to Joseph, and, as usual, he was dumbfounded.

"Don't just stand there, Joseph. They're waiting for us! Give me the baby." And obediently he packed up and loaded the camels.

The Bedouins led us through valleys and paths no maps record. We journeyed until an hour before sunset. Then, in only a quarter hour of organized flurry and activity, we made camp in a semi-circle of mountains.

I did not know what hospitality was until that night.

The women prepared a feast such as I have never tasted. Salted lamb and rice. Fresh unleavened loaves. Dates and rich camel's milk. Coffee spiced with cardamom and ginger root. We ate to bursting.

Izel, the beautiful interpreter, brought scented oil for our aching backsides and feet. She gave me a soothing balm for my painful breasts and made a great fuss over my babe. Her son, Omar, came with her to see Jesus. As Izel bade us goodnight, she again raised her tattooed palm in quick salute.

We slept soundly that and every night amongst the Bedouins.

I found occasion to be alone with Izel many times on our journey. Mercifully, Joseph left me in our tent each night to drink coffee and smoke with the men. Then Izel would come by for tea. She taught me how to rub the baby's body with oil and salt to protect Jesus' skin in his swaddling. She administered to my tender breasts, brought hot water for bathing, and inspected my still-tender nether regions.

"There was some ripping, Mary, but you are healing nicely."

"Where have you learned these healing arts, Izel?"

She held up her left palm. "I have been trying to tell you these several days."

Suddenly, I remembered the five-pointed star tatooed on Jez's plump left shoulder. I felt foolish.

Izel laughed aloud. "Have you not seen the star before?"

"Once. But usually some cryptic message is given me and that is how I recognize a friend."

"Many women, some men, wear the star. Not always on the palm. But always on the left side of the body. When we recognize a Sister, we embrace, so."

She kissed me on the forehead and each cheek. Before she pulled away, she whispered, "Sister."

"I must get such a tattoo when we get to Egypt," I said, thinking my mother would kill me when I got home. Such desecrations of the body are forbidden. But if all the other Sisters of the Star have them, I should, too.

"Yes, and then you must greet others as I did you."

"How did you know I might be a Sister?"

"Rumour of you and your miraculous child reached me in Hebron. But I was not sure of you at first, so I was cautious."

"Izel. I must tell you. Jesus is beautiful and a miracle to me, but he is as mortal and ordinary as you or I."

She smiled. "Sisters of the Star find ways to keep alive. So it has been my way to use my wits since I was widowed."

"I'm so sorry, Izel."

Her face darkened. "My husband, Ali, died shortly before Omar's birth. A knife fight in the streets of Tyre, fool that he was. So to assure my family that I was still a good woman — useful, marriageable — I turned my hands to healing. My tribe cannot do without me now;

relatives come from far and wide to receive my touch and my balms."

"And you learned your art from the Sisterhood?"

"Yes, from my mother and grandmother, and from the women of the Eastern Star wherever I find them on our travels. When we get to Tanis, I will take you to a woman if you, too, would like to learn."

Three nights later, Izel summoned me to assist her with a birth. My first experience as midwife. Izel's skill and confidence were inspiring. She calmed the young mother, Rasema, with gentle words. Uttering encouraging sounds, I massaged Rasema's legs and back and shoulders. Izel kept her eyes on Rasema's eyes, communicating and coaxing. The crown of the baby's head appeared. Izel massaged the mother's opening with olive oil. Rasema pushed once more and the baby's head emerged. I struggled to hold back tears and felt a sympathetic contraction in my own womb. Again Rasema heaved at Izel's request, and the shoulders emerged without a tear in the mother's flesh. And finally a last push and the baby girl was caught lovingly in Izel's hands. We were three weeping, exultant women.

Izel inspected the baby, rubbing the white mucus into her soft pink skin, and instructed Rasema how to encourage her infant to take the nipple. The tiny girlchild was suckling at her mother's breast within moments. I watched as Izel tied a piece of boiled string tightly around the umbilical cord and cut it from the baby.

Later Izel and I walked arm in arm back to my tent.

"I like your work, Izel."

She smiled.

"I wish I'd had such help when Jesus was born."

"You did, Mary. You had yourself."

"I would like to learn what you have to teach, Izel."

"And I will learn from you, Mary. Good night."

And she left me, wondering what I could possibly teach her.

"I think you know how to marry well, Mary." Izel was decorating my hands with henna. "I shall follow your example."

I snorted. "You're joking, Izel."

"I am most serious." She did not look up from her painting.

"It shouldn't happen to a dog! I was desperate. You are young and beautiful."

"You do not even know what you have. I will tell my father of my interest in Gamaaz when we get to Egypt."

"Gamaaz of the missing teeth?"

"Gamaaz of the hundred camels!"

"Gamaaz of the crooked right eye?"

"Gamaaz of the great jewels."

"Gamaaz of the gammy leg?"

"Gamaaz of no wife, no sons."

"Gamaaz who nears sixty?"

"Gamaaz who is very rich and very ugly and very lonely and very old and not too bright and most receptive to a woman of some youth and charm who has her own aspirations for her life's work."

She laughed at my expression as finally, finally I took her meaning.

As I write tonight, I wonder why I have never thought before of my own life's work. Too caught up in the heat of Jeremiah and in saving my skin and in having this child suckling at my breast. Too spoiled by a rich father, pampered by a rich mother to think beyond the moment or myself. If I am in such enviable circumstances, as Izel insists, how best to use them?

I think of Rasema and her baby, my small part in her birth. I look to Jez and my mother, their saving of me. I think of Izel, the healing artistry of her hands. I look into the face of Jesus, sweetly asleep. Somehow, what I want to do in this world is woven in circles with all of these people.

June 25, Tanis, Egypt

I begin to get used to this new role. Jesus is seven weeks old. He grows plump and more gorgeous daily. I cannot take my eyes from him, and I take him wherever I go. I love to watch him suckle and move his little fists about. When he concentrates, he has this little scowl that is quite adorable. Already I can see he takes after his mother: so clever. Jesus loves to smile at me. He is the love of my life.

I have decided to clean up my language, attend to my grammar as I was taught. Swearing shocks Joseph, which is one reason that I like to curse. I also feel that the power of such words is restricted to men, like so many words. Like the arts of reading and writing and study. I will have these gifts that men hoard. And I will teach my son.

But I do not want Jesus' first word to be "shit." Or worse.

Of course, I hope it will be "mama." Smarmy, I know. But I feel these sentimental rushes lately, and I can cry at the slightest provocation. Izel says it was the same for her after Omar's birth. Perhaps it is so for all new mothers.

Izel, who stays with her relatives several blocks from here, brings Omar to visit daily and she teaches me much about motherhood and babyhood. I am very fond of her.

But I miss my mother and family — and even Nazareth — terribly. Tanis is a little hick town in comparison. It is dry and without trees. The water in the town well has a funny taste. Ah, but we are safe here from Herod's murderous hands. I always thought of Egypt as a marvellous place, full of wonders and secrets of the ancients. But I find it is much like anywhere else when you have no roots. I wonder if Jesus will be happy here. There is only a small community of Jews and no temple school. Here I go, getting well ahead of myself.

Joseph has already found work as a carpenter. He hung out his shingle, and business began the second day. It has been steady ever since. He works in a small shed in the back of our three-room dwelling. I told Joseph the cheaper house down the street would suit, but he insisted that I need a room to receive guests, as has been my family custom. I must admit I am thankful for his consideration. At times, I allow myself to grow fond of him.

I have, of course, fulfilled my conjugal duty. After the birthing tears healed, after forty days of purification, after two turtledoves, I had no more excuses. I finally acquiesced. What? I lie there. It happens. I feel nothing, but Joseph feels better. I can do no more. My body is my body; I cannot will it to feel for my husband what it felt, still feels, for my lover. But I can try to be kind and patient with Joseph. I owe him my life and that of my child.

July 2, Tanis, Egypt

Jesus will be two months old in five days. Daily he grows more beautiful. I love his little smiles and the way he grabs hold of my finger. He isn't a fussy baby and sleeps several hours each night and again after I nurse him. I adore the little gurgleburbles he makes and the sighs and the faces. Often I check if he's still there in his basket, still mine, still safe. I am quite in love with my little man.

July 30, Tanis, Egypt

I am sick. Aghast at the cruelty of men. My stomach heaves. My head whirls. I have been sick for days.

Herod has put to the sword a thousand thousand babies. All boys. All under the age of two.

And all because of me. That stupid angel story.

Is this Yahweh's punishment of me? What kind of cruel God watches this from heaven and is unmoved to stop it?

You can part the Red Sea, but you cannot save these innocent lives?

I shake my fist at you, Yahweh. I find it hard to love a God like you.

They say Herod heard the story of Jesus, the Messiah. They say Herod is a jealous, evil man. I know it is true. He taxes the people to their last shekel. He is luxurious. A swine. Covetous. He has power and lusts for more. A man jealous of a baby. A man who fears he will be deposed by an infant. And so he murders.

At first the Roman soldiers did their heinous duty by night. Cowards all. But as murderers will, they acquired a taste for blood and grew more ruthless, more thirsty. I heard that they brazenly marched into town squares, into villages, markets. In the open air, in daylight, under Yahweh's open eyes, they took their mannish weapons and speared child after child after child. When mothers shielded their infants, the soldiers skewered two bodies. If fathers or brothers or grandfathers interfered, their heads rolled in the streets. When the mothers and grandmothers and aunts and sisters wept, the soldiers laughed and spat on them.

They drank in celebration, as Roman soldiers feverish with killing do. They left the bodies in the streets, raised their cups of blood-red wine in the taverns while the mourners raised their wails. To drown the sound, the soldiers sang raucous songs. Repeated their victory nightly between the legs of the prostitutes.

The keening of the mothers carried on and on. It grew in pitch and volume, and the chorus of voices rose. Ascended. Flew on the wind and screamed a way to Herod's palace, where he lay sleepless in terror. The whine of the thousands drove some soldiers mad, they say. Soldiers threw themselves over cliffs or onto their own swords. The hysterical refrain reached even Caesar, rutting in Rome. He consulted his statesmen, his doctors, his portent-readers. No one could stop the mewling, screeching, wailing.

Finally, the chorus shrieked across the desert and into Egypt and into my own open, wretched throat. My voice, shrill and shuddering, joins the others. Aghast at men. Aghast at myself. Aghast.

I feel dead. Or that I should be. This is my doing. My words. My words have done this. Mary has condemned thousands of babies to death across the land of Israel. To save myself, to save myself ...

What can I do? What reparation can I make? I will not bargain with you, Yahweh. I do not trust a God like you.

For the rest of my life this blood crime is on my head. Those innocent lives for mine. Their mothers' sorrow, mine.

I am frail and weak and stupid and selfish and ...

I am so ... sorry.

October 31, Tanis, Egypt

Finally, I write. I did not think I would ever do so again. I am afraid of my words. I will begin again. Slowly. My hand falters. The page is hard to fill although my heart is full.

November 2, Tanis, Egypt

I try again. If I write, I feel better. I write my grief on this page. I write my love. For Jesus. My beautiful boy.

November 14, Tanis, Egypt

The winter sun is warm on my face. Jesus bit my nipple today. Teething. He has two teeth. He lies asleep beside me as I write.

I never dreamed to be alone and a mother. Of course, I have Joseph, but I am apart from my family. I have written to my mother. I told her of my pain over the deaths of all those babies. My grief for their mothers. Fathers. Bubehs. Zaydehs. She told me to forgive myself. To go on. Herod would have killed the babies anyway because the stars told him so, the stars and his meshuggeh astrologers. I suppose so, but Jeremiah wrote that Herod feared a king ...

Still my mother's words are comfort. Words again. A mother's words.

December 20, Hanukkah

We have much to be grateful for! Our friends Izel and Gamaaz are married. We feasted and danced. Joseph's business is good. Jesus is an active, happy baby. There are bonfires tonight!

January 13, Tanis, Egypt

Today, Izel took me to meet Magda of the Eastern Star. She is a very large woman, perhaps the largest I have ever seen, and she lives in a rather run-down quarter of Tanis, where I am afraid to go on my own. Her curious shop is very dusty and full of things! Bottles of potions and ointments collect cobwebs on crowded shelves. Amulets and stones and amulet purses and parchments with strange writing lie in smeared glass cases. Pictures of strange animal gods adorn her walls. Murky jars of what seem to be body parts and organs — I try not to look too closely — clutter the counter. Her place is forbidden and fascinating. I love and am loathe to go there. If there are Egyptian secrets to be found in Tanis, they are surely in Magda Makimbim's curio shop.

Behind the beaded curtain are her living quarters, where Magda smokes a water pipe or her strange-smelling cigarettes. Izel and I tried one last week, but they made us giddy and silly and so Magda sent us reeling home.

Magda has the same tattoo as Izel's and she has heard of Jez back home in Nazareth. The incense of her private rooms often confuses my thoughts.

"So a new initiate to the Sisterhood, Mary?"

"I would like to learn more."

"More. More of what?"

"To heal. To treat."

"Ha."

"I can read and write. Aramaic, Hebrew and Greek."

She drew a deep draught from the water pipe. "Most women are forbidden such an art."

"I ... know."

"Much of what we teach is forbidden."

"Yes."

"It is a matter, of course, for you to determine what it is you will come to know. Your Jez, I suspect, knows enough to keep herself and a few vagrant girls alive. Izel there knows midwifery and healing." Izel nodded, but said nothing. "What will you know?"

I drew myself up and tried to shake the cobwebs from my thoughts. "I will know everything you will teach."

Magda laughed and her fleshy girth seemed to shake the room. "You are young and foolish, too."

"I am fifteen. I am a mother and a wife."

"You have had a lover."

I gaped at this woman.

Her throaty laughter rang in my head. "I myself have had many lovers. I intend to have several more before this great body withers in the dust. But love is a different matter. Love can betray the Sisterhood. And it can betray you. You love this man."

"Yes."

"And he you?"

"Yes."

"It is well that I know. And so, Mary who will know everything I will teach, welcome to your training." With that, she opened a jar. Took my left palm and applied a strong-smelling ointment that numbed my skin. Dipped an instrument — part needle, part stylus — in an inky substance and began to draw on my palm.

"There is, of course, a price to be paid for my teaching."

"We are of humble means here in Tanis, but I can send for money from my home."

Magda snickered. "The price is more than gold or silver can buy."

"What price do you ask?"

"That will become clear to you as you learn, my dear.

"The arts of the Sisters of the Eastern Star are not only the arts of life and life-giving. They are also the arts of death and death-dealing. Sisters of the Star are creators and destroyers. Life coexists with death. Sometimes it suits our purposes to give life, sometimes to take it. For the sick and the infirm, the very young and the very old, the weak and the helpless, we try our best. But there are times when one lies writhing in the final stages of some disease and it is better to help the soul to a place of souls. There are times when our herbs and spells are impotent. And there are those of ill-heart whom we never help; in fact, we may seek to make them sick or worse. Each instance requires wisdom and forethought.

"Always we seek to help women and their children. We are, after all, a Sisterhood. Women alone are powerless. But together we have more power than men of power care to admit. Some of us have died for our secrets. We try to keep ourselves hidden. Many of us live on the margins of towns with outlaws, whores, lepers. In this way are we safe."

A five-pointed star stained my left palm. It's not even the Star of David. My mother will be scandalized.

Once again Mary of Nazareth transgresses. Well, I am Mary of Tanis now.

"Every Sister, at some time, risks her life. The greater good is before safety. Sometimes your family, your child, will be at great risk. This is a given you must accept."

"I do." I looked over at Jesus asleep in his basket, near Izel.

"There are safe havens where you may flee, alone or with your family, should need arise. Always look for the star and the eye."

I looked into my palm and saw a large open eye staring from its centre. How? When was it drawn? Or by Magda's magic, did it just appear?

"And so, initiate, you are begun. Why do you want to know, Mary?"

Again I looked to the babe. "I saved myself from stoning and my infant from Herod. Many are not so fortunate. For fifteen years all I am has been about Mary. Now I see I can be more; I must be. For those who helped me to live. And for my child." And for those who died and mourn the dead, I thought to myself.

Or at least that's what I think I said and heard and thought. The incense was puzzling my brain. But the tattoo is looking at me as I write, willing me to inscribe the truth.

February 5, Tanis, Egypt

Life is very full between caring for the baby, keeping house, washing and cooking meals. Several hours a week Izel and I bundle up our babes and go off to Magda's shop. I am learning about medicines and ointments, how to make them, how to use them, what prayers to recite in their preparation and use. There is much I have to learn.

Last week, Izel and I helped Magda set the broken arm of a woman past bearing age, a woman with a fallen face and stooped shoulders. Her name is Martha and she is a regular client. She is my mother's age. Her husband beats her. Like so many women, she must endure mistreatment. Or be turned out into the streets.

"Can she not run to her relatives?" I asked after Martha limped from the shop, her arm in a sling.

"Her parents are dead. Her daughters are married and scattered. She has no sons."

"Is there no place else for such a woman?"

"What place is there for such a woman?" Magda snorted.

"A shelter? A sanctuary?"

"There are brothels. There are leper colonies."

"No temple?"

"For women? Temples are for virgins and priests."

I am troubled. It never before occurred to me that there must be many such women, with nowhere to turn. I am indeed fortunate to be with a good man. Joseph would never raise his hand to strike me.

March 18, Tanis, Egypt

The days have leapt away from me. I have so little time to write what with nursing and the house and my lessons. Jesus is always hungry. He is a good baby, and we have settled into a kind of routine — I understand his moods and his feeding times and his fussing times — but some days I am overwhelmed with motherhood. I wish my own mother were here to help me.

March 28, Tanis, Egypt

I can only write in snatches. Today at Magda's I learned how to stitch together a wound. Martha came again, her arm still in a sling, this time with a gash on her forehead. I have never seen so much blood. It fell in great drops and thickened before my eyes. My stomach heaved from the sight.

Magda, who moves with surprising deftness for so large a woman, saw that I would soon be senseless and useless, so threw a rag over the pool of blood.

"A wound to the head always lets much blood. Run a needle through a candle flame."

This I did, glad to turn away and collect myself. Izel and Magda held Martha firmly, while Magda instructed my sewing lesson.

"A cross-stitch works best. Taut, but not so tight that you pucker the skin to worsen the scar."

Fifteen stitches later, Martha headed back to her sorry life. Jesus began to squall. I picked him up and rocked him as I watched her slight figure sink into the afternoon shadows of the narrow street.

April 17, Tanis, Egypt

I am learning about poison. In the right amount, some herbs heal, some kill. It all depends upon what you need to set aright.

Besides drying plants, Magda has shown Izel and me how to extract venom from the fangs of an adder. Dangerous work. And Izel and I nearly bolted one afternoon last week when we saw the serpent Magda had caged in a wicker basket.

Momel, her halfwit, cross-eyed brother, was in her shop and played upon a tinny-sounding horn that caused the serpent to rise and sway upwards out of the basket. We stood mesmerized by the nasal tune Momel played; the snake seemed as if charmed. Then faster than anything I have seen, Magda looped the creature's head with a snare on a stick. The reptile thrashed and whipped its tail, but Magda held fast. Izel and I clutched each other, terrified from the charmer's trance.

Magda forced venom from the adder's fangs by pressing them through lambskin stretched across a bottleneck. This venom so deadly, Magda assures us, in the proper dosage can be used as a curative.

Izel would not touch the creature, but I did. Its skin was not slimy but dry. In a burst of foolhardiness or courage, I offered to extract some of the venom. The creature resisted, but could neither escape Magda's coil about its neck nor the pressure from my hand. It gave up the poisonous juices, several drops at a time.

Together, we returned the adder to the wicker basket and locked it, hissing, inside. Later Momel returned it to some arid desert bluff.

"We do not kill those that help us," Magda explained. She looked at me with something new, almost admiration, in her eyes.

I felt very brave, I must admit. I have dreamed three nights of the adder.

Passover, Tanis, Egypt

I eat your lamb and your unleavened bread according to your old decree, Yahweh, and your food is gall in my mouth!

Exiled in Egypt, the very land Moses and your people escaped. Today I remember the babies Herod slaughtered. Their mothers' empty arms. And today, in this land, I think you are not so different from Herod. He slaughtered the boychildren by the thousands. You slaughtered the firstborn of every family of Egypt. Innocent babies and children of these people, their ancestors, killed by your tenth plague, by your might, by your will.

And you said, Yahweh, that never again would there be such a cry throughout the land. You said, Yahweh, that not a dog would move his tongue against the children of Israel.

And yet you allowed Herod, the dog, to do just that.

You and Herod are very alike. What is it about our rulers and our God that they so fear babies and children?

I have marked my door with the blood of your lamb, but I will sleep no more soundly with you watching over us all.

May 7, Tanis, Egypt

Happy birthday, my son!

May 12, Tanis, Egypt

Jesus took his first steps today! We are such proud parents! If only we knew an artist who could capture the moment. My words will have to do.

He was so pleased with himself. Giggling and laughing. You'd think he'd walked on water, the way he carried on!

June 1, Tanis, Egypt

I have a toddler on my hands! Jesus is now scampering about the place. We must watch him constantly. Yesterday he swallowed a shekel. Everything, everything goes in his mouth! I am always on the run.

June 14, Tanis, Egypt

My lessons with Magda continue, but learning is difficult with a baby bent on exploration. Izel and I take turns watching the children and then watching Magda.

July 1, Tanis, Egypt

I try to write, but my son ...

July 2, Tanis, Egypt

Today I will sit down for a minute and write ...

July 3, Tanis, Egypt

Jesus is ...

August 4, Tanis, Egypt

I have never until this day come close to a leper.

Fearful for Jesus, I hung back and would not enter Magda's shop until she thumped to the door. "Foolish girl! You claim to want to heal and yet fear the sick!"

I entered meekly, my son in my arms. Izel reassured me and took Jesus into the other room with Omar. Magda resumed rubbing a young boy, around six or seven years, with oil. He had swollen and angry-looking lesions all over his body.

"Chaulmoogra oil," Magda pronounced and nodded towards a dark-clad figure in the shadows. "This is Nefri and her son Nagjib."

The small figure sank further into the corner of the room and said not a word. Neither did I.

"If you intend to help at all today, you will find a basket of food in the larder. Bring it for Nefri and her son."

Stumbling over my fear and my foolish feet, I descended into the dank cellar and retrieved the basket. Magda was helping Nagjib into his clothes, mostly rags, and speaking to Nefri in their mother tongue, still so strange to me.

"Give her the food!"

I stepped towards the woman and lifted my face. Hers was a nightmare. I drew a shaky breath and managed a smile.

"Food for your family." I offered her the basket, as Magda translated. "And I am sorry for my rude manners earlier."

With bowed head, Nefri accepted the food and a flask of the chaulmoogra oil and muttered soft thanks. As she turned to leave the shop, I noticed she was with child. She and Nagjib hovered at the doorstop, waiting until the narrow street was clear of passersby, before scurrying away.

"I cannot imagine such a life."

"Harrummph! There is much you cannot imagine." Magda lit the eucalyptus incense to purify the shop. "Right now I cannot imagine what I will do with Nefri's infant once it is born."

"She will give it up?"

"She will and she must. Her son Nagjib has fallen to the disease just as his parents before him. The only hope for the babe is to be removed from the lepers. But there is not an orphanage from here to Cairo, and I am not going to raise a child at this stage in my life!" Magda slammed things about the shop in frustration. She was too upset to instruct us further that afternoon, but she lent me several parchments about the ailment leprosy that I will read aloud to Izel.

Tonight I can't get the thought of Nefri's baby from my thoughts as I nurse my own healthy infant asleep. And again tonight I miss my own mother. There are so many wrongs in this world. Beggars and lepers, the innocent afflicted with disease, wives beaten by husbands. Where is Yahweh for his people? It makes me as angry as those welts on Nagjib's body.

September 15, Yom Kippur

Well, Joseph and I are finally talking again after our enormous fight several weeks ago. He was being completely unreasonable about my lessons with Magda.

"People are beginning to talk, Mary."

"Let them."

"These are our neighbours. Your deeds will affect our livelihood."

"There is more work than you can manage now! What are your worries? Besides, just watch as these yentas run to Magda when they need her medicines and herbs or her lovecharms for their straying husbands!"

"You are not to go to Magda's shop again, Mary."

I looked at him, dumbfounded. I gathered gall into my mouth and spat at Joseph: "Who are you to tell me when and how much I will learn and from whom? I learn the arts of healing with Magda. The arts of medicine. She is no witch. Neither am I nor Izel. Someday my knowledge may save our son's life. Someday my herbs may save your own miserable life!"

Joseph's eyes blazed into mine. I had never before seen him angry.

"You are a willful woman who does not know her place! You must live according to the examples of Ruth and Ester and ..."

"I live my own life, not that prescribed by dead and buried prophets and martyrs! I aim to stay alive, Joseph. To keep my family alive. And to take care of others who need care."

"Does that include that swine, Jeremiah?"

I did not think Joseph capable of such nastiness. I raised my chin. "I care for anyone who comes to me in need, but if you wonder whether I will share my bed with him, the answer is no. That cold sterile place is reserved for you alone, old man."

He left me then and we did not speak anything of import to one another until this day of atonement. After temple, Joseph walked with me. Jesus was fussing because he is cutting another tooth. We set him down on Joseph's robe and sat amusing him.

"I do not want this coldness between us, Mary."

"I have not changed my mind, Joseph."

"I know."

"Knowledge is a good thing, Joseph."

"But Eve wanted knowledge and look where it got us."

"I think you should not listen so closely to that rabbi. He infects your mind. And didn't you once tell me that you weren't a man to deny me knowledge? Think of this, Joseph: maybe someone didn't want Eve to have knowledge. Why is that?"

"God knows, Mary."

"Precisely. God. When my mother insisted that my father teach my sisters and me to read and write, he listened to his wife. Many frowned on his teaching. He knew knowledge was power, and he would not have his children — any of them — powerless and ignorant."

"But it is risky, Mary."

"What risk? Life is risk, Joseph. But knowing helps to outsmart risk."

He was silent, but nodded. "I am swayed by the traditions of my father and his before him. I forget that you are an unusual woman. And he is an unusual child." Jesus was smiling and gurgling up at Joseph. I had rubbed some mint oil on his gums and he was in better spirits. Joseph put Jesus on his knee.

"You are a good mother. And wife, Mary. You may learn all you wish to learn."

I almost retorted, but thank God, held my tongue.

"Jesus looks a little like me, doesn't he, Mary?" He gazed into Jesus' grey-green eyes.

In your dreams, Joseph. "A little."

Tonight the bed thawed. At least for my husband.

November 1, Cairo, Egypt

"I must go to Cairo and you must take me," I told Joseph, simply.

He sighed. "Why?"

"If I am to be more than a village idiot, I must continue to learn, Joseph. There is much to see in Cairo, much wisdom I am only beginning to glimpse. Your shop will be well enough on its own for a fortnight." Joseph had a young apprentice, Baruk, who could attend to the business. My mind was firm.

Magda had told me of a wise seer and healer in Cairo, a distant cousin of hers, who knows much about the arts of life and death.

So we made the preparations and journey. And here we are in Cairo, mystical metropolis of antiquity. It is the largest city I have ever seen. I am frequently frightened by its mysterious inhabitants, its worldly air, its noisy, labyrinthine streets. Even when it is sleeping, it is awake.

I have been in many shops and smelled spices I've never before known, tasted teas pungent to my tongue, heard music foreign to my ear.

Jesus has been a remarkably good traveller, even though he continues to cut his back teeth. They are willing their way through his sore little gums.

Joseph has been wandering about the city, following me with his mouth agape, what else is new? I had to tell him to close it or the flies would take up residence.

We have been to the great pyramids. I am awed and astonished at the ingenuity of the ancients. Truly, they worked wonders. I heard aged footsteps, imagined the business of making such structures, and puzzled over the paintings and writings and gods of the people. I will go again to marvel before we leave this land. The place reminds me how small I am. I only wish Jesus would remember our time here, but he is even smaller. Nevertheless, together we will see again the sunlight and shadows of the pyramids.

Mehmet and his wife, Fatima, cousins to Magda, are gracious hosts. We stay in a room in their home.

In the cellars below their dwelling are their secret rooms of healing and death arts. I learn from Fatima how to prepare a body, how to drain its fluids, how to use spices to make concoctions of embalming. These are sacred, secret arts and rituals, and I must write no more. Everything I learn I commit to memory.

Meanwhile, Joseph sits in the square with the other men, or with Jesus on his knee, in the fall sunlight. I dwell in the dark with the dead. Sometimes I come to the surface to find the sun has set.

Joseph shakes his head in wonderment at me. But I can say this: when he watched me bring a woman, who had seemingly fallen dead, back to life in the square, he looked at me with astonishment. And not a little fear.

She was not dead, but prone to fits. Joseph and the ignorant onlookers drew back in awe. I admit I enjoyed my moment of power. But I must be mindful not to succumb to pride. Later I told Joseph the truth about the woman. He nodded with respect as he listened.

And I must remember this most important lesson: though I am learning to tap the mysteries of life, of healing, of medicine, of poison and of death, I really know very little. I need only recall those pyramids …

November 7, Cairo, Egypt

I have begun to read Aristotle and Hippocrates from the fine collection of writings that Mehmet has in his underground library.

I know it is dangerous for a woman to know such things. I don't care. I am hungry to know. Like Eve. No wonder she reached for that forbidden fruit. Wouldn't any woman reach if such a prize dangled tantalizingly before her? Grab it with both her hands?

Think what I can teach my son, already so clever and so responsive.

I study the dangerous art of abortion and twice have helped Fatima prepare the herbs that will bring a child to premature birth. I learn when this practice is too great a risk for the mother, and I have seen women — desperation in their eyes — turned away from Fatima's careful hands because the birthing time is too near.

I pity them. I have been desperate and fearful. But for luck and scheming, I would have faced their lot. Will they end up dead under some butcher's knife? Stoned by the unforgiving mob? Or will their ditch-delivered babes be strangled by the cord of life and left to rot in the dust and blood?

Again and again I ponder. Why do the suffering have no safe place? After all the learning, will I only provide at best a temporary balm? And where is Yahweh?

I put these riddles to the great Sphinx, but she did not answer.

December 3, Tanis, Egypt

So we are returned to Tanis. I have the gift of more knowing, and I have the gift of the great wonders of the pyramids, and I have the gifts of Aristotle and Hippocrates given me by Mehmet.

Nefri is very close to her time. After several sleepless nights, I have devised a plan to save her child.

I will adopt the child, if Nefri will consent.

Joseph does not know this.

It doesn't matter what he thinks.

I will simply bring the babe home. I have more than enough milk for Jesus and his new sister or brother.

Secretly, I hope it is a girl.

December 25, Tanis, Egypt

It's a girl! Happy Hanukkah!

January 3, Tanis, Egypt

Magda urged me to take the baby quickly after her birth. So I stood at the edge of the leper colony with open arms. An old woman, wrapped like the bodies of the dead I shrouded in Cairo, hobbled towards me with the infant. I took her and left behind what I could. Food.

Medicines. Maybe some shred of hope.

Sol, my daughter, was quick to suckle and is so easy to love. Just like Jesus. He is curious about the new little girlchild, who is olive-skinned and dark-haired like her new mother. I thought for a moment of calling her Mary, but that would be a sick joke. Jesus tends to cry in sympathy whenever she cries, and the two of them are wearing me out.

So my life is very busy with my apprenticeship to Magda and three children to raise.

Yes, three children.

Jesus, Sol and Joseph.

Joseph Schmoseph! Aiiiah! That man.

"But she is not Jewish, Mary!"

I shot that down with one withering look.

"Whose child is she? A leper's? You have brought leprosy into this family!"

"Joseph, don't be a stupid! You know nothing about the disease! This child is as healthy as Jesus! And she is beautiful and she is ours; we cannot send her back! I will not give her up!"

"She is not *my* child!"

"Ahh! There's the crux of the matter! She is not *your* child. Jesus is not *your* child! You cannot father a child, Joseph! I have known this for some time. Your seed is spent or never could give life. Either way, you will not produce a child in my womb."

"Sarah and Abraham …"

"Sarah and Abraham, rubbish! Sarah and Abraham is a nice story, but that is all. No woman who is eighty or ninety or one hundred and seventy-two has a fruitful womb. This is wishful thinking! This is dreaming!"

"This was a miracle, Mary! I do not like how you scorn the ways of God."

"Sol is a miracle, Joseph! Jesus is a miracle! Life is its own miracle. But no, I do not believe that Sarah conceived Isaiah when she was ninety. And I know for a fact that you cannot sire!"

Both babes were squalling from our harsh words. I turned to them and turned my back on my husband.

Hours later, I saw Joseph bent over Sol, asleep in her makeshift crib next to Jesus'. He was touching her fingers and there was that softness to his face I have come to love.

Late the next evening, he came in from his workshop with a new cradle for our new baby.

"Every child should have a warm and comfortable bed."

I like him best when he is simple. When he tries to think, his brain becomes addled. I will try to cure him of this.

February 7, Tanis, Egypt

Women's work is all-consuming. More and more as these days pass of babies, and diapers, and croup, and cleaning, and cooking, and learning, I appreciate my own mother. How I wish she could visit.

We had a message from home that Herod the maniac is still raving about some Messiah born in a humble stable, about prophets and angels. He, who put thousands of children to death under the sword. May some evil spite the villain!

So we will not return to Nazareth this year, I think. This makes me weep.

The people of Tanis, of Egypt, are familiar and foreign. Although the women at the well and in the market are friendly enough, sometimes I catch them staring. I feel a chill in the air here. People view Izel, Magda and I with suspicion. It is always so for healers, Magda says. We are ever at the edge of the world, looking in. It is a lonely place to be.

I have my babes. And there is Joseph. But I long for company, for friendly banter, for all my relatives. I miss community. I miss our temple back home.

I miss Jeremiah. I miss our passion. I miss …

Ah, but here is Izel at the door, my Sister and my friend, just in time to save me from myself.

February 17, Tanis, Egypt

The entire household is sick from some grippe. First Jesus, then Joseph, then me and finally Sol. I am exhausted from nursing us all. Izel tried to help, but I don't want her family visited by this illness, so I shushed her away.

For all my knowledge, I can find nothing to rid us of this coughing and sneezing and snot. I've searched Hippocrates in vain. My herbal concoctions are at best an ointment for breathing or a tea to help us sleep the night in less misery.

Someday, I hope to find a way to heal this malady that seems to strike each winter.

March 3, Tanis, Egypt

Today the sun broke through the clouds, and we are reminded that spring is somewhere in the air. Jesus, Sol and I spent a fine day in the nearby hills, picking sage and other herbs from amongst the scrub. Magda's supplies are low and I would like to repay her for her lessons with some small offering.

I have asked Joseph to make repairs to her weather-beaten shop and, though he is clearly frightened of the great woman, he has begun in earnest. Have I said before that the schlemiel is a good man? Perhaps it is time.

A sad thing happened in the past weeks. I have not been able to write about it until now. Martha is dead. Her snaggle-toothed husband, Kerim, summoned us to breathe life back into her broken body. I saw the bruises about her neck and knew she would never again know life's breath. As Magda closed her eyes, I said a silent prayer. Asked Yahweh for the thousandth time for justice. In Martha's face was a curious peace.

I spat on Kerim on my way out of his dwelling. Magda said something to him that I did not hear, but the man now walks with a painful limp.

June 2, Tanis, Egypt

Has it been so long since I've written? I am shocked at the passing of time. Jesus had his second birthday and I my seventeenth. Joseph doesn't know when he was born, so we celebrated his, too. Sol's croup seems to finally be over, and so she enjoyed the festivities. I prepared a fine meal for all of us, for Izel, Gamaaz, Omar, Magda and her newest lover whose name escapes me. Truly, I can't keep up with the names of all the men she has known. We felt like a large family and the eating and drinking, singing and dancing went on well into the night as, one by one, our children and then our men dropped off to sleep.

We sprawled sleepily on cushions and rugs, and Izel told me sad news. "Gamaaz and I are leaving Tanis."

"I feared this day would come, Izel, but I hoped that because Gamaaz is old, he might be weary of the road."

"We are Bedouin," she smiled, "but I think this will be his last journey."

"Where do you go?" Magda asked drowsily.

"We will follow the River Nile and seek our relatives farther to the south."

"When will you come back?" I asked.

Izel smiled. "I don't think Tanis will be my home again, Mary, but I know we will see one another again." She embraced me, and we wept together.

So my heart has been heavy ever since. Beyond my daily work, I try to spend what scant time I have with Izel.

She is my Sister of the Star and she leaves in ten days.

June 21, Tanis, Egypt

I am trying to keep my spirits up by reading Aristotle and Hippocrates and learning from Magda, but since Izel has left, the sun is too bright and my tears come often.

Joseph made a toy for Omar, and I gave Izel a gift of a necklace made of beads I traded for in the market. I watched the family caravan disappear along the horizon, long after Joseph had returned to his shop. A part of my heart has gone with Izel.

I am so very homesick. Missing Nazareth, the town I'd longed to escape. Missing my mother. My father. Even my brothers and sisters have become dear to me with the passing of time. Who would have thought I would ever miss Deborah? Or Samuel? Spend time wondering what Joanna and Ruth might look like after two years? Wish for Passover with my cousins? I'd love to visit Adi, to know how her marriage with Aaron fares. To sneak over to see Jez, just to share a joke or two, tell her how I've changed, who this Sister is becoming.

I should be happy that summer is here. I should be grateful for Jesus, who is chattering my ears off, and Sol, who is such a plump and happy baby. Jesus watches her so closely and so seriously. She will gurgle some baby comment to him and he will smile or laugh. They are adorable together. I am blessed to have such children.

My latest studies are of the tinctures of flowers for medicines. I work with Magda whenever time permits. But I also gave a simple village goose girl a love knot with cubeb berries tied in it. Now she thinks her man's head has turned towards her, so she brings me eggs every other morning.

Joseph's shop is always busy; at least these folk recognize a fine craftsman.

Yet I feel so alone.

July 14, Tanis, Egypt

Herod is dead! I have word from Mama and Papa that Herod the Great was found in his magnificent bed, choked on some crust of bread, and purple in the face!

Joyous news!

Joseph and I prepare immediately for our return! Jesus does not know why we are so happy, especially his mother, but he shrieks in delight when I pick him up and swing him around. Sol, too, laughs at my delirium of happiness.

I will leave word with Magda for Izel, should she pass this way, that we will be in Nazareth.

Nazareth! In just a short time!

I cannot believe my good fortune! Our good fortune! Soon I will embrace my family. And they will come to know Sol and Jesus!

I am so excited I cannot sleep or eat!

July 25, Tanis, Egypt

Finally, the packing is finished, and we have sold what we do not intend to take with us. We have a caravan of camels, and are far more seasoned travellers than when we first set out from Bethlehem. Was it really just over two years ago? It feels as if ten have passed.

Magda has been filling in as many gaps as possible in my herbalist education these last weeks. I take careful notes, but know I must study and investigate the properties of flowers, roots, herbs and plants the rest of my life. I hope that Sol and Jesus have a desire to learn what the great she-earth can teach them. I so want them to grow up with purpose, not silly and naive like I was.

I look back at my earliest writings and wonder who that girl was.

When I look in the mirror, I am the same Mary, but I feel changed.

And Jeremiah? Now that I am a mother of two, where is he in my heart? I sometimes check to see. There he is still, somewhere in my secret chambers. I feel, from time to time, torpid stirrings of my flesh, especially when I read my earliest scrolls and when some thought or mood or fragrance reminds me that I am a woman with a woman's passions. I do not know if I will taste rapture again. This saddens me.

For now my passions must be my children and my return to Nazareth. Jesus and Sol are my true loves.

"What will you do when you return?" Magda inhaled her strange smoke deeply.

"I do not yet know."

"All this learning, this study, these books you read … will you take your knowledge anywhere?"

"I pledged to you that I would."

"Then you should think carefully what it is you plan to do with the rest of your life."

Magda's words are a seed in my soul. I have been carefully musing for a week now. I approached Joseph with my latest idea.

"Joseph," I began, "what is the largest structure you have ever built with your carpenter's hands?"

"A house, I guess."

"Was it a house of many rooms?"

"For a rich man, yes."

"When did you build such a dwelling?"

"Many years ago now, Mary. I am given to crafting and working wood these days."

"I know. But could you build such again?"

"If I had the workmen. Why do you ask?"

"Because when we return to Nazareth, I want a very large house, Joseph, greater than that of your richest client."

He raised a hoary eyebrow. "Mary, this seems not like you."

"I want a mansion with many rooms, Joseph. Would you deny me such a dwelling?"

"I … no, Mary. The business has done well here."

"So it's not a matter of money."

"No, but I do not understand you."

"Ah Joseph. I have done well here, too. I take home with me my knowledge for healing and caring. It is my dream to have a home for many, a house of cures. A refuge for the sick and dispossessed. In this way, I can continue my life's work."

"But your life's work is to be a mother and a wife, Mary."

"Yes, but I have told you that I wish to extend my care to others."

"You cannot adopt the world, Mary."

"Perhaps not, Joseph. But I can try."

Poor good man. He looked quite perplexed, but I know he will build my house of cures. We will look for a healing spot when we return to Nazareth.

Magda is quite impressed with my idea. "Your heart is a good one, Mary."

"Will you come to live with us, Madga?"

"And leave my home and my people? No."

"Who will care for you as you grow older?" She is already gaining on sixty winters.

Magda laughed. "I will, my novice. I have always cared for myself. And I always will."

I believe her.

July 30, Tanis, Egypt

Today we depart. The sun is just going down over the horizon and I must pack away these scrolls. Many full pages, and I will have others to begin when we get home to Nazareth.

I love to read over the lines of who I was and who I have become. Who will I be when the book of my life is over?

Jesus and Sol are bundled with me. They are so well-behaved and eager. I don't pretend that travelling with children will be easy. But we are going home and nothing can dampen that thought.

Magda came to say goodbye tonight. I had nothing to give her but a simple woven cloth from my mother. Any herb or potion that I can prepare, she knows better how to make.

"Thank you, Magda, my teacher, for your wisdom."

"You have been a good student. Learn well all your life, Mary. Sorrow will come to you, but you will endure and wax strong. You are, after all, a Sister of the Eastern Star."

Tonight we follow the star that will lead us home.

Part Three

Hysteria

April 25

Who was that boysick, lovesick goose of a girl? Who was that little imbecile? That naive mother and reluctant wife?

I don't even recognize her.

Five years have flown since Tanis. And with them my nonsense.

I am busy with my growing family and, of course, Wellhouse. There is, in fact, a wellspring beneath the foundation. We draw our pure and purifying waters there.

Joseph is an amazing craftsman. We have a house with many rooms, the Star and the Eye above the gate. Our living quarters, a huge kitchen, a hospital, and dormitories; a home for the homeless. In the midst of the dwelling, a garden with fruit trees and fine soil for growing things. A place for peace, and for the children, play. We are known throughout Nazareth and beyond.

Jez spent her dying breaths here, with women to give comfort. She died from too much love, a disease I've come to know well. Many of the sick and homeless we treat are prostitutes. Ours is a last refuge.

While I have known healing, I have known too much death. For the poor, there are no doctors. Only women healers. Though I know much about herbs and much more than those charlatan half-wizard doctors, I cannot cure what ails so many. My own bubeh died from something I could not understand. Perhaps I will never be wise enough.

What brings me to write today? After all these years, and so much living that there has been no time for writing words?

Perhaps it was the way my mother looked so aged in the spring sunlight today. She is not as spry as she was. She forgets things sometimes; her thinking stumbles.

And I too will go her way.

I recall her life of toil and caring for children and my father. In many ways it has been a noble life. She has suffered the loss of her parents, a dear brother, two stillbirths. Quietly she rose each morning to make our bread, clean our clothes at the river, draw the water, sweep the dust that always threatens invasion, tend to the animals, work in the market, mend the clothes, minister to my father's every need. When we were sick, she was at our bedsides, touching our foreheads, calming our fears.

She has always seemed tireless. But now, she stoops at the ovens. Is slow to rise. The ache of joints hinders her every move, no matter what bark of willow I prescribe. Pain makes her wince. And sometimes, like today in the sunlight, I can see death's promise in her face.

I am sad. Loss of my mother seldom enters my thoughts because she is always so alive. Even as the moment passed and the smile came back to her face, so too did life's colour. But still I saw that she will die. One day gone without a trace. Except that her heart will beat on in mine, in Deborah's, Joanna's, Ruth's, Samuel's. And in Jesus'. But who will know her? Who will remember the remarkable woman who is my mother? She will die, and with her the story of her life.

I will pass on her life to my children; I will tell them tales of my mother and I at the well. I will tell them about the softness of her hands. I will tell them how she knew me too well. How she helped to write the story of me. How she saved me. And after I am gone, perhaps they will remember to tell their children. And perhaps not.

In five generations, who will remember any of us? Maybe that is why I write today. So that in five generations, some great-great-great-grandchild may pick up this scroll and be moved to think of her own mother through reading words about me and mine.

I suppose it is a silly thing. Vain, even. I am not a great Pharisee or magistrate. But I do the labour of saving lives. I have seen wonders worked with the juices and extracts of plants. I have watched women, my mother included, heal and cure and soothe. We welcome the sick, the infirm, the elderly, the abandoned, the starving, the wretched at Wellhouse. What more important work is there? What more important story?

May 30

Jesus is seven. Sol is going on six. They are a handful. Sol is petulant when she cannot do everything that Jesus does. She even insists on helping Joseph in his shop. Joseph says that Jesus could have a hand for carpentry. I hope he does. It is good work. But Jesus is a difficult child.

My family has spoiled him. They indulge his whims and fuss over his dark curls, his grey-green eyes. He is a son. *The* son. And Deborah, damn her, told him that ridiculous angel story which, Yahweh help me, I will never live down. So now he entertains grandiose ideas, which he sometimes shoves in his sister's face, that he is the Messiah and she must heed his every word.

I overheard him at it last night and gave his ear a tug. Of course, that immediately led to a tug-of-wills.

"Ouch!"

"You'll get that and more if you don't mind your wagging tongue. Sol is crying, under the pomegranate tree. Go to see her, and mend your ways.

"You can't make me. I'm the Son of God."

"You are a little boy, a nasty little boy to hurt your sister, who loves you and wants only your love in return."

"I hate you!"

"This to your mother? The one who feeds you and plays with you and tends to you? You repay her love with your hate? Fine. Then live with your choice. Be hateful."

And I was silent for the rest of the night. He knew he had overstepped his limit. I watched him from the corner of my eye make amends with Sol and pay her special attention. But I gave him none of mine until this morning when I took him on my knee.

"Jesus, you are a special boy."

"The Son of God."

I sighed. "In a sense, just as Sol is a daughter of God. Just as I am. But to lord it over your sister ... or your mother ... is not right. It is not what I want from you. It is not what your father expects of you. All children are gifts, and you are precious to us. But I want you to forget the notion that you are God's Chosen Son. I want you to treat Sol and me and your Papa and the children and mothers in Wellhouse with kindness."

"And Bubeh and Zaydeh?"

"Yes. Everyone, if you can manage it."

"You pulled my ear."

"I am sorry for it."

"I'm sorry, too, Mama."

And off he ran. Children's troubles are so light, their grievances so easily forgotten. Why can it not be so with adults?

June 14

Late last night there was an urgent knocking at the door. One of the women, Lydia, came to our room, whispering of an injured man, a bleeding man.

Joseph helped us carry him in, half faint.

It was Jeremiah.

I felt all my carefully constructed walls threaten to crumble. I could hardly breathe at the sight of him.

Joseph said nothing as he looked down at the man bleeding on the pallet. Lydia and I examined the wounds. Joseph caught my eye. I pulled him along with me to get fresh water.

"So, he is back."

"It would seem so."

Joseph sighed, and I took his hand. "You have nothing to fear, my husband." And I smiled at him.

He touched my face with his carpenter's hand. I sent him back to our bed.

When I returned with the water, Jeremiah was moaning. Lydia and I sewed the gashes, knife-cuts all. I wiped the sweat from his brow. He was very pale from loss of much blood. Lydia left us to prepare a salve for the dressings.

"What fight was this?"

"I was jumped in the street."

"An innocent victim?"

He could not lie to me. "No. Someone in Nazareth bears me a grudge."

"I see."

He grimaced in pain. "I'm sorry, Mary. I stole into town. To see you and the boy." And he looked at me with those beautiful eyes.

"You may rest here. A week, perhaps."

He took my hand. Even though he was weak, his warmth, his pulse made my own leap.

"Then you should leave Nazareth."

"For your good or mine?"

"For us both."

Lydia returned with the salve. I let her dress his wounds. My hands were too shaky.

I want to find this foolish part of me where the idiot dwells and take her out and shake her! Why does this man have this effect on me? Even now I am drawn to the part of the house where he sleeps. I look in on him every hour. Try as I might to mask how I feel, I am sure that I give myself away.

Joseph, gentle, uncomplaining and uncomplicated. He deserves better than me. I just now brought him his midday meal. He asked no questions. But how can he not know?

Know that after seven years this man, Jeremiah, still holds my heart prisoner. This man, this rogue breathes fire into my veins. Know that only a thin promise keeps me from locking the door and dropping my robe before this man, Jeremiah. Know that I am weak. A woman. Weak. And stupid.

My mother? What will she say when she comes this afternoon? She will know. "Ayi, such a daughter was I given! This I need in my old age? Mary, I am telling you, as your mother, get rid of him, this Jeremiah. He is nothing but bad news. And I'll tell you another thing. Get rid of him for good because he's a hanger-on. I know one when I see one."

She tires me out before I even see her. Maybe I can preoccupy her with her grandchildren. She keeps after me to have more. If only she knew how dangerously possible that is!

June 16

My heart is a peculiar organ. It has been bounding about all day.

It lurched when Jeremiah darkened the door of my workroom. I felt him before I looked up to see.

"Mary?"

Although weak from his injury, he is the same, only more handsome. He has a streak of grey through his hair. His eyes are the eyes that caught me before. Trim and fit, he carries his body like a man who knows he looks well.

"May I … see the boy?"

"He is playing in the garden." I left my work and helped Jeremiah to the courtyard, conscious of his nearness, his breathing, my own, my hair, my plain clothes.

We watched from the doorway. "Would you like to meet him?"

"Not yet. Perhaps tomorrow." Fatigue was showing in his face.

I helped him back along the hallway.

"I've meant to come to see you before."

"Have you? We've been here five years, Jeremiah."

"I know it. Only I have ... my wife. And my business often takes me abroad."

"I see."

"I couldn't come, Mary! Couldn't risk it. Seeing you. Not having you."

"You are seven years too late, Jeremiah." I turned away.

He gripped my shoulders, spun me around. "You are always in my mind, Mary. You rule my thoughts." And he kissed me.

And in that kiss, Mary melted away, into the nights of passion, the hunger for him, the months, years of pain in not having him. The terror of being alone, and the enormous lie of my life that saved my life.

"Come to my room."

I pulled away to collect myself. "What? Are you kidding? Jeremiah, you cannot have me! My child, my children play and live under this roof. I am married. You are married. What are you thinking? I bargained my life away seven years ago and have built it anew. I will not destroy the happiness of those I love or my own!"

"You are happy with him?"

"Him? Joseph? I am content."

"Content."

"Happy, even. Look what I have! Look at who we are and what we do in this house. I have a family. I have love. What do you have, Jeremiah?"

"I thought I had you."

There was a silence between us. "In a way, you will always have me. I have longed for you. You are the father of my child. I have never stopped loving you."

He reached for me again.

"But! That doesn't mean we can be together."

"Until he dies!"

"That is an awful, hateful thought. Leave me."

"Mary ..."

"There is no room for hate or violence in Wellhouse. There is enough of both out there in your world."

I left him. But he has not left my thoughts.

June 19

Jesus has met his father.

Jeremiah grows in strength daily. It is the healing power of this place. He says it is the healing power of Mary. I laugh at that.

I took our son to him the second day.

"Jesus, we have a guest for you to meet. He has been hurt, but is healing."

Jeremiah sat against the wall, on his mat. He had trimmed his beard, dressed himself in borrowed robes, discarded his bloodied ones.

"Hello." His voice was thick in his throat.

"What happened to you?"

"Some men jumped me and stabbed me."

Jesus' eyes widened. "Cutpurses?"

"You could say that."

"Was there lots of blood?"

"Yes."

"Mama, did you see the blood?"

"Yes, Jesus. Lydia and I tended to the wounds. But Jeremiah is getting better. Already the colour is back in his face."

Jesus turned back to the man who is his father. Their eyes locked in mirror image. "What is your trade?"

"I am a ... salesman."

"A merchant, like Zaydeh?"

"Not really. I travel."

"My father is a carpenter. He built Wellhouse. He can build anything! I'm learning to be a carpenter, too!"

"It's a good trade, Jesus."

Perhaps he heard the catch in his father's voice. "Jeremiah. That's a prophet. Are you a prophet?"

"No."

"I'm going to be a prophet."

"That's enough of that, Jesus. Say goodbye to Jeremiah. Go on and join your sister in the courtyard."

"Goodbye, Jeremiah."

"Goodbye, son."

We were alone then. The air was heavy. I moved to leave him.

"Don't go yet, Mary. Sit awhile with me."

"I have much to do." But I sat beside him, cautiously. "He looks so like you."

"I see it, too."

"He is learning to read."

"Good."

"He believes that angel story. It goes to his head, although I try to convince him he is just a boy."

Jeremiah smiled his beautiful smile. "You have a daughter now?"

"Sol. She is adopted. She and Jesus are very close, but also enemies. It is the way with children."

He smiled again. "Will you and Joseph have other children?"

"He cannot."

"We make beautiful children, you and I, Mary." He touched my mouth.

I sprang to my feet. "You are healing well. Lydia or Rebecca will be in to change your bandages.

"I'd rather you did."

"I cannot." And I fled the room.

June 22

I resisted going to Jeremiah these past days, but tonight I brought him his supper. He stood looking out the window of his room.

"My husband wonders how you are doing."

"He wonders when I will leave this house."

"Yes."

"Tell him that Lydia has taken the stitches out of all but one wound. When the last is removed, I'll go."

"Good."

"She's very pretty. Lydia."

"Is she? I hadn't noticed."

"Yes."

"Enjoy your meal." I placed the platter before him and turned quickly.

"Mary." He caught my wrist. "I'm teasing. It's your face I want to see. You I want." He pulled me against him.

"It doesn't matter. There's nothing I can offer you."

"Nothing?"

"Except food and refuge." I willed myself from his embrace and closed the door behind me. I braced myself against the wall, my heart floundering between relief and desire.

I returned to our living quarters to inform Joseph of Jeremiah's plans for departure. Joseph sighed and nodded. I went about the evening pretending to be Mary, wife of Joseph the carpenter.

June 23

He held a knife to my throat. There is a red mark still from the point. I can smell his sour breath. Wellhouse has been violated.

My hand shakes as I write.

Joseph knows none of this. And never will!

Just before we lock our doors, late night visitors. We have them often. Children, old men, wives seeking refuge. At the door, a woman huddled under a mantle. Bent as if in agony. I could not see her face. I let her in.

And she became a he. With sudden force, one hand covered my mouth in a grip so strong, I could not break free. Before my terrified eyes, the other hand unsheathed a huge dagger.

"Not a sound, see," he hissed warmly against my ear.

I considered my options. Joseph was abed hours ago. Only one other woman still awake. I nodded and he let go, his dagger poking the flesh of my neck where my pulse throbbed.

His free arm shifted to a vice around my chest. He grabbed my left breast and squeezed it painfully.

"This and more if you don't take me to the bastard."

Stunned, I wondered who he meant as I fought to clear my thoughts. Jesus? Surely not Jesus. And then, of course, Jeremiah! This evil was visited upon me because of him.

A four-legged beast, we walked the darkened corridors towards Jeremiah's room.

The summer moon through the window cast everything in a blue glow. Jeremiah lay on his mat, so vulnerable in the surrender of deep sleep.

The brute thrust me from him and lunged towards the man I love.

"Jeremiah!"

He woke instantly just as the assassin moved to slit his throat. Jeremiah bit the man's wrist. I don't know how Jeremiah reacted so surely, so suddenly, but the cur screamed in pain, dropping the dagger. Then two men became one. They rolled over and over, swearing and cursing. A pair of growling tigers. Their two bodies locked in battle — one clothed, the other almost naked. The killer had his hands about Jeremiah's neck.

I stood shaking in the moonlight. I don't know if I screamed or cried out, but no one was roused to come to aid.

"Oh God, oh God!" The fiend succeeded in locking Jeremiah's head. I heard choking sounds. He meant to snap Jeremiah's neck.

And then I had the dagger. And I raised it in both my hands, above my head. And then I heard, felt the sickening plunge of blade in flesh. And the man fell forward onto Jeremiah, dagger thrust in his back to the hilt, the point of the blade clear through his chest.

He died as men do, with that surprised and open-eyed gaze.

Still panting, Jeremiah looked up at me.

"You've killed him, Mary!"

I collapsed. And my world collapsed with me. And Jeremiah was there, touching and holding me and kissing me. And I let him. I responded. God forgive me. We made love next to the dead man. And I knew what I was doing. And I did not.

It doesn't matter. Because I have killed a man. Broken the commandment.

Afterwards, Jeremiah held me in his arms. "You are a strong, strong woman, Mary."

"I am a weak and wretched woman."

"No, no. You have saved me."

"And damned myself."

"Shhhh. It's over."

I wept.

"I must go, must take care of this body, vanish for a while. They'll know I've left Nazareth and you will be safe. But I'll come back when this trouble blows over. I'll see you and the boy again." He kissed me and I knew he wanted me again. And again.

Instead, he dressed quickly, and took the dead weight of the body across his shoulders. I led him through the passage. He staggered out the door and into the shadows of the empty Nazareth streets.

I locked the door. Returned to the empty moonlit room of my murder and my lust. Cleaned the blood as best I could, but it has left a stain and I will never wash it away.

Then I crept, repentant and miserable, back to my marriage bed. Sore between my legs, sore in my heart. I wept myself to sleep beside Joseph's snoring form.

August 1

Nothing in the summer sun delights me. My children and husband try to cheer me, but I am sullen. I cannot rid myself of the nightmares. Every night I kill and kill again.

It is always the same. I take the dagger in both my hands and stab a figure in the back with all my woman's might. The figure falls to the floor, dead. I turn it over. Only then the dream varies. I lift the mantle to reveal the face. Sometimes it is Joseph, sometimes Jesus, sometimes Sol, sometimes Jeremiah. Sometimes Mary of Nazareth.

I bolt awake with a cry, face awash with tears. Joseph tries to comfort me. It is no use. I will not be comforted. He watches me at the supper meal. As I say the prayers for Sabbath. As I go about my days. He knows something is amiss, but cannot tell what.

Jeremiah is gone and not heard from. That, at least, is a relief. I go through the motions in my marriage bed, and Joseph is oblivious to the fact that I am not really present. Thank God.

And I am not pregnant. Thank God.

Or don't thank him. Not the God of the Rabbi ben Aaron. I cannot turn to such an angry, vengeful God. If he exists as the rabbi paints him, I am damned already. I do pray, ask for forgiveness and strength. But I don't know from whom. Yahweh long ago forsook me.

After all, I am just a woman. What would he have to do with me, his errant handmaid?

Tomorrow Jesus and Sol want to go into the hills to gather herbs and wildflowers. They try to distract me. Perhaps it will do me good.

August 2

Today, when we returned from the hills, Joseph greeted us at the door, a bundled baby in his arms.

"He is James. His mother has died. He has no one in the world. I thought maybe we ..."

I took the wee thing in my arms. He is maybe fours months old, but jaundiced and scrawny. Sol and Jesus dropped their bundles and gathered round.

"Oh Mama," Sol said, "can we keep him?"

"Yes, Mama. Papa wants him and so do I!"

"Jesus, Sol. This is a baby, not a puppy!"

"But Mary, you are so good with children. You are a good mother. We have room at this inn. Why did we build this Wellhouse, if not to care for such as he?"

James began to cry, pathetically. I looked at Joseph, his face lined with worry. For me. He brought this child to our house for me. Curse men with their simplistic answers. As if a baby could cure what ails me. As if all a woman needs is another baby.

"Let us find Rebecca. She gave birth in May and will have milk for two."

And where once were four, now there are five.

Yom Kippur

I have much to atone for. Dead babies. The killing of a man.

At the synagogue tonight, all the women of Wellhouse were once again behind the screens listening to Rabbi ben Aaron. I, too, listened to his words, tried to hear wisdom in them. But I thought of all of us there together, apart from the men. Apart from their world. Apart from their God. Yahweh, I wondered, what in this place of worship speaks to me? Where do I belong in a faith wherein the men thank you daily that they were not born women?

We returned to our house of hope. I tucked my children, Jesus, Sol and James, into their beds. Where do they belong in the worship of a God who smites the firstborn?

Lydia, Rebecca and I made the rounds, checking on the ill and dying. Where do these figure in Yahweh's omnipresence?

Who will keep Lydia and Rebecca safe from those who would keep them harlots? Harbour their children, Joses, Juda and Anna? Offer sanctuary to babies like James, abandoned or orphaned? Why do the cries of these not move Yahweh in his omnipotence?

But then, Rabbi ben Aaron reminds me, I am a woman unschooled and untutored in the Torah. He thinks me illiterate and unknowing, my questions naive. He calls me willful when I protest. He does not know the daughter of Joachim and Anna. He would be scandalized if he read my blasphemous words, indeed, if he knew I write and read at all.

I have much to atone for. I know it. I wonder if you, Yahweh, stoop to atone with us, your wretches, in this, your Israel.

PART FOUR

Eros

May 24

Time is curious. It does not feel as though eight years have passed since I wrote my last words. Today is my birthday. I am thirty. My hair has streaks of grey. When I smile, the lines crease at my eyes, and when I sober, the lines remain. My hands are red from so much washing, wiping of brows, wrapping of swaddlings and shrouds. I grow older.

Joseph says not. But then he is very old. He has seen sixty winters, if not more. His hand shakes, and he can no longer saw and measure with a sure eye. Jesus, fifteen, and daily more a man, works with Joseph in his carpenter's shop. Joses, too. James and Juda are learning. So is little Simon.

I worry about my husband. His breathing wheezes. His steps slow. I lost my mother three years ago. My father only months later. I know I will lose Joseph soon.

He and Jesus have added several rooms to Wellhouse. Our walls were bursting. These days the sick and the infirm come from as far as Sidon to seek our healing ways. Most are women.

Women, lost and forsaken, some with children, some without, find another life behind our doors. Women who have no other choice, no story to save their lives. Women great with children, women who seek to empty their wombs, women shunned or raped or left for dead.

I have twelve who work with me and are learning my arts. The Eastern Star, our symbol, is a beacon of welcome above Wellhouse's sturdy gate.

And we have a reputation. Some like us. Some do not. Herod Antipas has raised our taxes. We pay: I want no trouble. Rabbi ben Aaron died here, and now his son Caleb comes to talk with Joseph and Jesus. They discuss the Torah. Caleb has his eye on Sol, my beautiful daughter, who serves the men wine and figs. She seems not to notice his attentions, but I think he will ask for her sometime soon. Sol is so good, so well-behaved, much older than her years. She is a comely daughter with none of the wildness of her mother.

Among those who don't like us are some of the Pharisees and Sadducees. There are good men among them, but also busybodies who spy jealously on the work we do. They resent that we help gentiles, people who worship false idols, Egyptians. They resent that we consort with lepers and prostitutes, fugitives and widows. One day a Pharisee, Micah, joined Caleb to break bread with Joseph and Jesus.

"Mary, you break God's commandment," Micah accused.

"And which one would that be?"

"You work on the Sabbath."

"Yes. I do."

Joseph moved to protest, but I cut him off. "The sick and the dying do not pause in their suffering for the Sabbath, and so neither must I. We must feed them. And so we must sift, grind, knead, bake, clean, carry ..."

"God expressly forbids —"

"God isn't here to do our dirty work. And I'm sure he is not offended that I am tending to the helpless and the infirm."

"In His name!" Joseph offered.

In the pause the men variously stared or glared at me. I dropped my head, gritted my teeth. "Yes, of course. In God's name. Always."

Caleb seemed mollified, eager to be cheered, and cited some appropriate proverb in support of our healing work. Micah was not appeased, however, but I noticed he did not refuse our food. He ate well that day.

I have filled these years with work. We all work hard. But I have worked to forget. Or try to. It is folly. I cannot forget.

There was never a ripple about the man I killed. Never a body found. Never a word from Jeremiah in all these eight years. Maybe he is dead.

But I know he isn't. My heart knows. And also, several times a year, a woman brings a bag of silver to our door. The woman is mute. Her tongue has been cut out. But I know who sends the silver. It is blood money. And I accept it.

Since that long ago night, I have not been the same. Oh, I have known joy. The joy of my work when we heal and cure. The joy of my baby sister Ruth's wedding and the birth of my twin nephews. The joy of my children. The growth of my family. Our health.

But I have found these years hard. Aside from my great crime, and the murdered babies still on my conscience, I mourn my parents.

Especially my mother. I hear her voice sometimes and wonder where she is, if Yahweh has prepared a good place for her and my father. I wish she were here so that I could go to her in the cool of the evening and lay my head in her lap and she would stroke my hair. I miss her touch.

I wept when Lydia and Rebecca left us. In the night, like thieves. Back to their men. I heard that Rebecca works again in her trade; I do not know what became of Lydia. But I have their three abandoned children. Peevish Joses, Juda who stutters, and lonely Anna, now mine along with Jesus, James and Sol.

Simon came half crawling to us. A man with a cart had run over him. The boy told us he is the child of a Roman soldier. Simon's mother died two years ago, and he was forced to beg in the streets. I set his leg as best I could; Joseph tied the splints as I have taught him to do. But the bone was crushed beyond repair. Still, Simon is a happy boy, though small for his age. He limps gaily after his brothers and sisters, trying to keep up. We will never let him go back to his wretched life. I spend many sleepless nights worrying about the other urchins who beg at the city gates and in the square. Where are their mothers? Who are their fathers? I eye the Roman guards suspiciously for any sign of Simon in their faces.

Jesus is much on my mind these days. He is so clever. With wood. With words. All too often, with his mouth. Once he told me everything. His joy. His dreams. And too often, his hurt. He is different from the other boys, different from his brothers. He does not like the rough and tumble. Jesus likes words, music, the company of the girls and women of Wellhouse. He is a fine craftsman, but is not made for rough carpentry. In frustration, he carps at his schoolmates, making himself even less popular with them. He watches his brothers at their games, sometimes joins in, but leaves when they turn aggressive. He prefers the little children of the orphanage or will seek out Sol and Simon. I love this about my son. I love his way with words. It was I who taught him to write. But now Jesus writes in private and his scroll is closed to me.

I grieve for him. And wonder why I have no cure for this disease between us. I can pinpoint when things started to go wrong. It was when we held his bar mitzvah, when he turned thirteen. We took him to Jerusalem that year for Passover. As we returned to Nazareth, we thought he was with my sister Deborah and her family. Only later in the afternoon did we discover him missing.

His father and I hurried back to the city. My heart was in my throat. And where did we find him? In the temple! Debating with the rabbis.

Joseph called him out of the synagogue. Several of the teachers followed him. Jesus, who is not terribly popular with his peers, revelled in the attention of the elder scholars.

"We have been worried sick about you!" I spat, and grabbed him by the arm. "This is the way you treat your poor father? Look at him! He is grey from the stress." And indeed, Joseph was. In addition, the heat of the day coupled with a nasty bowel ailment were taking a toll.

Jesus shook me off.

"Don't you know what I am doing?" He spoke loudly, turned and gestured to the temple retinue on the steps behind him. "I am about my Father's business, woman."

Shorter than Jesus by several inches, I can nevertheless assume my mother's imposing posture. I drew his chin to within inches of my own.

"Upstart! I know who you think you are. But know this! You are nothing but a little bastard. And if you do not, this very moment, come down these steps with me and Joseph, you will live to regret it!"

Jesus and I locked eyes. "You're hurting me," he said.

"And you," I hissed through clenched teeth, "have hurt me."

We stood there for perhaps a minute, perhaps only a few seconds. I saw the tears in Jesus' eyes and dropped my hand. He followed meekly. None of us spoke a word the entire trip home.

Since then we have been estranged, Jesus and I. Our communication consists of single words and slamming doors. Jesus slams around the kitchen every morning, slams out the door to the carpentry workshop. He slams in and out for lunch. Slams back in for supper and out in the evening. The only time he doesn't slam is when he returns after midnight, but I hear him anyway. He has slammed the door of his heart.

June 13

Jesus has run away. Anna and the boys are worried. Simon is inconsolable. Sol is despondent. Joseph has taken ill.

I have run myself ragged throughout Nazareth, sent word to Jerusalem. Queried relatives and friends. Asked his old schoolmates.

No one has seen him. He slipped away quietly into the night.

I looked for his scrolls, for a note of some kind. He left his room neat. But empty. Took his mantle and sandals. Some food from the larder.

Since that time in Jerusalem, he has kept to himself. Everyone excluded from his secrets. This is all my fault. I do not know why he has left or for whom. Yahweh knows if we ever will see him again.

Yahweh, hear my prayer. Be a God of forgiveness, this once. Forgive my sins; bring me back my son.

June 20

We grind. We clean. We tend to our children and the animals. We take in new patients. The cured leave us. The dead are buried. I feed my family. We say our prayers. Always for Jesus. I minister to Joseph, who cannot work for weakness. Joses and the older boys try to keep up with the work in the shop. We sleep. Or some of us do. We rise. Pray. Begin again.

God has forsaken us.

July 3

Caleb, in an effort to cheer us, came to make a dowry offering for betrothal to Sol. Joseph was well enough to rise that morning and welcome our visitor. I brought Sol to the young man. The scene was so familiar. I saw myself fifteen years ago, sick at the thought of marrying Joseph. Sick for love of Jeremiah. Sick with his baby in my womb. Jesus.

Caleb is ten years older than Sol, a handsome man, a rabbi once he is married. But I wanted Sol's word.

We left Joseph and Caleb to their talk.

"Do you love him?"

"Mama, I don't know him."

"Could you love him?"

"I don't know. Maybe. He is a good man."

I looked at Sol. And then I understood. "Do you love someone else?"

She didn't answer, at first.

And then she showed me. A letter. A poem. Then a box of letters. All written by Jesus to his sister. Full of love. Full of want. Full of never having.

"It is why Jesus left," she whispered.

I went back to the men.

"Caleb. We thank you for your generous proposal. Joseph and I will talk together."

Of course, he was surprised, but Caleb has good manners and willingly left without an answer.

I will tell Joseph nothing of what Sol has revealed to me. The shock would kill him.

Later

"For a year we have loved each other as more than brother and sister," Sol told me quietly, when we were alone.

"You are not blood."

"No. Even so, I believe we are brother and sister."

I sighed. "So would the rest of the world."

"He talked to me about what happened at the temple after his bar mitzvah. It changed his life."

"He hates me."

"No. He is full of remorse and full of anger. He is passionate. And confused."

"He was thirteen. He is only fifteen now! All teenagers are confused and angry and rebellious."

"I am not."

"No, you are not."

"He asked me to run away with him. I told him, no. I couldn't leave you and Papa. I cannot love my brother as a husband."

"So he left alone."

"Yes."

"Where did he go?"

"I don't know. He wanted to flee to a great city. But he left in the night without a word." And Sol began to cry. We spent an hour together crying. Mother and daughter, in anguish over a lost son and brother.

July 17

She came, red-eyed but certain, to Joseph and me the next morning.

"Mama. Papa. I have decided I wish to marry Caleb."

Joseph, bedridden, was visibly cheered. "This is wonderful news!"
I searched Sol's face. "Are you sure, my daughter?"
"I want to marry. I want a family."
Afterwards, when I found her alone, she assured me, "Jesus is gone. I must act now. We all must go on."
Caleb joined us for the Sabbath meal that night. There was light in our house for the first time since you left, Jesus.
And tomorrow they will marry.
I live in hope and fear of your return.

July 22

Jesus has come home. He has been gone forty days and forty nights. In the desert.
The day he arrived, I paused my digging in the garden to see a bedraggled Jesus turn down the street. I dropped the hoe and ran out the gate.
I threw my arms around my lean and sad prodigal son.
"Jesus."
"Mama."
I held his beautiful face in my hands.
"We thought we had lost you. That perhaps you would never return. That misfortune or worse had claimed you. Me, Papa, Anna, the boys …"
"Sol?"
"Jesus," I swallowed. "You need to know ... Sol is married. Has been married these past five days."
I dreaded saying the words. Thought he would push me away. But I did not expect that he would crumble so. I gathered him in my arms and held my child, trying vainly to shield him from the sun and all the world's hurts.

July 25

I went to see Sol today. We talked about her wedding, the gifts. She had been such a beautiful bride, although hers was not the wedding I'd hoped for my daughter, clouded by the absence of my son. Still Sol had been brave in her resolve.

She and Caleb live about a mile away. An adept at weaving, Sol is already putting her touch on their home.

It lifted my heart to see her, but it sank again at the purpose of my visit.

"He's back."

Sol turned her back to me and fussed with the loom on which she was crafting a rug, but could not hide the shudder of her shoulders.

"When?"

"Three days ago."

"So soon after the wedding."

"Yes."

"What ... what can we do, Mama?"

"Do? Why, daughter, we go on as we have always done. We live. We endure. Jesus will survive. In time, like you, he will begin anew."

"How can I face him?"

"With love."

"When?"

"When we are all ready." We embraced. We wept. This life seems rife with tears.

August 10

We tread gently around Jesus, not to lose him again.

Joseph's appearance shocked him. Tearfully, Jesus greeted his father, his heart full of remorse for leaving. He blames himself for Joseph's failing health and works to exhaustion in the shop, trying to catch up with the customers' demands.

Simon seldom leaves his brother's side and is a bit of a pest, I fear. But Jesus will not send him away.

Sol has not called. Jesus has not asked about her.

Tonight Jesus and I walked beyond the city, together in the evening dusk.

"I have missed you, son."

"I should have said something before I left."

"I have missed you these past two years, Jesus."

He nodded.

"It is time we spoke of this. That day at the temple, in Jerusalem, I was cruel. I was hurt."

"I showed disrespect to my parents. To my mother."

We listened to the whispers of the desert, then sat on the crest of the hill. He spoke again, "Who is my father, Mama?"

I sighed. "You have met him. His name is Jeremiah."

Jesus puzzled over a vague memory. "The man with the knife wounds all those years ago?"

"Yes."

"Where is he?"

"I don't know. Capernaum, I suppose. He has a wife there."

"What does he do?"

"He is a criminal. A drug dealer. Maybe worse. He consorts with others like him."

"I don't understand how you met up with someone like that."

"Like you, I defied my parents. I would have run away. Would have traded my virtue, family name, everything to be with him. Like you, I couldn't have what I most wanted ..."

Jesus stared at me. Jeremiah's looks, but truly my son. I told him the whole story. I spared him nothing, not even my sins. When I finished, the stars were spying on the two of us, weeping on the hill.

"Do you love him still, this vagabond? Do you love him more than my father, Joseph?"

It was hard to answer, but by then I'd told him everything. "He will never leave my heart."

August 21

We returned three nights to our hill, and Jesus told me about Sol. How she comforted him the night of his return from Jerusalem, heard his frustration at not being allowed to stay in the temple to learn and debate further. Brother and sister grew closer. And he began to write to her. Gradually, he loved her more and more deeply. And realized with greater desperation that he couldn't have her.

"You might have turned to me," I suggested.

"How could I confide such wicked thoughts?"

"They are not wicked thoughts, Jesus. Love is not wicked."

"I will never love again."

"Yes, my darling. You will."

"You have not."

How does a mother argue with such a son?

September 11

Sol and Caleb came for dinner. I delayed until I could wait no longer. My son-in-law and daughter were overdue for their first family meal.

So tonight with bread and wine and chicken and sweets, we ate together. Jesus, pale and quiet, barely looked at Caleb and Sol. Simon chattered. James and Juda teased Anna, who is turning eleven and becoming a young woman. Joses ate three helpings of everything. Sol tended to Joseph, who was able to join us for only a short while. Caleb said the blessing. And I held my breath.

After supper, Sol asked Jesus to help her ease Joseph back into his bed. Brother and sister were at last alone. Later they talked in the garden together. Jesus wept.

Finally, they returned to the main room where the rest of us listened to Caleb's stories. Sol sat near her husband. I was holding Simon asleep in my arms, and Anna was sprawled across my legs, when Jesus came to lay his head against my shoulder. In that moment, I gave thanks to Yahweh for returning my son. Even though we are in pain, we are in pain together.

As Caleb and Sol left us, she embraced Jesus and made a gift of the small rug she had woven. My son, great of heart, then embraced Caleb and wished him shalom.

It was a hard night, but we endured.

Hanukkah

Joseph is dying.

And now it is the Festival of Lights. But we light the lamps with grief instead of joy. I do not know if he will survive the lighting of the final lamp.

Jesus, still suffering for loss of Sol, is beside himself. He begged me to use my arts and medicines to cure Joseph.

"He is my father! He is your husband! Save him!"

"Jesus, I try! I have tried, but his is a wasting disease devouring him from within. There is little I can do except to ease his pain."

"Why does God make him suffer so?"

"I do not know, my son, how God works or why he acts as he does. I only know God does as he wills. He has little time for his suffering people."

"But Papa is such a good man! Can't Abba see?... "

"Yes, Joseph is the best of men. And no. I don't think God sees. Or if he does, Yahweh doesn't care."

Jesus looked at me in alarm. "You have blasphemed!"

"You forget, Jesus — that is the least of my sins."

"Perhaps that is why God takes Papa from us now. Because of you."

I tried to ignore the sting of the words. "Perhaps. Or perhaps your Papa has just grown old and sick. And none of this has anything to do with God. But everything to do with our ignorance about sickness and disease, old age and dying."

"But you know everything there is to know about healing!"

"No, son, I know only too little."

"Then it must be God punishing us for something ..."

"Look at the people who fill this house. Look at their suffering. Broken children. Beaten women. Old people worn out by life. Are they evil? Sick and bewildered because of sin?"

"Yes. That is what we are taught. God is angry at his people. They are visited with illness for their sins."

"The baby who died last night? The old bubeh, forsaken by her sons? Simon, crippled by God?"

Jesus dropped his eyes.

"Jesus. I don't pretend to understand Yahweh. I don't believe in that God of the rabbis, such a punishing and cruel father. Maybe God does look down at us right now. Maybe he is sad to see your papa so sick. But maybe he can do nothing about it at all, despite what the Torah tells us. Maybe he expects us to do the thinking, find the answers, save one another. Do you not think that possible?"

"I think ... that I want to know what you know."

"What I know?"

"About healing."

"You are a carpenter."

"Let me also be a healer."

January 5

We all sat together as a family, watching the shell that was Joseph take its last breath. It caught raspingly in his throat. And we ripped our garments. Anna, Sol, and I covered the mirrors, bathed and wrapped

Joseph's body. Jesus sat through the night in vigil. The next day, Ruth, Joanna, Deborah, Samuel and their families arrived. Together we placed my husband in the hillside tomb just outside of Nazareth. We ate a meal of consolation and my family remained with us for seven days and nights.

I am a widow.

I think back on the many harsh words I once thought and spoke about Joseph. How I tricked him into marrying me, pregnant with Jeremiah's child. Joseph amazed at the miracle of Jesus' birth, believing all of his life that Jesus was the Son of God.

Or perhaps not. Perhaps that is only wishful thinking on my part, generosity of spirit on Joseph's. I will never know.

I recall our adoption of Sol, of James, whom Joseph brought to me. The others who followed. Joseph loved and accepted them all. He taught the boys his trade. He loved the girls, although he little understood them. Or me. Yahweh help him. He loved me.

And now I am a widow.

I remember our arguments, heated words, stoic silences. How eventually he always acquiesced to my stubbornness as I pushed to learn the craft of healing, continue the Sisterhood, raise my girls and boys in literacy, defy the laws of our traditions. And always his admiration of me.

I remember my infidelity.

I was not, am not prepared to be a widow. The surety of Joseph, the security of Joseph is gone. Nothing in this life is meant to last, I know, but somehow I saw Joseph as mine forever.

I am an erring woman, full of vanity.

I miss him. Even his snoring was a comfort. Now the night is empty. No one reaches for me. Even though he never moved my body to passion, I miss his longing. Though I set my heart against it, I loved the man. My man. Gone.

March 16

Jesus is an apt pupil. Such a quick study. Such a caring young man. He softens his carpenter's hands with olive oil before he touches the babies. He has such a way with children, and their mothers adore him for it. His knowledge of herbs and plants is growing. He is ever hungry to learn more.

I wanted Sol to learn the arts of the Sisterhood, but she has neither the interest nor the time now that she is the new wife of a rabbi.

Jesus will visit their home now, sometimes with Simon. Then he returns moody from heated discussion with Caleb. Or sore-hearted because Sol is too busy to talk with him. He and I turn to our studies. We seek a remedy for his jealousy. And his longing.

Today we may have found one in the market square. A group of Pharisees brought forth a young woman. Her dark red hair blazed in the sun; her dark eyes burned with anger and fear. I knew her plight immediately. I know too well so many of her sisters.

"This woman was taken in adultery!" Amoz the Pharisee's gruff voice rang out, silencing all those in the square.

"She was discovered with Samson the tailor!"

And where is Samson, I thought. And how much did he pay this young woman for her troubles? And what does his wife think about it all?

Amoz droned on about the law and sinning women and crimes of the flesh. I felt my ire rising. Too many stonings. Too many dead women. Where is men's guilt in all of this? As he stooped to pick up a chunk of rubble, I spoke up.

"Let he who is without sin cast the first stone."

Amoz froze. So did Jesus beside me. So did everyone in the square.

"Who spoke now?"

"Mary, widow of Joseph the carpenter. And I say ..." I stepped forward, "let he who is without sin cast the first stone."

Amoz straightened and peered across the square at me. "What right have you?... "

I walked steadily towards him.

"No. What right have *you?"* I took the young woman by the shoulders, away from his murderous intent, and led her back to Jesus. The crowd parted like the Red Sea. My face felt hot beneath their stares. The young woman shuddered.

"Jesus," I said. "Close your mouth. The flies will get in."

We walked home quickly. I knew there would be trouble. But this young woman's life would be spared.

When we arrived, I shut the gate and locked it. We went immediately to our living quarters.

Jesus and I scrutinized our guest. She wore expensive garments meant to show the woman. Her deep red hair was thick with curls and scented with myrrh. Her face was painted. Several earrings pierced each ear; bangles adorned her wrists and ankles. A ring on each finger. Her hands were adorned with henna, her face with cosmetics.

"What is your name?"

"Mary."

I might have known. "How old are you?"

"Twenty."

"Hmmph."

She lifted her chin in defiance. "I am. Ask Jake."

"Jake?"

"Jacob."

"Who is Jacob?"

"My ... brother."

"Your pimp."

"That's an ugly word."

"For an uglier trade."

"He protects me."

"Really? Where was he just now?"

"I ... I don't know."

"Jesus, close your mouth. You're drooling. Get Mary some clothes, something to drink."

"You can't keep me here."

"You're free to leave."

She made no move. Jesus shuffled off.

"I have my own clothes."

"I see that. But if you intend to stay within our safe walls, you need to dress like one of us."

"Why?"

"So that when they come for you — and they will — they won't know you from any of the other women who live and work here. So that you will stay alive for another night, at least."

"Who are you?"

"I am Mary of Nazareth." I showed her the palm of my left hand. "This is Wellhouse. Here we cure. Here we provide sanctuary. Here you may stay. Or go. But if you stay, you must earn your keep. In a new line of work."

"Like what?"

"As a nurse or a cook or —"

"Who are *you?*" she asked Jesus, just returned and unable to remember his name.

"He is Jesus. And fifteen."

Mary and Mary looked at each other. Then she tossed her hair.

"Hello, Jesus." She took a drink from her cup and a drink of my son.

"Enough. Where do you come from?" I asked.

"El Mejdel. Although I was born in Cana and raised in Bethany." She would not take her eyes from Jesus.

"El Mejdel. I know of the town and its reputation. Your Jacob comes from there, too?"

"Yes." Still she stared at my son.

"No doubt he's been drummed out of Nazareth back to el Mejdel."

She shrugged. Jesus seemed in a trance.

"Well, Mary el Mejdel. You may room with Hannah, a Sister near your age. Give me your clothing and your jewellery. I'll keep them hidden and safe. Bind up your hair and cover it. Wash that muck off your face and try to look humble, if you even know how." I drew her through the door. "Close the door and your mouth, my son."

The men came tonight, after our meal. We were ready. Jesus had recovered his voice and answered the door. He brought my son-in-law and several Pharisees to see me, Amoz and Micah among them. I put down my mending and stood to greet them.

"Mother," Caleb addressed me, "these men say that you stopped the stoning of an adulteress today."

"I didn't stop anyone. I challenged any non-sinner to cast the first stone."

Caleb looked at Amoz.

"Of course, there were none to be found, as well you know, son-in-law."

The men drew together and began whispering fiercely. Jesus, too. I knew that they were arguing the finer points of the Mishnah, of which I, a woman, am ignorant. Jesus winked at me.

"Still, this woman is harbouring a whore!" Amoz' exasperation ended the conference.

"Many women who have left the profession live here with us. You know this, Caleb."

"Yes, but Mother, this woman was a harlot this morning! Is she a convert so soon?"

"Where is she? I demand to see her!" Amoz was apoplectic.

"She left this afternoon." Jesus' voice was mild.

"I don't believe you." The Pharisee cast a shadow across my son.

I moved to stand by Jesus. "Her home is el Mejdel. Seek her there if you want her. Her pimp is one Jacob."

"We will search this house!" Micah thundered.

"You will not!"

"Woman, out of my way!"

"If my father were alive, you wouldn't behave so rudely!" Jesus shouted. The men stopped before my son, who barred the door. "I myself will lead you. But we have guests and we have sick patients. Therefore, you will speak softly and tread gently in our home. You will respect the memory of my father. You will respect his wife."

Caleb, ever the peacemaker, bowed and set the example. "As you bid us."

We led the men through the halls of Wellhouse. They looked in on the nursery and the orphanage. Barely put their noses into the rooms of the sick and the dying. Wandered through the kitchen, past the well, in and out of the women's rooms. The women of Wellhouse stood humbly, heads bent, each dressed in the simple linen cloth of our work.

Mollified, the men left us. But Amoz, not without a bitter glance of parting. I must take care when next I unman him.

Jesus and Mary are in the garden as I write this. They do not know that I watch them. That I take note each time Mary laughs. Oh yes, Jesus has certainly recovered his voice. And perhaps his heart. But I hope with my own that he will not lose it again. I don't dislike this Mary. But neither do I trust her. She is too old for Jesus. She knows too much about men. And he, not enough about women.

March 25

I have a new carpet, my first major purchase since Joseph's death. The colours — deep red, blue, gold — soothe me.

A carpet salesman was in the neighbourhood, and on a whim, I invited him into our home. His two boys worked up a sweat over the next hour and a half, unfurling carpets before my careful eyes. They made quite a show of it, throwing the rugs up in the air and snapping them open, smoothing them down, whipping back the corners to show me the workmanship. I know quality when I see it, of course, so I was not fooled by the display. I chose the finest among them. The salesman, probably my age, a balding man with hunched shoulders, eyed me admiringly when I struck our deal: ten shekels and some willow bark to cure the toothache. As the man left, he proposed marriage, but I declined. I laugh to think of it. But it is good to know I haven't lost my touch.

So the children and I have admired the carpet all day. They, too, appreciate its pattern. Anna, especially, is fond of stroking it. Truly, it is the grandest thing we own. Perhaps it was vain of me to buy it. But the money continues to come in from the carpentry shop where Jesus, Joses, James and Juda fill the orders and work their father's craft. And the bag of silver still arrives faithfully. Tonight as my children sprawl across this new luxury, Simon already asleep, I am warmed by the sight.

March 28

Mary el Mejdel has found a way to be useful. She makes bandages for the hospital and cares for the orphans in the nursery. At last she is helpful! Mary cannot cook. The sight of blood sickens her, so she is useless stitching wounds. The girl is inept at cleaning as she does not care to break into a sweat; Naomi complains she must clean rigorously again after her. Tending to the cow, the goat, the chickens makes Mary sneeze. She cannot tell vegetable from weed.

It is not that she is witless. Jesus, after all, delights in teaching her to read. The little children love her. My own family, too.

But she knows so little of the practical side of things. Her mother died when Mary was a baby, living in Cana.

"And my father when I was eight."

"Then who raised you?"

"My brother, Lazarus, and my sister, Martha."

"In Bethany."

"That's where they live, where we moved after Papa died."

"And did you not learn to cook and weave from Martha?"

"I tried. But I never took to it. You know. It's not me."

"So you left your family?"

"Yeah. When I met Jake five years ago."

"You ran away with him."

"Kinda."

"He put you to work?"

"We needed the money. He was down on his luck. The numbers weren't going his way."

"The numbers?"

"Jake gambles. Camel racing. Dice. That's how he made his money. Except sometimes he loses."

"So you worked to pay off his gambling debts."

"Off and on at first. Then more and more."

"Were you the only girl working for Jake?"

"Hey! He's my boyfriend. Of course I was the only girl working for him. I loved him and stuff."

"Loved?"

"Yeah." She cast her eyes away from me.

I looked at this young woman. Twenty going on forty going on fourteen. Stupid, love-starved.

"What changed your mind?"

"I don't know. Working the circuit, you know, the towns, was different. Dangerous. The mob that day. Then you brought me here. I kinda like it here. And then there's Jake. It was dumb to trust him, I guess. He ... he could be mean."

This seemed only too true. I always examine the working girls who come to Wellhouse; we have to be wary of head and body lice, festering sores, any ailments of the profession. And I had found bruises on Mary's back and shoulders. She wouldn't tell me what from. But I know enough of her cruel trade.

My voice softened. "Why didn't you leave him? Return to your family?"

She shrugged. "I couldn't."

"Why not? Were you ashamed?"

"That. And something else."

"Mary el Mejdel, what else?"

"I left Bethany in the first place because I didn't want to marry

Zachariah the bricklayer. I ran away with Jacob. And they, Martha and Lazarus, think I am married to Jake. Married and living happily ever after in Magdala!" And then the poor thing burst into tears. I took her hand. And thought of all the traps that are set in this life for women.

So I was relieved she could earn her keep.

That is all we ask of our women. That they keep their hands busy. Idleness breeds trouble.

My son is smitten. He rushes through his work to be with Mary. Joses grumbles that Jesus leaves him more than his share of the work. But then, Joses likes to grumble.

Still, I worry at my son's eager heart. His mind seems hardly on his lessons. Jesus senses her footfall and I put away Aristotle. He hears her voice in the garden and Hippocrates is abandoned. Together Jesus and Mary go to find herbs in the hills, where before he and I would walk. I am a jealous old mother, envious of youth and a young woman's hold on my son.

He is made anew in her presence. The tears he shed for Sol are forgotten. Jesus has found a new soulmate. And I am sad it is not me. I wonder if other mothers feel as I do now. Mary talks to Jesus in such earnest. She listens. She has taught him to laugh again. I should be grateful. I should stop spying on them. I should be gracious. But my spirit sinks when I see their two heads bent together over some secret. I want him to share his secrets with me. I am a foolish woman.

March 30

Five days old! Five days!

So angry I could spit!

I'll throw that worthless girl out on her ear, that's what!

On my carpet! My new carpet!

What are they, some kind of animals?

The two of them. Naked. Shtupping like goats in the barn.

Middle of the day. Middle of the carpet!

I want to throw things. I want to throw them both out, my son and that ... that whore. But they don't even give me that satisfaction.

They have run off!

My son. That's right. Go ahead. Run away again. May your backsides both be burning!

My carpet! Five days old.
Such a son I have!
My new carpet!
Jesus!

Passover

I am calm again as we prepare the Seder: the women of Wellhouse; my sisters Ruth, Joanna and Deborah and their daughters; Bernice, my brother Sam's wife; Sol and Anna; and yes, Mary el Mejdel.

It is my first Passover without Joseph.

And I am glad he was not here to witness the behavior of his son.

Jesus came to me, meek as a lamb. He and Mary had only hidden themselves, embarrassed, like Adam and Eve hiding from Yahweh in the garden.

"Mama, I am so sorry."

I said nothing to him. My tears were answer enough.

"We ... I was an idiot. Caught up in my own passions. I ... I wasn't thinking."

He listened to my soft sobs, muffled against the pillows of my bed.

"I have hurt you."

"She has taken my son from me."

"No, Mama. Never. I am always and ever your son."

"You will leave me."

Jesus sighed, "I may move into my own dwelling, Mama. Someday, yes. But I will not leave you."

"Yes, Jesus, you will."

"How can I tell you I won't? Even as I love another Mary, you are still my mother. Always the first Mary."

"She betrayed my kindness."

"No, Mama. We were ... I should have known better."

"She has taken your heart captive."

"She has freed my heart. I thought you would be glad of that. But there is room enough in my heart for two Marys."

"Two?" I looked up from my misery.

"At least." He smiled his father's beautiful smile.

I took him in my arms. "It's time we have that lesson about birth control."

"Mama!"

Since then, thankfully, Jesus and Mary are keeping a modest distance between them. And she, too, apologized to me.

"You must think I'm still a whore."

I looked at her, keenly. "The thought crossed my mind."

"I didn't touch your son for money. I don't want that life."

"Or Jake?"

"Or him. I want your son."

"So I noticed."

"I mean, I love your son."

"So do I."

"We did a lousy thing to you."

"You did." I watched her face for signs of duplicity. It is a soft face, one that should have had more mother's love. "I know your profession well. My closest friends lived by their bodies. I cannot judge them in this harsh world, as I did not judge you that day in the square.

"I do not think you were whoring with my son. I think you are both young and beautiful and took occasion on my carpet to say so to one another. And I was unlucky enough to eavesdrop on your conversation."

"I am sorry, Mary."

"I only ask one thing of you, Mary el Mejdel."

"Yes?"

"Take care not to break his heart."

She met my eyes. "I think he is more likely to break mine."

So tonight this great family of mine will join in the Seder meal. All the patients and residents of Wellhouse will eat matzah and drink wine. We will pray together, talk together, ask the four questions together, tell the story of the Exodus and sing together.

Later, the immediate family will retire to our quarters. As we recline on pillows upon the carpet of infamy, I will think of my husband and how hard it is to be a parent, alone. I will remember the deaths of innocent children and the slain man. And I will recall when I was a younger Mary, foolish in love.

April 16

Mary el Mejdel is gone! Either run off or taken. She went to market this morning and has not returned. The streets are empty after dark; I have been to the brothels. No one has seen her.

Jesus has made off for Bethany this evening to find her family. Ah, my son. You know so little of the world.

I talked to the young women of Wellhouse, those like Mary whose livelihood was harlotry before they came to us. Especially Hagar who still has an ear to the underground. They all shook their heads. None seem to know this Jake Mary spoke of.

So I pace and wonder what to do. A secret part of me is glad that she is gone. I hope that she never returns. My son will be my son again! But like his mother, he is an ardent young man whose passions, once stirred, are not easily distilled.

The better part of me is worried for Mary. This pattern is too familiar. I have seen other girls, other women, seemingly born anew into a safer life, leave us to rejoin their pimps and masters. We here at Wellhouse have wrapped too many shrouds about such unfortunates. And after all these years, I still cannot understand why women return to such men. But these brutes have some power over their chattel, some hold over their women's will. And Yahweh help me, I cannot save them all.

But the better part of me wants to save Mary el Mejdel.

April 24

In Bethany, Lazarus and Martha knew nothing of Mary's whereabouts, and were suspicious of my son inquiring after their married sister.

Now Jesus is a man possessed. Talking of running to el Mejdel, confronting Jake the pimp, stealing Mary back.

"Jesus, are you certain that she did not go willingly?"

"How can you ask that?"

"Because I am your mother. Because I have seen so many women go back, to their peril."

"But you have seen as many stay here where it is safe! Look at Naomi, Sarah, Hagar!... Besides, she told me ..."

"That she loves you."

"Yes!"

"Then search el Mejdel. But, my son, be careful. Do not confront her pander. Such men are dangerous and they keep murderous associates. Watch your back."

And so he leaves again tomorrow. In quest of the girl who will elude him. Mary is not in el Mejdel. I feel in my bones that she is back on the circuit, travelling from town to town, Yahweh help and protect her.

Jesus will return. Downcast. Defeated.

What does a mother do with such a lovesick son?

She writes to his father:

Dear Jeremiah,

I have no idea how this letter will find you, but I hope you are well enough to assist me. Your son searches for a young woman, a prostitute, who works for a pimp named Jacob in the village of el Mejdel. But the pimp has taken her elsewhere and sells her body against her will. Her name is Mary and she loves Jesus. Help us to find her. This I ask of you.

Mary of Nazareth

I will take this message and a pouch of shekels to the back market streets, to Özgür the daggersmith, who has a reputation for dealing more than daggers.

April 30

Today I met Mary's brother and sister, Lazarus and Martha of Bethany. They stay the night with us. I have told them all. If we are to find Mary, there can be no secrets.

Of course, they are shocked and upset. Lazarus sees his sister as irredeemable. Martha simply weeps. Lazarus says that no one will want Mary's damaged goods. I told him that, in fact, someone very much wants Mary.

"Who?" His voice was gruff, unbelieving.

"My son, Jesus. The one who came to you."

"He is just another customer."

"He loves her. We ... we love her."

Lazarus looked doubtfully at me. "She will shame your family."

I kept my voice mild. "She will be a cherished member of our family, my greater family of Wellhouse."

"Do you consort with whores, then?"

"Yes, I do." And I stared at him, frankly.

Lazarus was silent.

I told him about our lives, the work of Wellhouse, the many who seek our shelter. I told him about our healing, our hospital, our orphanage. I told him that Jesus is learning the curing arts, and with them, the art of compassion, which, I added ruefully, this world could use more of.

He nodded, finally, and bent his head to pray. Martha joined him. So did I. We can use your help, Yahweh, if you're listening.

May 1

Jesus is returned. As I predicted, no one has seen the pimp, Jacob, in recent weeks, or is willing to admit to seeing him. Mary is not in el Mejdel.

"But there are so many women in her trade, Mama."

"Yes."

"They are unashamed about offering me their bodies." He flopped down beside me on the carpet of infamy.

"That is how it's done, Jesus. They see you as a potential customer. They must make enough money to eat and to pay their masters. Some work in brothels kept by other women. Some boys also work. Sometimes, when you are desperate or hungry or both, your body is your trade."

"Never me! Never Sol! Never you, Mama!"

"Ah, Jesus ... watch what you say, my son. But for the grace of Yahweh you might have trod such a path. There was a time even I briefly considered it."

"Seriously?"

"Well, perhaps not seriously." I smiled at him. "I found another way to save you and me. I found a story."

"I can't stand that Mary is selling her body!" He jumped up in frustration.

"It is a dangerous life and we will do all that we can to find her. Save her. But you will need patience."

"I feel so helpless!" And he left the room and the house, presumably to walk in the desert alone.

Wherever you are, Mary el Mejdel, be as well as you can.

May 7

Jesus is sixteen today and what an unhappy sixteen-year-old he is. We are miserable with him. We are miserable when he leaves us. Routinely, he searches the nearby towns and villages, the streets of Nazareth for Mary. Sometimes he disturbs our sleep working until late hours in the workshop; at other times, abandons projects half-finished, leaving the burden of completion to Joses. When Sol or I try to comfort him, he shrugs us off, and escapes to the desert. Caleb, as his rabbi and his friend, has tried to talk with him to no avail. Even little Simon has felt his rebuke. At times, Jesus will fitfully tell me everything he has learned and seen during his forays; at others, he is sullenly closed-mouthed. To date, he has found no real trace of her, although several people have claimed to have seen someone of her likeness.

I have heard nothing from Jeremiah. Perhaps I never will.

May 24

This morning, Jesus turned a moment from himself to ask what I would like for my birthday.

"That you return to your learning. That we somehow get on with our lives while we search for Mary."

He said nothing then, but later came back from the hills with early summer herbs and flowers. I found him grinding roots this afternoon, and tonight he helped Joses finish a table for Ezekiel the publican.

Just now, he kissed me goodnight and wished me a happy birthday. I will sleep well tonight.

June 16

Two months Mary has been gone from us. Jesus is a madman, bent on working round the clock or nearly so. Tracing desperately up and down the Sea of Galilee on a pointless quest. I try to convince him that his efforts are wasted; I tell him that I have sent word to those who know her trade.

"My father? What can he do? What has he ever done for us?"

"He is a part of the underbelly of our world. And from his unseemly work comes some of the money that funds Wellhouse."

"We can support ourselves." Jesus raised his chin, defiantly.

"Not entirely. We feed and clothe and house so many these days. We can always use more money."

"Money from sin."

"Yes. Call it a sin tax, if you like. But I am not too proud to take it. The publicans, the Romans, the patriarchs do not see fit to help us help the helpless. So I take money where I can get it."

"Sometimes ... you sicken me, Mother."

I hate when he calls me *mother*. "Do I?" I said to his back.

Sometimes I sicken myself, Jesus, but I do the best I can to lead a good life. I ask myself the hard questions about whether what I do, what I've done, is or has been for the right reasons. I ask myself how I've come so far from the innocent girl born in Nazareth over thirty years ago. And life answers me. With its hardship. Its sorrows. Its losses. The only way I know is to go on trying to preserve and celebrate life. Because life, no matter how hard or how empty, is still better than death, health is better than sickness, breathing is preferable to suffocating. Which is what I would do in my misery at my mistakes if I allowed myself. So my son, judge me, but not too harshly. Life will have its way with you, too. And you will make difficult, even loathsome choices. That is life's promise.

July 10

The woman with no tongue came to me today. She brought more silver. Much more. And she took my arm as though to pull me with her into the street. I mistook her meaning at first, but finally consented to follow. She led me to Özgür the daggersmith.

"Ahhh, Mary of Nazareth." Özgür's mouth struggled with my name from beneath the ugly knife scar that divides his face.

"You have news of Mary el Mejdel? Is she alright?"

He lit one of those foul-smelling cigarettes. Instantly, I was back in Magda Makimbim's shop. I tried to clear my head and focused on the items for sale. A curved dagger and its sheath inset with hammered bronze. Knives made small for concealment. All weapons. No tools.

Özgür drawled, "You could say that." His look made me uncomfortable.

"I have much to do and we are eager for this news."

"How eager?" He leaned forward.

"I can pay you good money."

"Not interested in money."

"I have nothing else to give you."

"Nothing?" His voice was lazy.

"No." I raised my woman's eyes directly to his piggish own. And I did not move my stare.

A minute passed. I felt the woman with no tongue flinch.

Özgür spoke, "The whore is gonna be in Jerusalem by next Sabbath. In the east quarter, near the Bazaar. Pentateuch Street. Number 2. Ask someone the way."

"I can read."

He raised an eyebrow. "I've heard you're Jeremiah's."

"I belong to no one. What is her name?" I nodded to the woman with no tongue.

"Sheol if I know." Özgür shrugged us from his shop.

"What is your name?" I asked her again when we reached the gate of Wellhouse.

She pointed to me.

"My name is Mary," I pronounced carefully, although the woman is not deaf.

She nodded.

"Your name? What are you called?"

She touched my chest, then hers.

I snorted in recognition. "You are called Mary?"

She smiled her closed-mouth smile. From beneath her tunic she produced a sheathed dagger, the one on display in Özgür's shop. She put it into my left hand. Then turned and left swiftly, as she always does.

Jesus, of course, was fired up to leave immediately. The entire family, even Sol and Caleb, wanted to go to Jerusalem. I told them that only Jesus and I would risk it. We need to maintain Wellhouse, which I'll leave to Sol's care, and the shop, which the boys can handle.

I spoke to my son privately. "We must be careful, my son. We cannot simply run in and steal her away."

"Why not?"

"Use your head. Jacob has means to keep her with him. Weapons. Accomplices. The trade is a dangerous one. Have you not seen how the girls and women come to us? Afraid? Battered? Bleeding? Desperate?"

"Then how?"

"I have a ruse ... another ... story." And I told him. Tomorrow we leave. Three camels. One trunk. All the silver.

July 14

We are in Jerusalem at the Solomon Inn. City of wonders. Holy city, where before I have only prayed, not delved into the underworld. Once I thought there could be no underworld to this, the City of David. But now I know that wherever there are men, even in the holiest of places, will be corruption.

Tonight we go to shul and will take our Sabbath meal together. Tomorrow we will need to be strong. And sly. Yahweh grant us this.

July 16

"M-mother? Mama, is that you? You are beautiful!"

"Thank you, my son." I looked at the brightly coloured silks that adorned my woman's body. My skin still retains its glow and I rubbed it with essence of frankincense. Every ornament I own — my mother's rings, my bubeh's earrings, the baubles my father gave me in my youth — I wore. My hair I'd rinsed in henna to give its blackness a reddish sheen, and to cover the grey. I'd wrapped some tendrils with silks bedecked with coins. Made up my face as I did when I went to Jez's to dance for Jeremiah those many years ago. Even I had to admit my own shock at my comely disguise. I felt painted. Wild. Young.

Jesus wore the merchant robes of his grandfather. He carried two bags of money. He was to pretend to seek the services. I was another kind of buyer.

We set anxious foot into the dark streets of Jerusalem, and headed east.

Into the torchlit corridors of the city's night bazaar, crowded with leering men. Hard-faced women. Foul smells mixed with those from outdoor grills. Music shrill, thumping of drums, one discordant strain unblending with the next. Shouts from the gamblers. Laughter spilling into the streets from the brothels. Jesus and I walked closely until we reached Pentateuch. Here he was to wait on the corner, haggle the price of a prostitute, later meander into Number 2.

Alone now I entered. The outer room was dimly lit with oil lamps and smelled of men and hashish. On pillows and carpets, a number of young women reclined. When my eyes adjusted, I could see that theirs were glazed or half closed in delirium. In the corner, I saw a water pipe.

"Jake?" I asked an Ethiopian girl. "Where is he?"

She gestured limply towards a beaded doorway at the back. I jangled through and found several men in discussion over a game of dice. They stopped abruptly. One man stood and came forward.

"Who're you?"

"I'm lookin' fer Jake." I worked to still the tremor in my voice. Stood with a hand on my hip.

"Maybe you should get back to work, honey." The man tried to guide me out of the room.

"Are you Jake? No? Then git your hands offa me! I wanna talk bizness with Jake." Underneath my layers of silk, I felt perspiration between my thighs.

"Let her alone, Ziba. I'm Jake. Who are ya and whaddya want?"

I looked at the man, Jake. Rakishly good looking, trimmed beard, expensive robe, bad manners.

Drawing myself up, I spoke. "I do bizness in private."

"Sure ya do."

"I got silver. Lots of it. But I won't be talkin' with anyone else in the room."

"These are my buddies."

"Sorry. I thought you were a wise guy." And I held up my left palm, before turning to go.

"Wait! Ziba, Agag. Scram." Jake waited until the men left us. "I am a wise guy. Better believe it!"

"Well, that's what I heard ..."

"You got that star."

"Yeah. Me, I'm part of a Sisterhood. That's why I'm here to talk to ya. I'm in bizness, same as you."

"You a whore?"

"*Was.* 'Til I figured out there was more money in it fer me working girls than working off my own tail." I laughed and Jake laughed with me. "I got a little place outskirts o' Sepphoris."

"I never seen it."

"That's right. Ya ain't suppose to see it. Y're suppose to be invited to it, see?"

"Oh."

"I only attract certain customers. I specialize in serving Romans, if ya know what I mean. Have about twelve girls workin' right now. Had a thirteenth, but she got knocked up. Had to retire her 'til after the kid comes. Now my numbers're off. And that's why I come to you."

"I'm listenin'."

"Heard you got some fine flesh fer trade."

"Ya heard right."

"An' I'm wonderin' if you got any fer sale."

"Hey, hold on. I only got about ten girls myself. They support my other bizness: camels. Racing. I need all my whores for steady income."

"Look. I'm not tryin' to leave you short-handed. But for the money I'm offerin' you could have yer pick from the brothels in Jerusalem to make up the loss. I don't have that luxury. I'm in and out in one night. Gotta be. I'm a woman in a man's world."

"What kinda money you talkin' about, sister?"

I steadied myself. "For the right girl ... two hundred pieces of silver."

Jake's eyes bulged. "You crazy? No whore's worth that!"

"Mine are!" I smiled. "Call me a generous woman."

"Who told you about me? How come you want one of my girls?"

"Know Jeremiah?" I held my breath.

"Sure I do. Everyone knows him in the circuit. He sent you to me?"

I nodded. "In this bizness, a gal's gotta rely on her associates. Jeremiah's mine. Said your girls were fresh. Clean. Good teeth."

"He said right." Jake studied me. "I got an Egyptian I could let you have."

"Nope. Sorry. I gotta do the pickin'. My girls hafta have a certain look. The right appeal. If ya know what I mean."

"Well, they're out there in the lobby. Go have a peek."

I obliged him, even though I knew Mary was elsewhere, pausing to scrutinize each girl carefully. I was halfway around the room when Jesus entered the brothel and engaged Jake in negotiations. He paid

Jake and sat down next to the Ethiopian. His eyes flickered over me without recognition; he turned his attention to the young woman. My heart lurched at his performance.

Jake came back to my side.

"Uh-uh," I pronounced.

"Whaddya mean? These are great girls!"

"Maybe so. But not for my place. Guess I'm outta luck. You, too." I made as though to leave.

"I got a couple girls upstairs ..."

Jesus did not even flinch, but began kissing the Ethiopian.

"Oh yeah?"

"I'll take ya."

Jake led me up a narrow stairwell to a dingy second floor. There were three rooms. He flung the first door open and surprised a huge bellied man who protested vehemently when Jake pulled a young girl from atop him.

"How 'bout her?"

Not Mary. "Nope."

We went on to the second room. A woman lay asleep amongst the bedclothes. Jake slapped her face to rouse her. She sat up weakly and blinked at me.

"Too old," I said, silently asking the woman's forgiveness.

Mary was washing up behind the third door. I prayed that she wouldn't recognize me. But I had little to fear. She turned to Jake and put her arms around him.

"Now this one's special. I kept her for myself until she ran off."

Mary el Mejdel smiled weakly. Jake unclasped her arms and she fell back on the pallet.

"Not too steady on her feet."

"She doesn't need to be in this bizness."

I chuckled, trying to still the revulsion rising in my throat. "Let's see her face."

Jake took Mary's chin and turned it a cruel angle towards me. He brought the single candle in the room towards her face. I kept my own very still. And observed. The languor of her expression. The fading bruise around her left brow. A cut on her cheek. A dullness to her eyes.

"Opium?"

"Had to tame her, didn't I? Once they run ..."

I nodded, pretending to be the discerning buyer.

"Now she's sweet as an angel."

"Her face don't look too hot ..."

"Shoulda seen her before. Besides, sister. You know about makeup. So does she."

"With a bit a work, she might be okay."

"Okay? She's great! On her back, on her face, on her knees. Mary'll do it all, I swear! I trained her myself."

I resisted the urge to spit on him. "I'm not interested in payin' for someone else's habit."

"A few days in the cold and she'll be clean."

"Maybe."

"She's young. Got lotsa miles in her yet."

"Well, I'll offer ya one hundred fifty."

"Hey! The deal was to start at two hundred."

"Not for an opium addict."

"She ain't no addict. She's a user!"

I pursed my lips. "One seventy-five. 'Cause I'm gonna have to buy her drugs until she's weaned."

"She's my best girl. Two hundred or no deal."

I looked at Mary. She smiled simply, spittle pooled in the corner of her mouth.

"She ain't worth two hundred. I'll have my hands full." I felt rather than heard the approach of Jake's two goons in the hallway. My mouth went dry. "Shit. It's gettin' late. She the best you have?" Sure enough, the goons were at the door. "Fine. Two hundred. Because I'm generous. You boys make yourselves useful. Pick her up!"

Ziba and Agag jutted their chins resentfully at my bark. I faced them, my arms crossed, mainly to stop them shaking. The moment seemed an hour. Finally, Jake nodded.

"You heard the lady. Bring 'er down."

Agag, the larger, hoisted Mary's dazed form over his shoulder; Jake followed. And behind me, I felt Ziba's hot breath on my neck as we descended the stairs.

A hundred years passed before we re-entered the small back room.

Agag dropped Mary to the floor.

"Hey! Tell your goon to watch the merchandise!"

Jake ignored me. "The silver?"

Ziba and Agag were poised at the door. None of this felt good.

I raised my voice and called my father's name, "Joachim!"

Jesus shook off the Ethiopian and pushed between Jake's two thugs to enter the room.

Jake's eyes narrowed. "You? Y're with her?"

In answer, Jesus pulled the two bags from beneath his robes and handed them to me.

Immediately, the goons grabbed my son and pulled him back to the door.

"Lay off my assistant! C'mon Jake! A woman's gotta be smart. I can't walk around this city with two hundred pieces of silver in my skirts can I?" I swallowed. "Yer boys got bad manners." I made my voice a menace, "Let 'im go!"

Jake nodded to the goons.

Jesus yanked free and shot a gob at Agag. Ziba slugged my son in the stomach. He coughed and doubled in pain.

"Hey!" I barely contained my maternal rage. I wanted to scratch their eyes out, but held in my claws. No time to be impulsive. "Call these hounds off, right now, Jake! Or kiss the deal goodbye."

I held the bags of silver tantalizingly beyond his reach. He gave the command. Jesus leaned against the grimy wall, catching his wind. I turned my face to stone.

"Count it," I dropped the bags on the table and stepped deliberately behind Jake, seated. I wanted my back away from his brutes.

Jake greedily set to his task. Mary lay slumped on the floor. I stood still, wary.

"… one niney-eight, one niney-nine, two hundred. Yup. It's all there. She's yers."

"And in fine shape, too," I added as Jesus bent to pick up the lolling form that was Mary.

When he did, she smiled at him through her stupor. "Jesus."

"Who?" I answered for all of us. A dull roar began in my ears.

"Some john," Jesus suggested.

But Agag and Ziba were on him, a knife pressed to his heart.

I had foreseen their treachery. From beneath my skirts I'd deftly removed Özgür's dagger from its sheath tied to my leg and palmed it. The men moved. But I was a swift tiger. The keen edge found Jake's throat; its curved blade pressed his pulse, quickening in fear. He had no time to protest.

Agag and Ziba stood open-mouthed.

"Let Joachim go!" My blade pressed white the skin of Jake's neck.

"Let him go, you bastards!" I looked at Jesus' blanched face, his arms pinned painfully behind him. "Or I'll slit Jake's fucking throat!"

I pulled the pimp's hair and brought his head back sharply. His Adam's appled bobbed grotesquely. I'd felt more pity for the goats I'd slaughtered in just this way.

"Let the boy go," Jake's voice was hoarse.

And they did.

"Get rid of them, Jake!"

"Beat it!" Jake dismissed the two, who made as if to stay. "You heard me! Get lost!!!"

At that moment with just the three of us and Mary lost in a torpor, I was tempted to draw the blade across his miserable neck. To put an end to his excuse for a life. Yahweh knows why I released him to ruin other lives.

Jake rubbed his throat where my blade left its mark.

I sniffed. "I'da done it, too."

Jesus picked up Mary.

"I know," Jake rasped.

"Now. Show us out."

Still stroking his neck, Jake led us over the lounging bodies in the lobby to the exit. It took everything I had not to break into a run. Jesus carried Mary out into the darkened street. I followed.

"Nice doin' bizness with ya!"

"Right." I turned away.

"No hard feelin's?"

East Jerusalem was quieter than when we'd begun this vulgar task. Dawn was only a few hours away.

"Give my regards to Jeremiah ..."

Jesus and I began to pick our way through the debris of the leftover night.

"Hey!"

I stifled a scream.

"Don'tcha even wanna know her name?"

I held up my tattooed palm. "Don't matter who she is," I said mildly. "She's mine now."

"Hey!" Jake called to my rigid back once more. "I don't even know yer name!"

"Jez."

Silently, we scurried through the grey shadows and rounded the corner. Breathless and half-mad with terror, we tripped back to the inn with our burden. No one followed, and there was nothing to fear from sleeping beggars and stray dogs. With each step nearer the inn, I felt the quelling of my nausea.

In a rush of relief, I threw open the door of our room, stripped off my costume and washed.

"You were amazing, Mama." Jesus' voice was touched with awe.

"I was terrified."

"I, too. But you, my mother, did not seem so. You were so brave. The bravest woman I know." And he embraced me.

I touched his stomach tenderly. "Are you hurt?"

"I'm sore, Mama, but I'm all right."

Then Jesus bent over the barely conscious form of Mary.

"What's wrong with her, Mama?"

"Jake has filled her with poison."

"Poison?

"Opium."

"A narcotic." Jesus looked at Mary, pale and small against the cushions of the bed. "Will she die?" Jesus' eyes filled with tears. Despite my anxiety and my fatigue, I tried to reassure him.

"She will sleep ... for now. We must hurry, son. Change your clothes and pack our things. Pay the innkeeper. We must leave before dawn."

We did not want to rouse suspicion, but I wanted to put distance between Jake and ourselves. Clad in simple travelling robes, Mary rode with me before an hour had passed.

The desert was torturous and we had to stop in the shade of an oasis to pass the heat of day. Mary woke briefly and slept fitfully. Jesus and

I bathed her forehead and forced her to drink. She saw us and did not see us. We ate and waited for the sun to set before resuming our travel. Finally, the beacon lights of home blinked on the horizon.

It was an arduous journey. But the one ahead is harder yet.

Day One

Patient is suffering nightmares and waking hallucinations. Hot and cold sweats. Sleep is fitful and brief. Severe agitation.

Pulse is quick. Patient experiences palpitations. Has a low-grade fever.

Patient's colour is grey. Eyes dull. Skin clammy.

Food intake minimal. Fluids only. Water must be forced into patient at regular intervals.

Stools are loose, foul-smelling. Urine is frequent and dark yellow.

Lucidity in intervals. Patient seems disoriented.

Prescription: bedrest, fluids, frequent cool baths, intense supervision.

Prognosis: uncertain.

Day Two

Patient worsens. Grave hallucinations: visual and auditory. Claims serpents crawl over her skin and seven devils pluck at her eyes. Hears loud braying of animals and harsh laughter.

Forced to restrain patient with ties to ankles and wrists as she has self-inflicted scratches about her face and arms.

However, intervals of severe stomach pain attacks necessitate periodic release as she seems to derive comfort only in a curled position. Hence, patient must be under constant supervision and sometimes we are required to physically restrain her.

During episodes of stomach pains, patient vomits (mainly bile) and is incontinent. Unable to keep any fluids down.

Patient is very irritable and hostile. Threw bowl at attendant (Anna). We must not turn our backs when she is free of restraints. Patient cries incessantly.

Pleading for opiate has begun in earnest.

Prescription: fluids whenever patient is free of stomach pains,

heated stones placed near stomach to alleviate distress.
Prognosis: uncertain.

Day Three

Pleading for opiate continues. Patient broke free today while attendant dozed. Ransacked the pharmacy and was about to ingest tincture of licorice root when discovered. (Luckily, I had the foresight to remove all narcotics to my own quarters.)

Patient has begun incessant sneezing, sometimes for two continuous hours, three bouts so far today. Mucous is green and yellow. Nose and mouth are irritated.

Severe stomach pains continue at frequent intervals.

Waking hallucinations continue to make patient dangerous to herself and others. Periodic restraint continues.

Pulse is at times rapid; at others lethargic. Fever is periodically very high.

Colour continues to be poor. Patient has broken a blood vessel in her right eye (presumably from sneezing or vomiting).

No food and little water intake. I fear patient is suffering from lack of fluids. We are forcing water into her, but she frequently refuses and abuses us.

Patient is belligerent to all attendants.

Blood in urine today. No bowel movements.

Periodic vomiting of bile continues.

Prescription: balm for nose and mouth irritation, frequent bathing, forced fluids.
Prognosis: condition worsening.

Day Four

Patient is very weak. Lethargy in all limbs.

Eyes are dull. Fever high. Have attempted small doses of willow bark, but she vomits what she ingests.

We force spoonfuls of fluid into her every few minutes, but this too is vomited up.

I have not left patient's side in twenty-eight hours.

Violent sneezing continues at intervals and patient has developed a cough. She is further weakened by these attacks. Stomach muscles are very aggravated from sneezing and vomiting.

Patient is wracked with fits of shaking as in a palsy.

Her agitation with attendants has subsided. She is too weak to fight.

Pulse is erratic.

Prescription: water, however we may get it into her.

Prognosis: condition grave.

Day Five

Patient is unconscious.

We have immersed her in a cool bath to lower her fever.

Water is forced into her.

The vomiting, sneezing and coughing have stopped.

Patient is unresponsive.

Prescription: constant supervision by a number of attendants.

Prognosis: Yahweh, spare her ...

August 1

What a trial we have been through. Mary's eyes opened in wakefulness two nights past.

I thought I would have to bar Jesus from Mary's sickroom, but finally, finally a calm came over him, and in our most desperate hours, he was there, caring and curing beside me. It was a supreme act of love. I am moved to tears as I write.

I have never heard such foul language and insults as he, Anna, Sol, Joses and I endured those first nights. Mary was a hellcat and difficult to love. But love her we do. Mary el Mejdel is a survivor. Despite the ugliness, she has been very brave.

She is still, but the nightmares, the daylight terrors have passed. Her mouth and nose are healing. There is light in her eye. Her stomach ailment has subsided. She thirsts. For water and for life.

Tomorrow her sister and brother arrive from Bethany. Until then we sleep in peace, in this house where tonight, at least, all are well.

September 30

I write by candle flame. It is very late or very early, depending how you look at it.

Jeremiah is asleep in my bed. He will leave with the dawn.

Yesterday my son married Mary el Mejdel.

And because my flesh is weak and so is my heart, I led the father of our child to my room and I spent my pent-up passion on him. Again and again.

I, a widow of not yet one year.

And I am without shame. For tonight, at least.

No one need know but Jeremiah and I. And, of course, Yahweh.

The wedding was planned shortly after Mary's recovery. Since then, Jesus and Mary have been inseparable. Martha and Lazarus joined us, and Jesus received the brother's permission. We gave the family a dowry. The date was quickly set, and Mary grew stronger with each day.

She insisted they marry in Cana, home of her parents. And so the plans were made. Caleb was to marry them, our families to attend.

I broached with Jesus the subject of inviting his father.

"No!"

"Jesus. He may not come. His wife ..."

"I don't want him to come. And neither does Mary."

"Does she even know about him?"

Jesus stared sullenly at the ground.

"I thought not. Here is the truth, my son. He is your father. His money helped to deliver this young woman, your future wife, safely to us. His spies found her whereabouts."

"I don't owe him a thing. Because of him I am a bastard."

"Because of him you have your life."

"No, because of Joseph, my father. You said so yourself."

"Yes, Joseph, too."

"Joseph especially."

"All right, Joseph is your father. Joseph saved you and me. Jeremiah helped to save Mary. He might want to see you married."

"No."

"I am the hostess of this wedding."

"Fine."

"I don't want this unhappiness between us. If you really don't want him there ..."

"Why? Why do *you* want him there, Mother?"

I paused to consider. "Because I am grateful."

"For his sin tax?"

"No, my son. For you."

He stormed away in sixteen-year-old vehemence. But he came to see me later, as I tilled the garden.

"Go ahead. Invite him."

I leaned on the hoe and wiped sweat from my forehead. "Are you sure?"

"I should know him. This man. My father."

"As you wish."

And so word was sent but none received back. I assumed Jeremiah was not coming.

Yesterday when the sun rose and the excitement began, I didn't stop to think of him. We bedecked Mary. We preened Jesus. I made sure the children were presentable. I wore my beautiful new robe and adorned my hair. Deborah, Ruth, Joanna, Sol and I saw that the food was ready, the lamb turning on its spit. I had the boys bring extra vats of wine for the feast. Like my mother before me, I insist on too much food and drink for any festive occasion.

The day was bright and gay, a fine one for a wedding. A canopy was erected; Caleb was in place. My large family stood weeping beside Mary's small weeping family.

And then Jeremiah touched me on the arm. "Where should I stand?"

How can so many years pass and my heart still leap to his touch, to his voice? My cheek hot, my skin damp, I led him past the curious gaze of my family to my place beside Sol. Jeremiah stood just to my left, his body touching mine.

So the ceremony began. Under the canopy two younger versions of ourselves were joined, as once I'd dreamed for us. Their beauty was ours. Their vows were spoken aloud in testament, before their watching families and you, Yahweh.

When the music and dancing began, I lost sight of Jeremiah in the revelry. An hour later, I saw him speaking with Jesus and, still later, my brother Sam. Jeremiah and I supped opposite each other, a laden table between us. Pomegranates and cashews, roasted lamb, fresh breads, honied sweets, flowing wine. I could barely taste the food we'd prepared for days.

The bride and groom, so happy, sat together at the head of the table.

Caleb rose to say Mazeltov so often that Jesus drained his glass too many times. Slightly drunk, he rebuked me for running out of drink, but I had the help bring out the other six water vats full of wine. He was surprised but appeased, and by the time Mary led him off to their room, Jesus was quite silly with happiness and sentimentality.

My Sisters and my daughters helped me clear the debris of the feast after the men had gone to bed. But even as I washed and swept, I knew he waited for me. I saw his silhouette under the olive tree in the moonlight.

And then I went to him.

I opened to my beloved. I rose up to Jeremiah. We came at last in this enclosed garden. And the banner over us is love.

I will suffer his absence. Perhaps I will never again see him after this night. I want never to let him go. But having him was not in your plan, however this plan of yours works, Yahweh. So I will let him go. But not before I drink his honey again, taste the sweetness of his flesh. Live another hour in his embrace.

Dawn will come. Dawn will lift the shadows. Come dawn, I will seek him in my bed but find him not.

Part Five

Metamorphé

October 26

"He is not the Messiah." I had to raise my voice to make my point. "He is my son. A good man. A carpenter, healer, gardener. A sometime fisherman; a sometime shepherd. A husband and brother. A teacher. But not the Messiah."

I shut the door and shut out another hopeful believer. These days there are more and more of them trailing to the door of Wellhouse. As if I don't have enough to do, what with the poor staying poor, getting poorer. There are ever more sick, more dying coming to me. Unwed mothers, desperate prostitutes. Beggars. Street children. Lepers from the colony in the hills beyond the town.

The family of Joseph has had to take on extra tasks. James and Joses now work the carpentry shop. Juda fishes with my brother Sam along the coast of Galilee, and returns weekly with a catch of fish and a small sum of shekels from the fish markets. Simon tends our goats, sheep and cows. Daily, Sol brings over my three beautiful grandsons. Moses is still in swaddling, so she helps as she is able whenever he is not at her breast.

Of course, there is Anna who does little or nothing. Anna, my daughter, born of Rebecca, who left Wellhouse some years past. I love the girl, but Yahweh help me, she tries my maternal patience.

Much of the work is left to the Sisterhood. In these eight years we have grown too great for Wellhouse. So some of the Sisters of the Eastern Star have moved on to other towns to continue the work they learned here. We send them a little money when we are able. The twelve who remain toil endlessly to salt the fish, till the soil, draw the water, wash the garments, harvest the vegetables, crush the grapes, grind the flour, bake the bread, card the wool, spin the thread, dress the wounds and on and on and on. I sometimes wonder why they stay with me amidst all their schlepping and my kvetching. They are dear to me, my Sisters: Eve, Hannah, Lilith, Naomi, Sarah, Salome, Hagar, Abigail, Bathsheba, Sophia, Delilah and Sharon.

Jesus offers himself wherever and whenever he can. He is indispensable to Wellhouse, but he is a man pulled in many directions. His studies continue with me over our medical scrolls and with Caleb over the great books of rabbinical learning. Mary el Mejdel is often with him, learning and listening; she teaches the children of Wellhouse to read and write, just as Jesus taught her.

They themselves have no children although Mary has been three times pregnant. Miscarriages. Despite my best efforts. Mary seems unable to carry a child. Each loss has cost her dearly.

And so to cheer her, Jesus has taken to travelling about with Mary. She is his helpmeet and dear to him, so she grows dearer to me. It is only rarely that I can visit my sisters beyond Nazareth, and so it falls to Jesus and Mary, who often seek the women of the Eastern Star in Acco or Bethany or Cana or elsewhere. Moved as he is by the misery of this world, Jesus seeks to comfort those in need. Mary has taken up his cause. I admire them both for their efforts.

But I worry.

Zealots congregate where Jesus wanders. He has many followers such as the man today. Everyone these days is eager for a sign that Yahweh is with us, that he will intercede for his Chosen People. Against Caesar. Against oppression. Against poverty and suffering. It is an uncertain time, this new era of Tiberius. And damn me! That blasted angel story has resurfaced around my son. Everyone is looking for the Messiah. Jesus talks to them. And his words fill them with hope that he is the One. Of course, it doesn't help that he heals the sick and performs other feats the simple call miraculous. Ah, my son. What have I done to you? What trap did my story set for you all those years ago?

And here I am telling stories again. My story. It always comes back to me. I had put my stylus and dreams well away, I thought. I have so many matters to attend to, so many people demanding my time and my patience. This writing is self-indulgent. What, am I crazy? Today I have no hour to myself. Yet here I am, selfishly writing away.

It feels so good to write it all out. Wring it out.

Speaking of wringing, I'd like to wring his neck. Jeremiah. Not a word since the night of Jesus' and Mary's wedding. Money, yes. He still sends the money. But would it kill him to send a papyrus scroll? Drop by to see me once in a while? But no. Nothing. My bed and my arms have been void of him for years. My body still hungers for the man who belongs to another Mary.

It's funny really. I grow older but no smarter when it comes to men. I have known Jeremiah. But I do not know him. Not like I knew Joseph, not like I know Jesus. Not like I know my dearest Sisters. Jeremiah is a stranger to me. And, fool that I am, I cannot seem to get over him. There is something I cannot resist about his skin against mine. Some would call this profane. When I am with him, when I was last with him, I felt touched by something sacred.

Like an idiot, I kept waiting for him to return. Denied to myself his other life. The other woman. Completely forgot she was me: I am the other woman. She is his wife. For weeks, months I kept an ear tuned for his footfall in the quiet street, his presence at my door, near my window. Listening for him hurt my heart with the strain. After a long while, I finally stopped.

Even now it hurts to think of him. After all these years wanting someone so. Having then not having. Bereft. Lonely. Missing him in my heart. Between my legs.

So I knew the magician was a bad portent. I should have turned him out with the first trick he turned two years ago. His coming and leaving should have been only too familiar. I should have been able to sniff out trouble. I guess I did and ignored it. I, especially, fell under his charm. Another trick of yours perhaps, Yahweh: eternal cosmic magician.

"Magicians are coming to town!" Simon burst in on Jesus and me as we prepared a eucalyptus poultice for an old woman's wheezing chest.

Simon pulled me out of Wellhouse and into the streets to the main where a bright caravan was passing, colourful people calling out their attributes and talents: soothsayers, contortionists, snake charmers, jugglers, all assortment of performers — some from Egypt, some from farther lands with names I cannot pronounce.

We promised to take Simon to the magicians, but they came to us in the form of Jamin, master illusionist, flame swallower and conjurer. His fellows brought him writhing to our midst, his throat burned by paraffin oil. Unable to utter a sound beyond a moan. An errant gust of desert wind had upset his usual brilliant performance, we learned. I gave him a sleeping draught to ease the pain. And he moved into our lives.

Still unable to speak when he awoke, he dazzled us with sleight of hand. Illusions with cards, shells, coins, birds. What seemed there, wasn't. What seemed vanished, reappeared. He might have worked in Pharaoh's court all those centuries ago. He certainly worked some kind of magic on all of us.

By week's end, we were all trying to emulate his trickery. Simon was completely seduced. Jesus, as in all he undertakes, engaged in serious study. Anna, our resident loafer, was eager to disappear into thin air. Even I had some luck at palming. But Jamin had another kind of instruction in mind for me.

I cannot tell how old he is because he himself has no idea of his age. But I am sure that I am old enough to be his mother.

He was not interested in my maternal side.

At first I thought he fancied Anna. But Anna takes no romantic interest in men. Then seventeen, now nineteen, she is looking for a life she cannot have. A freedom she cannot enjoy. She has tried various ways to shock me into this recognition. She got a tattoo. Not of the Eastern Star but of some design of Mithras. I told her this religion has nothing to offer women; best she should stay with us, the Jews. To follow Mithraism one must be a man: salvation is offered only to men. Anna retorted she would rather be a man. Then she pierced her body in ways and in places that repulse me. But I am older and wiser since my first teenagers. I merely shrugged and gave her ointments to ward off infection. She is always looking for a reaction from me. I work hard to give her none but support. Even when she shaved her head. I only told her to keep her pate out of the sun. I think I frustrate her.

She exasperates me. I marvel at the differences between Sol and Anna. I confess that I am playing at a guessing game with this daughter.

Anna announced that she wanted to be a renegade magician performer. Join Jamin's band. He had given her two cheap silver rings: one, a crescent moon and the other, a puzzle, a trick of a ring.

"What might you do with this band of reprobates?"

"Jamin isn't a reprobate."

"I withhold my judgement of Jamin. He has yet to speak a word to any of us."

"I could be an acrobat. A fortune teller. I don't know! I just want to go with them."

"You cannot. You are a girl and a silly girl at that. You would be devoured."

"No one has to know I'm a girl. I'll dress like a boy. Call myself Andrew."

I stared at her. "No."

"Are you gonna send Jesus after me? Juda? Caleb? Who's gonna stop me?"

"I will stop you. Because I am your mother and this is dangerous. Foolish."

"You're not my real mother!" And she stormed off.

This she throws in my face quite often.

I sought Abigail, one of my Sisters, for advice in this matter. She is several years older than Anna, but not so far removed as to forget what seventeen was like. Abigail paused at her kneading of dough at the kitchen table.

"You are right to dissuade her from this ... profession."

"Dissuade her? I forbid her."

"She sees what Jamin has, the liberty to do and travel as he pleases."

"To be a man. It is what she most wants. Anna wants to be Andrew."

"I think Anna would be happy being Anna. She's confused."

"*I'm* confused!"

"It's very simple, really. Anna is a woman who loves women."

I blinked at Abigail. I felt the pieces fall together in my brain. No wonder Anna set herself so willfully against marriage, threatening to bolt at the mere mention.

"Where have I been? What kind of mother would allow this? What have I done to this child?"

Abigail let me rant, then spoke softly. "It's nothing you did, Mary. It has nothing to do with you."

"Perhaps she is ill."

"Mary."

"We could try a medicine."

"She is not ill. She loves women. In a way, mother and daughter are not so very different. You, too, love women."

"I must think ..."

"Anna does not want to be wife to a man. She wants to join with another like herself. In sisterhood. In love."

"It is forbidden." I couldn't believe I'd spoken the words. As if forbidden crossed my mind when I defied my parents and my religion all those years ago with Jeremiah. As if forbidden crossed my mind when I made up the elaborate and blasphemous lie. As if forbidden made me cease toiling on the Sabbath, stopped me from learning what was purportedly not mine to know. As if forbidden kept me from adultery or stopped my hand from killing a man. Forbidden has been the theme of my life. Why now did I think of my daughter as transgressor?

Abigail sighed and sat me down beside her on the kitchen bench. She took my hand. "It will take time perhaps for you to understand. But I know what Anna faces. It is an ugly struggle in a world that doesn't accept deviance. There is nothing harder than defying tradition. There is nothing lonelier. On some level you and I share this understanding. Perhaps that is why you talk to me now. Like your daughter, I have no wish to be with a man. I seek the company of women. I want to be with a woman."

I looked carefully at Abigail who has seen so much. Several years earlier, on a midwinter night, she had come to Wellhouse. She had been running from her home in Jerusalem three days, and all of her life from a father who took her as wife. Her first sixteen years had been cruel. Here she found sanctuary within a family of Sisters. Abigail is dear to me. Too wise for her years.

"The law is very clear," I smiled at her, "but the law was written by old men."

She laughed at me. "I'll talk to Anna."

"I'll talk to our magician patient about his influence around here."

When a mage does not wish to be found, I have learned, he has ways of becoming invisible. I sought the day long, but could not find Jamin. Not in his room. Not in the garden. Not in the carpentry shop. Although I had the feeling he was always near. Watching somehow. I could almost smell him. It was that trouble I was sniffing.

He came to supper as if he did not know I had been looking for him. Jamin took his evening meals with us largely because Simon, so fond of him, wore me down with pleading.

As usual, Jamin said nothing. Jesus said the prayer, as he often does, being the eldest son. Mary el Mejdel and Anna, for once cheerfully, served the meal. The family chatted idly, affably. Jamin smiled and looked at me. I'd often caught him so since his arrival. I did not understand what it meant, the intent behind the sly smile.

When the meal ended and the fruit was passed around, Jamin took a pomegranate, threw it up in the air. Used to some nightly show, we watched the fruit spin upwards. Jamin caught it, and as he made to throw it again, the pomegranate burst into a flash of white, and a dove took flight about the room. Finally, the creature settled back on Jamin's shoulder and cooed in his ear. Everyone applauded. Except me. I was beginning to tire of his tricks, my patience worn thin that day with Anna's latest antics. He noticed my subdued reaction, took the bird on his hand and offered it to me.

"A dove for Mary."

"Jamin!" crowed Simon, "Your voice is back!"

Amidst much mayhem and cheering, I set the dove back on Jamin's arm, and Mary and I began clearing the supper bowls. "I trust this means you'll be on your way," I tossed over my shoulder. I could hear my children begging him not to leave — except Anna, who begged Jamin to take her with him.

Once Simon was in bed, Jamin seemed to have once again slipped from Wellhouse. I walked out to the hills to see the starlight. It was a crisp evening. From the shadow of a hill the magician materialized and tossed something to me. I caught it. The pomegranate.

"You could frighten someone half to death doing that act."

"I'm sorry. I wanted to see you. Alone."

"Hmmpph. Well, I've wanted to talk to you. Where were you all day?"

"Always within earshot."

"Didn't anyone tell you I was looking for you, Jamin?"

"Yes."

"Well?"

"I wanted to save the surprise of my voice until supper."

"And when did you find this voice?"

"This morning, when I said hello to the dove you seem not to want."

"Your dove is a trained bird. There are doves enough in Nazareth."

"Ah, but none that would be so devoted to Mary."

"I have twelve women devoted to me. A family. The responsibilities of caring for many who are ill and in need, not to mention the chickens, cows, goats, lambs and sheep ..."

"And no room for any other?"

Suddenly, I took his meaning. My fickle voice shook. "No."

And then he kissed me. Very full on the mouth. Then I could not tell where his mouth and my mouth began or his or my body ended. So, in the chill air, under the stars and the indiscreet moon, I made love with the third man of my life. A boy half my age. A Gentile. And as I write this, my body tells me I would succumb again in a heartbeat. The flesh is weak. And pomegranate juice stains my shift to this day.

Afterwards, after I'd caught my breath and replaced my heart in my chest, I asked him, "Why me? Surely you could have your pick of ..."

"Girls? Why pick a girl? I want a woman. This woman. Ever since I saw you that day when the fire burned my throat, another fire has burned my loins."

I laughed because I didn't know what to say. But he did. And he repeated it half the night.

I returned to Wellhouse alone. James was asleep on a pallet by the door.

"Mother," he was cross and sleepy. "Where have you been? I couldn't lock up with you gone. I've been worried."

"By the sleep in your eyes, not so worried, my son. I lost myself in the stars, but I have my bearings now, I hope." I shooshed him off to bed and ambled along to mine, pausing outside Jamin's room. Magician that he is, he'd found some way past James and I and into his chamber.

"Goodnight, Mary," he whispered, divining my presence.

That night I slipped into exhausted, satiated dreams.

Magicians are a slippery lot, to be sure. I never asked him to leave. But leave he did. After a fortnight of teaching my body to respond to his and my teaching him what older women know of love, which is quite a lot, I admit now, he vanished. Left the dove behind to remind me painfully, daily of his absence, as if I didn't feel it exquisitely between my legs.

The children never knew I pined for him. Or that I'd known him. Still made love to him though absent. A woman alone finds ways.

Simon, depressed, tried to saw a kid goat in two. Anna pierced another body part, I forget which now, and puzzled over the solution to her silver ring. The others, less infatuated with Jamin, carried on with their lives as before, but for Jesus, who continued to perfect a number of illusions.

Two months brought us to Hanukkah, when a bedraggled troupe of performers, Jamin included, wandered back to the outskirts of Nazareth. I remember because Jesus and Mary, gone to Nain to heal and teach, were due home that day. Anna, who, true to her wishes, was now dressing as a boy, discovered Jamin in the town square. "Andrew" threw herself on the mage's neck and brought him to Wellhouse.

"Look! Look who I've found!"

I set my face. "Jamin."

"Mary. You look ... well."

I steeled my nerve. "I hope you have no intention of staying. We can't harbour sorcerers in this house. We have problem enough with the Pharisees complaining about our work, suspicious about the cures we perform."

"Ma!" Anna is easily scandalized by her mother.

"Don't mean to impose. You'll find me at the Hezekiah Inn." Jamin turned to leave.

"Ma!" Anna's eyes looked ready to rupture.

"What am I running, a boarding house? Fine! Fine! Stay for dinner, then."

Anna shrieked and hugged me. Then led Jamin off to perform for her and Simon his latest cheap trick.

I was sullen throughout dinner. Everyone in the family, even Mary el Mejdel, recently grieved by her third miscarriage, was happy to see Jamin.

After supper, the magician brought us out into the garden to show us his flame eating. It was impressive, I must say, although I refused to show my appreciation. A mouthful of paraffin oil, and he seemed to eat balls of fire. He touched the torch flame and his fingertips alighted, to no harm. He placed the lit torch into his mouth to douse the fire. Another gulp of oil, he relit the torch with his mouth, then blew out a flame large enough to set a bush afire. The family of Joseph were impressed. The wife of Joseph, too, although she feigned boredom.

"Time for bed." I ushered Simon off.

I left Anna, Jesus and the others engrossed with Jamin and tended to the patients with Abigail and Hagar. A woman, Mehetabel, was constantly slipping in and out of consciousness, and between us we could devise no cure for what ailed her. I turned my attention to my work and forgot Jamin.

Until I entered my room. Dropped my stained shift to the floor. Washed my face at the basin thoughtfully provided by Naomi. My yawn turned to scream, barely suppressed by Jamin's oil-stained hand over my mouth.

"Shhhhh," he held me tightly from behind.

"How dare you?" Freeing myself, I grabbed my clothing and held it modestly over my body. "Come in here uninvited. Spur my family to love you. Invest their hope in you. Deceive them with your tricks. Anna is ready to run with you and the ruffians you call your friends. And I ..."

"You, Mary? I left the dove. I thought you knew I'd come back." He stepped towards me.

"No closer. I don't trust you."

"Not trust *me?*"

"Anna ..." I stalled. "Anna wants to run away. Probably Simon, too."

"I will talk to Anna. And Simon." Jamin touched my hair. "I'll tell them the truth about life on the road. How lonely." Ran his hand down my neck. "How very, very lonely." He kissed the nape. My clothing dropped to the floor.

He stayed three weeks. In and out of Hezekiah's Inn. Daytime performances in the square, at night in my room. My shadow lover.

When I try to recall those days, weeks, I can see little. Hear little. We seldom talked, even though Jamin's voice was fully restored. What had we to discuss? The children? Wellhouse? His itinerant friends? The future? What future?

Whatever loneliness infused his soul, I eased with my body. Whatever my longings — for love or Jeremiah or Yahweh knows what — he quenched with his youth and ardour. There was nothing beyond that in our midnight coupling. And yet, there was a desperation, at least on my foolish part, that we never end.

When he left again, I was downhearted, but that passed in a week's time. I felt in my bones he would return. And he did. Months later, bringing trinkets from the far-off lands he had been to.

And more tricks.

Mehetabel with the sleeping fits now lived permanently at Wellhouse. One afternoon, Jesus, Mary and I watched Jamin raise this same woman, ill so many months, from her pallet. Her eyes flew open. She smiled in gratitude at Jamin, and rose to unsteady feet. From that day, she had no further fits.

Another man, Nabob, heard voices in his head. Jamin stilled them by putting him into a trance. He spoke to the man softly, as he had to Mehetabel. Our magician then snapped his fingers and Nabob awoke to leave Wellhouse completely cured.

I asked him what sham this was. Truthfully, I was awed and a little jealous. He told me and Jesus that this was no illusion or fraud. Jamin had travelled through many places in the world and had learned from teachers of many arts. He put me in a trance while Jesus watched. At Jamin's command I awoke from a strange state of waking and not-waking, feeling liberated and refreshed. Both my son and I learned this practice; it has proved helpful in dulling pain, calming a savage soul, restoring the mind's peace.

But Jamin is, nonetheless, a trickster.

Not to mention a thief.

Why am I attracted to such men? Rogues. Vagabonds. And Jesus is so like me in the kind of people he's drawn to.

I caught Jamin with his hand in our gold chest, the same chest Jesus received at his birth. One scorching afternoon, when our magician thought everyone slumbering or lazing or otherwise occupied, I found him pilfering our money. It wasn't enough that he held a key to unlock my door, he turned his tricks to spring the lock to Wellhouse's private room. Violated our house of cures.

I stood still at the door, waited for him to turn and discover me.

"Mary!" A snap of purple cloak and the chest that was there wasn't. I had seen this illusion before.

"I suggest you put that back." In a swirl of purple, the chest re-appeared.

"And that." I nodded towards the small sack of gold, hot in his left hand, concealed beneath his robe.

"I … I …"

"I'm really not interested in why you're stealing from us, Jamin. I'm interested in your returning what's ours."

Shamefaced, he handed the bag to me. I checked it carefully; his fingers are quicksilver.

"Now get out of our lives."

"Mary, I …"

"None your honey words. Get out."

"I meant no harm."

"I'm sure not. But you have harmed this family. And very nearly harmed Wellhouse."

"I'm sorry …"

"As am I. But not for you. You'll fare well enough in the world. I'm sorry for Simon, for Anna, when they learn you have a crooked heart."

He winced. Then stepped out of the room. I closed the door behind us and said to his back, "If you leave the dove, this time I'll wring its neck."

Simon wept. Anna ranted. But in a few days, Jamin's spirit was exorcised. We went on. And we did not forget all of his secrets. I certainly kept mine.

Even now, two autumns later, I shake my head at myself. At the spell he cast on me. But as I read these words, my amorous mishap makes better sense. When we are hungry, we eat. Sometimes the food disagrees. Sour grapes. Rancid meat. Jeremiah. Jamin. Both bad for my digestion. I must find food better suited to my constitution.

November 10

Today I rise before cockcrow. It is dark. I make my way by touch through the corridors of Wellhouse and down the stone steps to our well. Our centre. My centre.

It is the quiet time. It is my time.

I dip the bucket and rope into the still waters. I dip the ladle and drink. The water is pure. Everywhere in this underground cave, I hear the music of the water dripping an ancient tune.

To its music, I drop my robe. Pour the water of the well over my head. I gasp at the pure shock. The water is pure.

And so am I. If only for this moment.

I whisper a prayer. Hum it. Sing in tune with the water's dripping melody. Two voices. The water and I.

Today I pray for children, as I do every day. The poor, the sick, the orphaned. I pray for people oppressed by the Romans. People dispossessed. Those imprisoned or enslaved.

I give thanks for life. For this home. For my family. For the greater family of Wellhouse.

Today I pray for the twelve who make Wellhouse.

For Sarah whose body is cramped and bowed with age, our eldest sister. I wonder some days if she will make it to another spring. And then, on others, her spryness, her old woman's humour and quipping tongue convince me she will live forever. I pray for Sarah.

For Sharon, found half-alive in a Nazareth alley last summer, gang-raped by drunken Roman soldiers. Her broken body has healed, but what of her broken mind? Her broken heart? I pray for Sharon.

For Abigail, knowing Sister who loves women and teaches me daily patience with Anna.

For long-suffering Naomi, former prostitute in Acco, now scullery maid and gardener.

For Hagar who fled from a brothel in the dead of night from Sodom near the Dead Sea.

I pray for Abigail, Naomi and Hagar.

For Salome, rescued from the streets by Mary and Jesus on their recent foray to Sidon. Uncomplaining, she has assumed many duties here at Wellhouse and is a great favourite of my daughter-in-law. I pray for Salome.

For Hannah who was put away by her husband. Shunned by her family, she has found another here with us.

For Sophia, wise as her name, whose husband beat her from his home. She ran to us, children in tow, and has begun living anew.

I pray for Hannah and Sophia. For all women abused or shunned by their husbands or families.

For Lilith, once courtesan to Felix, a Roman. His brother, Max, poisoned Felix and claimed Lilith for his own. She could not abide Maximilian's caresses or his penchant for bedroom violence. Fearing his treacherous ways, she fled. I pray for Lilith.

For Bathsheba, never married because she was burned severely as a child and no man would have her. Scarred and abandoned by her family, she sought this one out. We see beyond the scars to the spirit within. I pray for Bathsheba of the beautiful singing voice.

For Eve. We do not know Eve's story. She has not divulged her tale. But then we all know Eve's story. Our Eve likes to read and is an avid pupil of mine. I pray for Eve and for all women who wish to, need to know.

For Delilah whose wicked name belies the manner of this, our gentlest Sister. Pregnant out of wedlock, like a Mary of long ago, she came to us several months along. She lost the child, but her family would not accept her back, so she remains with us rather than be stoned at the city gate. I pray for Delilah.

And for our lost women: Rebecca, Lydia, Jez. Gone back to the ways of the oldest profession or gone to the beyond because of it.

I pray for women. For mothers. Daughters. Grandmothers. I pray for all of us.

And when my song is sung, I bind my hair, dry my skin, step into the sandals of my day.

Naomi, Hagar, Abigail were already at the ovens. I ignored their bickering. So many women in one house, there will be bickering. I left them to it.

Shook a sleepy Simon out to milk the cows, while I gathered up the eggs, one of which I dropped. And I thought that lost egg seemed a lost day. A wasted hour. A soul lost to us at Wellhouse. I shrugged the thought away. Just a broken egg; I have a whole basket of others.

The Sisters took the food to the sick and ailing, the recovering, the healthy. And I made my rounds. Today alone. Jesus and Mary are in Bethsaida, so I am sole physician and healer. I touched the forehead of the infant, eight months old, dull-eyed and unresponsive, brought yesterday to us. I prescribed milk and much affection. The baby suffers the malady of neglect. He will thrive with our care.

In the men's room, I greeted John who has lost both his legs. His toothless grin has cheered me daily these past six months. He tried to talk to the burned man, whose face is swathed in bandages, who sullenly refuses to speak to any but me.

"How is the pain?" I asked.

"It was a hard night."

I did not touch him, but my voice did. "I will see to it that you are more comfortable today." And I wondered how I will ease his pain once the bandages are removed, once the scars have ceased oozing, once he finds only half a face.

Today three women and a child came with the cough that marks the fever that marks the pox that marks the end. These, too, I visited. The Sisters were busily changing rags that will be later torched. We cover our mouths in the sick room, change and boil our clothes, our linens. Keep the dying as calm as we can, remove the dead. Pray there will be no epidemic. Pray we will not succumb.

My last stop this morning was with the children. Today an earache. Hannah was already warming the olive oil. Noses run, but this doesn't stop running feet. The orphanage is a good place to linger. An alive place, a place for play. Lessons are taught, rhymes chanted. The hope of Wellhouse.

I broke my fast with fruit. Then entered the room where I crush and grind herbs, mix tinctures. Pore over my books. Think. Make notes to myself. Think. I am grateful that my concoction to stay conception has worked so well in my own experiments. I re-read my script: pine bark, rhus coriaria, both to equal parts, pulverized with wine and dipped in wool before coitus. I offered silent thanks to the herbs, to the earth from whence they come, and yes, to Yahweh, that I have control over my woman's body. I opened another scroll of my scribblings.

Frowned over my various failed mixtures for treating syphilis. A cure eludes me. I scratched away with my stylus: crossed out summak, made a note to try a combination of yarrow and yellow dock. Next I muddled through the writings, my own and those of the ancients, searching for wisdom about a pox that plagues so many in the town. I read about noxious swamps that emit pestilence. I know of no such swamp near Nazareth. Sighing, I quit my books and my room. Tomorrow, perhaps, will offer more light.

Joses and James were sawing timber in the afternoon light of the shop. Simon was at his lessons with Caleb. Anna sauntered into the kitchen, aglint with all the silver of her piercings and rings. Today she was Andrew. Presuming that neither Andrew nor Anna had begun the preparations for supper, I set to washing the yams. Cast her a meaningful look. She put down the apple she was munching and headed to the larder for other supplies. I lit the fire and set the water to boiling for stock. We danced silently about each other in the kitchen. I kept my tongue firmly between my teeth. Finally, Anna spoke, telling me the roasting chickens would be ready in time for the evening meal. Silently, I gave thanks for not being baited into a senseless argument. Aloud, I gave Anna thanks for her efforts. The tension between us dissolved.

In the garden, I picked cucumbers and endive for our supper. Picked at the weeds that seem ever ready to choke our vegetables. Checked the mended fence where the goats broke in at the beginning of summer. Then I returned to the kitchen, where Simon joined us, fresh with tales of what he has learned at synagogue school. He dreams of being a rabbi. But he is only a half-Jew, as Anna delights in reminding him. Today she held her tongue and let him dream.

Gradually, the family arrived. James and Joses closed the shop, washed their feet and hands and took their seats. Caleb, my squirming grandsons — Zachariah, Nathaniel and Moses — and beautiful Sol joined us tonight. We women served the meal. Simon said the blessing. We celebrated our bounty. Our health. Together, we ate.

After supper, the men gathered in the evening circle as men do. The women cleaned up after them, as women do. I did not mind. It was good for Anna and Sol and I to be together. To watch over the babies. To remember what strength there is in being women. Later, I will turn to my books of learning, if I choose. So will Sol. So will Anna. I have given my girls some choice.

Tonight we sang while washing, sweeping, straightening. Lulled the baby boys to sleep. We sang the songs of our mothers and grandmothers. Sol remembered a song about Ruth and Ester. I sang a love song from Song of Songs. Anna hummed along, then slipped away. She thinks I don't know that she has taken a lover. A woman in Wellhouse.

Leaving Sol to croon to her babies, I found Simon. We washed the grime from his face and I tucked him into bed with a kiss and a story. He likes to hear about Joseph and his coat of many colours. Another dreamer.

The women of Wellhouse had eaten their evening meal and were talking and laughing quietly together. I sat with them to hear the events of the day. Two of the sick had died. But more were improving. They told me which fevers were high, which patients needed watching through the night. I drank in their faces, some wizened, some soft, some careworn, one scarred. All beautiful to me. Tasks were divided for the night, for the dawn, for the next day. I left them to make my rounds amongst the sick and the healing of Wellhouse.

Some Sister had given the baby a rag doll and he clung to it in slumber.

John, the man with no legs, sat smoking outside the men's quarters. I bade him goodnight.

The burned man tossed in pain. Hagar will stay with him through the night. I brought a mixture of gall and honey which she will administer at intervals.

In the room of the pox, I studied the writhing, coughing bodies of the very ill and dying. Naomi and Sarah were tending as best they could. There was no more I could do.

Abigail had put the children of the orphanage to bed. She was rocking one reluctant toddler to sleep. We exchanged a smile.

Tonight was a normal night. Today a normal day. I give thanks for its relative ease. There have been times when we thirteen have toiled to exhaustion to ease suffering, break fevers, change bedclothes.

I slipped beneath the moon, beyond the gates of Wellhouse. The stars were an explosion of light across the sky. I said goodnight to my parents. To Bubeh and Zaydeh. To Joseph.

Then I traced my steps back to Wellhouse, where I secured the locks against ill fortune and the chill night air.

December 3

Anna now Andrew is learning to become a stonecutter. A mason. She has befriended village boys, fooled them into thinking she is a boy their age. Nineteen and willful. Such work could hurt her. I told her so, but it turned ugly between us. So all I can do is watch as she works at masonry in the yard beside the carpentry shop. As she scuffs her hands with the tools of her new trade. Drops the great hammer and blackens a toenail. Stubbornly she carries on; afternoons she apprentices with the other mason boys. Soon, she tells us, she will work in the quarry. She will contribute another wage to Wellhouse. But my daughter does not come to me to treat her blisters or bleeding fingers; she ministers to herself.

Her arms grow brown and muscled in the way that boys' arms do. Her shoulders are broad; her calves are thick. She has no breasts to speak of; those she has are bound with cloth. Anna cum Andrew has cut her hair in the style of the centurions. She is tall and sure. I find myself admiring my girl-boy despite my misgivings.

I am full of misgivings these days. Anna holds council with the men of Nazareth. It is a marvel how easily she slides into their midst and into their conversations. She is a bold actress, my daughter, like her mother. But the stories she brings home chill me. Disgruntled taxpayers, angry Gentiles, surly scribes, hot-tempered men who want to rise up in Yahweh's name against Caesar. And while they hate the yoke, they vie for power. I feel a rumbling underfoot.

And she brings back idle gossip about the man Jesus, son of Joseph the carpenter, about the woman Mary, widow of this same Joseph. Both break the sacred rule of the Sabbath. Both consort with thieves and rogues and whores. Some say mother and son are healers, others say sorcerers. And now the son preaches fraternity and sorority, humility and compassion, generosity and altruism. As if paying taxes to Caesar leaves us anything for the poor who deserve what they get, lazy asses. As if we Jews haven't got troubles enough, in the tight grip of the infernal Roman fist. Still others claim Jesus is vainglorious and self-promoting; some say he is a visionary, a prophet. The Messiah.

My God. The Messiah. What have I done?

Such a story should never have been started. Such a story will break a mother's heart. Such a story that saved us both may destroy us in the end. And I am the author of this story.

When Jesus and Mary el Mejdel returned from Korazim, I made them listen to what Anna has been learning these several weeks. When she had finished, Jesus shrugged.

"Let the idle gossip. Let the citizens grumble. We have our work to do. Are you prepared to give up Wellhouse?"

"No."

"Healing on the Sabbath?"

"The sick are sick every day of the week."

"Well, then."

"I think your mother means that you need to be less ... visible, Jesus."

Mary el Mejdel touched his arm.

"Are the sick and poor invisible?"

"No, son. But you need to be cautious. That story keeps rising to the surface."

"Your story, Mama."

"Yes, mine. And in desperate times, people will believe such stories. They want to believe. They see your ministering to the needy as Elohim's ministry. They see your healing as a miracle."

"Healing *is* a miracle, Mama."

"Jesus, you know what I mean."

"And tending to the sick and poor is Elohim's plan for me and for you. For us, our family. Our entire, greater family. It is our ministry. Guided by God."

"I'm not so certain as you, my son, of God's plan for us."

"I have faith in His plan, Mama."

"I'm glad for you. But I do not."

He left the room then, angry as always when I question faith and absolute belief. At twenty-four, he is still so young. How has his faith been challenged?

Anna and Mary el Mejdel cajole him, try to make him see the prudence in caution and anonymity.

But my mother's heart is heavy. I would like to know your plan, Yahweh. This is Mary, your wayward handmaiden, asking you for guidance.

March 23

What a time we have had! Jesus has gone underground.

I owe most of his safety to Anna. Beloved girl-boy of mine.

At least I can breathe easier. Get a good night's rest for once, even as the reality also saddens me.

Too many words about fair dealing and freedom. Too many good works. Too many cures. Now his healing must be covert.

What kind of a godless world do we live in? Despite the holy claims of priests and Pharisees and Sadducees, men are, after all, jealous and petty powermongers. One who dares to work in humility and compassion — with no thought for personal gain, and all thoughts for communal gain — threatens and insults them. Where are their mothers?

Where did they get such bad manners? Who taught them greed and avarice? What sickness makes them fear one young man? How small these, your men creatures, Yahweh, made in your image.

Three months ago, Anna came home at dawn. I had been up all night, tearing my hair, fretting over her. Devising punishments for her. Restrictions. No more Andrew!

I sent James looking for her. Then Joses. Even Simon.

Finally, I heard her climb over the locked gate. The sun was just appearing at the ridge of the hills.

"Where have you been? Such a daughter! Just think what the neighbours must think of you whoring around Nazareth! You bring shame to this family, you ingrate. You little slut!" I spat out other things, words I shake to remember. Words I regret.

She stood her ground. Hands on hips.

"What do you have to say for yourself?"

"To you? Nothing."

I slapped her then. So hard my hand stung. I would have kept on striking, had I not seen the look in her eyes. Hatred. I saw it flash there. As sure as death comes. Anna hated me.

"Anna ..." I searched for the right words, those that so often elude me when I struggle with this daughter. "I am sorry. I was worried. Sick about you. I shouldn't have hit you. I didn't mean ... shouldn't have said ..."

She was so calm when she spoke. And cold. "But you did. You said them. You hit me. And you can't take any of that back. I'm leaving."

"Anna! Don't leave. I'm your mother."

"You were never my mother."

"Where will you go? What will you do?" I called to her shadowy form leaping easily over the gate and away from me through the dim light. And then I collapsed in my wretched and failed maternity. There in the garden, sobbing in the dirt. Useless. Used up. A stupid and mistaken mother.

I could not eat for three days. I lay on my pallet. Stared at the ceiling. Did nothing for or within Wellhouse. Let my hair flow wild about my face. On the second day, Jesus and Mary returned from Bethany. On the third, he brought Anna to me. Her hair was shorn, and on her head, a new tattoo. The mark of the dagger. I shuddered.

"Well?" Her tone sickened my stomach.

"Jesus, leave us." I waited. "Sit, Anna." She refused. "You are right. I am not your true mother."

"She is dead."

"How do you know this?"

"I know many things. I have many contacts now. She is dead of the illness of whores."

I sighed and silently prayed for Rebecca, my troubled friend. "Have you told Juda that his mother is dead?"

She shook her head.

"She was a good woman. But lost. Do you remember her?"

"A little. She seldom smiled."

"Life sometimes does that to people."

Anna sniffed.

"At first, I was angry at her for abandoning you and Juda. And a little resentful. But she did the right thing. On the street, she would have lost you or seen you killed. There was room enough here, and I already loved you as family. And so, Anna and Juda became my son and daughter."

Anna studied the pattern of the carpet.

"I don't understand you, Anna. I try. Maybe we are wrong together, my nature and yours. I push and you push back. At times, it is hard to like you, and I know you feel the same about me."

She nodded.

"I said awful things the other day. Cruel words. And you are right. Words I cannot take back. And I hit you. I cannot take that back either. I must live with those words and that slap. I must look hard at Mary and remember that ugliness that is me. And I must try again. Harder. I must somehow forgive myself and hope you will also forgive me. It is hard to be a mother. Sometimes I am not very good at it. But you are my family, and I want you home."

"I have another family now."

I looked at the tattoo. "The Sicarii are a dangerous lot, Anna. Do they know you as Andrew?"

She nodded again.

"Have they a place for Anna?"

I watched a tear drip from her nose. She shrugged.

"Here is the place for Anna. With us. With the woman you love in Wellhouse; don't think I don't know about her. With your mother. Your family. Mary and Jesus."

"Jesus." Her voice was hoarse.

"What?"

"That's where I was that night."

"With Jesus? He was returning from Bethany."

"Not with him. Talking about him. Learning what they say. From the masons who are the Sicarii. We talked all night. I was gonna tell you ..."

"Ah. So I was doubly wrong about you that night. What do you know?"

"A group of Herodians and scribes are plotting. They spread a rumour that Jesus is guilty of sedition. It's only a matter of time before Herod moves, before the Roman hand strikes. I came that dawn to tell you that Jesus has to be silent or they will silence him."

"So it has begun."

"What has?"

I shook myself. "Nothing. I am superstitious. Go on."

"Because he's my brother, the Sicarii will protect Jesus. For a while, but ..."

"But he must not raise Roman ire."

"Or he's dead."

"Yes."

"He's pissed off a lot of people."

"Seems to be a family trait. I am frightened of the Sicarii, Anna. They are terrorists. Assassins. I have had ... dealings with ... such men."

She shrugged. "They are my brothers. As Jesus is my brother. I trust them."

"And so now you are a terrorist and assassin?"

"I am new and untried, if that's what you're asking."

"Hope to God you are never tried, Anna."

She revealed what she knew to Jesus and Mary. Jesus was adamant that he continue his work, and that Anna leave the Sicarii at once.

"Anna may do as she wishes."

Jesus looked thunderstruck. "You would allow your daughter? She's already half-boy, half-wild. Look at her! What kind of mother —"

Anna spoke. "A good mother. Mostly." And she left the room and Wellhouse.

Jesus moved to go after her.

"Leave her."

"Mama!"

"If I don't let her go, I will lose her. I think she will come back to us. Anna-Andrew is her own person. Let her be that person. Let us all respect that person."

I could see the resistance drain from his body. "As you say."

"And heed her words."

"Mama!"

Mary el Mejdel added, "Anna knows what she's talking about, Jesus."

"I'll be cautious, but no more."

So stubbornly he persevered, visiting the members of the Sisterhood, travelling Judea, stirring up dust and talk wherever he went.

Anna came back to live at Wellhouse. I was very relieved. But she was often absent or late. I went to bed and tried not to worry. No more harsh words, if I could help it. Daily I put the balm on the wound between us.

Several weeks ago she brought the news.

Usually she informed us who was maligning Jesus or Wellhouse. Which petty Pharisee had decried my son or me. Which citizen claimed to know Jesus as Messiah.

But her news that day was very different. Assassination. In Jerusalem. During the Feast of Passover, Jesus would be killed by a Herodian. No one knew the killer's name.

I begged my son not to go. Anna pleaded with him. Mary and Sol wept. But he would go. He would do. None of us would stop him. None of us could.

Sitting in the garden, I cursed the strong will of my children. I watched Deuteronomy the goat butt his horned head against the board Simon held playfully up to him. That goat was a kindred spirit. I looked at his goatish face and then I saw. Touched my chin and laughed at my willingness to commit another sin. Sent Simon for the knife. The poor child thought I meant to sacrifice his pet. No, I assured him. And I cut off Deuteronomy's beard.

Within the hour, I purchased coloured robes from the marketplace. That afternoon I hired three camels for the early hours of the next morning. That night Abigail and Anna helped fasten a beard and moustache to my face and dressed me in merchant's clothes. We packed the camel bags, kissed the Sisters and family goodbye. Andrew the stonemason with Mark the merchant set out near dawn for Jerusalem.

I had not been back since we rescued Mary el Mejdel from Jake the pimp. I had not wanted to return. Jerusalem, holy city for so many, means trouble and danger for me and mine. I am filled with dread when I enter her walls. Ill portent. I must will myself not to flee like a dog with tail between its legs. Yahweh forgive me, I hate the place.

We took lodgings as before at the Solomon Inn, and were lucky to get a room. Perhaps it was even the same room. They all have the same design. The same smell: the stink of Jerusalem. Anna and I slept fitfully through a tepid night of stale air. We arose and bedecked our male selves again as per our respective trades. I was developing a rash from the resin we used to attach the goat's beard. But no one would notice. And I had no time to care. This was the morning of the determined day. The Feast of Passover. Last night the angel of death had spared us; today, however, was another matter. Jesus and Mary el Mejdel had been in the city for days, presumably lodging with Sisters of the Eastern Star.

Swollen streets were festooned with bright stalls and colours of the feast, doors of homes and shops still painted with blood, to mark your mercy to the Jews, Yahweh. We munched on matzah while we assembled my makeshift merchant stall in the market square not far from the temple. Even in the early morning the din was unsettling. Nasal hawkers called out raucously. Shrill-voiced fishwives advertised their salted catch. Vegetable pedlars shouted the produce of the day. Roman soldiers, their jaws set at an ugly angle, marched dustily by the square and pushed through the narrow streets. Animals lowed and squawked and grunted. I did not feel right in my skin, but I began to sell wares: homespun linen cloth that we'd brought. I was turning a brisk business when Andrew slipped away to her Sicarii brothers and to find Jesus' whereabouts.

She returned shortly with a young bearded man. I was haggling the price of a fine linen tablecloth, woven by Abigail and stitched by Sol.

"You're killing me with this price!" The woman was shrewd and wanted a bargain.

"Such a deal I'm offering. Take it. Leave it," I rasped, in my most mannish voice.

Caught in the zeal of negotiation, I did not notice Anna or her companion until she spoke, "Mark. I have news."

The haggling woman ignored this interruption. "Fine. But I want you to know I think you are a crook."

"So? You think you can find something better elsewhere? Cheaper, yes. Better, not on your life!"

"Mama! — I mean, Papa!"

The woman and I stopped short. She eyed me and Andrew.

"I've found the merchandise you wanted." My daughter-as-son glanced meaningfully at her companion. Now I spied the bearded fellow standing a little away, scanning the crowds. Twitchy. "It will be dispatched at midday, right before the temple."

The woman sniffed. "Better linens at noon?"

"Not linens. Wives. I am looking for a new wife. They say the Nubians make good wives."

"You would marry outside the faith!" In disgust she handed me the money for the cloth.

"Well, yes. A man like me. Lonely. A widower. I'm not too fussy. Unless a woman like you were to come along." I smiled my most lecherous smile.

"Uggh! I am a married woman! And you are a scheming shtarker!" She snatched the cloth from my hands and hurried into the crowds.

"Apparently, I'm not her type."

"Apparently." We tried to smile at each other, mother and daughter in disguise. The weight of the news bore down upon us.

"This is Eli."

I looked him over. Unkempt beard. Gold earring in each ear. He lifted his robe to reveal the telltale dagger at his side and tattoo on his forearm. "Of the Sicarii?"

"Yeah." His voice was gravel.

"This Herodian. Do we know his name?"

"No."

"What he looks like?"

"Nope."

I turned to Anna. "Have you warned Jesus?"

"Can't find him." Her voice was miserable.

"Well, then. We must trust Eli of the Sicarii."

"You must pay Eli of the Sicarii." He smiled, his teeth crusted yellow.

"Pay? I thought Andrew was one of you."

"Him?" Eli shrugged. "He may be. He may not be. He may be a Roman informant sent to trap us. Or he may be what he says he is: a Sicarii wannabe from that nogoodnik village of Nazareth. I don't really care. We work for money in this town."

"But I thought we were on the same side!" Andrew protested.

"Maybe we are. Maybe not. This Jesus — I don't know him from Adam. Why the Herodians want him is anyone's guess."

"If the Herodians want him, then the Romans want him, and he's an enemy of Caesar and aligned with your cause."

"Who's to say?" Eli emitted a sour burp. "Shekels or no deal."

"How much?"

"Papa!" Anna never knows when she is bested.

"How much?"

"To save a man? Five hundred."

"Done."

"Papa!"

"Two fifty now. Two fifty when Jesus is safe with us."

Eli squinted into my face. "Deal."

I counted out the first installment.

"In two hours, in front of the temple. Have a plan to hide this Jesus. Be ready, greenhorn." He tossed this last over his shoulder at Anna, who stood fuming beside me.

Two hours are a very long time when you are waiting to save your son. A lifetime. Two hours to think about all the stupid things you have done. Two hours will make you sick to your stomach and sick to your heart. Two hours will fray your nerves to useless rope-ends.

But two hours pass. Here is what I remember. Or imagine. Or both. The bright day is hard on the eyes. It is unseasonably warm. Sweat trickles down my back and stomach and thighs beneath my three layers of purple merchant robes. The streets are glutted with pilgrims.

Shortly before noon, I abandon my stall, meander over to the temple where the priests are chanting and intoning. Where the lambs are bleating, terrified before the blade slices across their throats in sacrifice and thanksgiving to you, Yahweh.

Somewhere nearby, street musicians are piping and strumming, drumming and singing. Closer, a belly laugh. A woman wailing. Children screeching. Beggars crying hoarsely for alms from the rich passersby.

And right before the temple square steps, a whistle, shrill and piercing.

The signal.

There he is. Sun glowing around his dark hair. A troupe of followers listening intently to his impassioned speech. He is beautiful. He is Jeremiah. He is me. He is Jesus.

What does he say? Praise for you, Yahweh? Certainly. He bears you no grudge. Still believes you are good and just. As he is good and just. Anti-Roman sentiment? Sickened by slavery and oppression, he wants to see our people rightfully restored as governors and guardians and leaders of our own, your Chosen, Yahweh.

Perhaps he remembers the aggrieved and miserable of this, your world. Remembers our duty to one another, to love one another. As we do in Wellhouse.

As I try to now, in this moment. But I feel little love — no love — for them. I hate them. I hate them all for what they intend to do to my son. They are all one. They all are "they," somehow complicit in this plot on his life. And they are all you, Yahweh. You, who with a wave of your magus's arm could stay this awful deed. Instead you leave it to me, his mother, to hire an assassin to kill the assassin.

What if it doesn't work, Yahweh? What if he dies bleeding in this square? What good will have come of his life? Of mine? What glory will this bring you if he is a dead Messiah? What is the point? What is the point of a dead son?

Now he nears the steps and Mary is laughing beside him at some jest they share. And suddenly Anna-Andrew is no longer at my side. She disappears into the people. I catch sight of her there, in the crowd. And there. I move to the left. Push and jostle my way through the maddening throng, the din of this deadly day. The stench of sweat and sour breath. I soil my purple robes against the mob, because of the mob.

Because of you. And like Anna who is Andrew, Mary who is Mark is swept into this vortex of your design. This dance you have choreographed. The pitch and rise of your tempest. We swirl around and inwards towards the dark dot who is my only begotten son. Thunder is in my head, behind my eyes, in my throat. He is still too far from me, from my reach.

Then I see the Herodian. An ugly man. I know it is he. The flames in my breast assure me. Malice in his eyes; he is so close to you.

A raised arm, poised shoulder. And then I am swept frustratingly further away. But not so far that I miss it above the whirlwind cacophony: a death cry, simultaneous with another voice, "Jesus!"

He turns his head sharply. Beside him Mary el Mejdel ducks, disappears. Another hand raises. Another. I see a flash. Another. One hand. Two. Three. More than I can count. One with silver rings. Flash upon flash. During this spell, I am swimming, kicking, tripping my way towards the spiral of colour and shouts and flashes of silver, until I am at the epicenter, the middle of the incantation. For a moment all seems quiet. There on her knees, Mary el Mejdel. Beside her, barely standing, a man with terror in his eyes. My son. Jesus.

A magician's flourish of my purple robe erases him. Another erases Mary. They are disappeared. Seconds later, we are three panting figures darting in and out of the crowd. Hands joined, three purple threads weaving into the soiled fabric of Jerusalem.

We head towards the inn. An eon passes. Another. And finally we arrive. Locked in our close room. Only then do I think of Anna, of the silver rings. I must go back, leave Jesus and Mary weeping in safety and in each other's arms.

Mass panic has erupted. I try to work my way back to the temple. A man dead. Young or old? Middle aged. Disembowelled. Multiple stab wounds. He lies reeking in his own thickening blood, right before the temple square, Adonai preserve us. Assassination. In broad daylight. On the day of the Passover Feast. It's the Herodian. Terrible sacrifice to God. Only one? Only one dead? It is enough. Desperate men, desperate deeds. The Romans are marching, seeking the culprit. Culprits. Sheol is breaking loose.

Anna is safe, from death at least. But there is still the law. Roman law. If anyone saw her or knows ...

The Sicarii, people whisper. *Anonymous. Powerful. Ruthless. Sicarii. Sicarii.* Their sibilance is a kind of prayer. My prayer to you, Yahweh. Thanks be to the Sicarii. To the assassins.

My son, my daughter, they live!

I cannot go backwards, so I go forwards, to the inn.

And there is Andrew with Eli. I pay the man what he is owed while Andrew watches and Jesus and Mary, unaware and exhausted, sleep. I pay the sin tax willingly. Willfully. Thy will be done, Yahweh. I will pay for my sins for all of my life. Amen.

I look at Andrew's beringed hand. Do I want to know? I say nothing. Instead, I lovingly bathe her feet. Her hands. Her face, neck, shoulders. I bathe my daughter clean. Help her doff the stonemason's dress and don the woman's. I cover her head with a scarf, hiding the tattoo and short cropped hair. In the early evening dusk, she is lovely. My Anna.

Then she helps me remove the goat's beard and moustache, applies salve gingerly to my raw, reddened face, brushes out my hair and helps me to plait it.

And we, daughter and mother, are disguised anew.

We order food to our room, a modest Seder meal. I rouse Jesus and Mary, and we eat together. We ask the questions, different than last or any Passover. My son gives his account. We give ours. He is wide-eyed, grateful, humbled. Finally nods his assent. We drink deeply of the Passover wine and give thanks. To Anna-Andrew, and yes, to you, Yahweh. For another day of life, for sparing Jesus. We think of the Herodian's family and offer a brief prayer. It is a prayerful, thankful evening, our last together for much time to come. We talk until the early hours before we embrace each other goodnight.

At dawn, Jesus and Mary head for sanctuary on one of our camels. They will live simply with our friends and allies. Survive by hiding. Jesus will teach and heal covertly. He and Mary will never stay anywhere for very long, and they have agreed to send spies and emissaries before them. Jesus must keep a check on his arrogance and self-righteousness. He has so much to do and teach, if he lives. For now, for today, he chooses life.

Anna and I watch them go, my mother's heart a mix of relief and heaviness. As we mount our camels, homeward bound, I know we will never be the same family. We are all changed. My son has a price on his head. I, his mother, paid a man to kill a man. And my daughter had a hand in the killing.

So the angel of death passed us over. This time. Just barely.

PART SIX

Epistles

January 31

Dear Jesus,

It was so good to see you again, my son, if only for a fortnight. Nine months is a long time not to see your mother. Nine months without word from you.

Sol is now well along with child. Soon she will be mother of four. We are all hoping for a girl as the boys are more than a handful for your sister. Perhaps you noticed Sol's ripening during your visit, but we hesitated to share the news, as you and Mary are still trying for your first. However, I think you should write your sister with your blessing and good wishes.

And I don't mean to offer advice where none is wanted, but we can speak frankly about these matters, you and I. Have you tried alternative methods of lovemaking? A woman on her back is not always the surest way to a baby. I don't mean to embarrass you, son, but you might consult the Greeks on these matters. There are other than the traditional positions by which to conceive a child. Might I also suggest that Mary raise her legs above her head after coitus and remain in said position for twenty minutes to half an hour. I have read that this aids in conception.

Just a few helpful midwifery tips. Now don't get all scandalized that your mother knows a thing or two. Neither of us was born yesterday.

I'm glad to know your itinerary for the coming months, son. I will, of course, be prudent and discreet in sending messages to you. I have formed many alliances with traders and shepherds and magi and such over the years. My letters will find you, and yours me, without arousing suspicion.

Seeing your face, and Mary's, brought me much joy. I hope I will see both again soon.

Much love from all of us at Wellhouse,

Mama

March 12

Dear Jeremiah,

Our son, Jesus, has been living in hiding for almost a year to avoid further arousing the wrath of Rome or the hypocritical Pharisees. You may be interested to know that he was nearly murdered last year at Passover in Jerusalem. Still he continues to carry on his life work of teaching and healing. But he must do so quietly and under cover.

I'm sure you know something of such tactics.

As we have not heard from you in over eight years, I have no idea if you are well or even inclined to help us or even care. However, to be brief, your son is short of money. He has written home twice for funds. I give him what I can spare, but I cannot starve Wellhouse. We generally make do. But only just.

So I'm writing for money, plain and simple. Can you afford to help your son?

I hope so. And I hope you are well, whatever you are doing with your life.

Mary of Nazareth

April 4

Dear Jesus,

I am not having this tiresome argument with you for the rest of my life. Stop your kvetching! I asked your father for money with no regrets. All right, already, I know you disapprove. But come to your senses, my dear. We cannot function without the funds that Jeremiah provides Wellhouse. Revenue from carpentry, fishing, goatherding and stonemasonry goes only so far in feeding a house of near a hundred. Not to mention the poor. Get off your high camel. Money is money. So it soils my already soiled hands — I wash them and continue my work.

And so, my son, must you.

Do I like it? I try not to think of it.

Should you like it? Who asked you? Just accept the money and launder it to good and compassionate use. God knows, it could be used for ill instead. Regenerate, that's what I say, Jesus.

Sol is doing fine, by the way. The baby is due in the next few weeks. I'll give Sol your love. Sometimes I wonder what you did with all that passion you once carried for your sister. Is it all visited on Mary, your beloved wife? Distilled into your teaching? Your cures?

Where does love go, Jesus?

Before I get caught up in some foolish sentimental web, I'll close for now. There is much to do in the kitchen today; Anna is home baking bread, and we never know what might happen.

Write soon.

Love,
Mama

May 12

Dear Jeremiah,

Thank you for the money. I received it safely from Mary with no tongue. We are as always grateful, and I have sent it on to your son and daughter-in-law.

I am sorry for the tone of my last letter. I am resentful and hurt that I never hear from or see you, other than via the silver you send annually to Wellhouse.

All these years, and the hurt persists, a dull ache in my heart. But perhaps you do not feel the same way. Perhaps you are happy in your life. With your wife. And indeed, the years have taken something from me. You might not wish to see the girl you knew now an older woman. After all, my fortieth birthday approaches. Forty. Such an ancient number. How did I get here?

Still, I would like to see you. It would be a wonderful birthday gift. But I don't dare to hope.

Love,
Mary of Nazareth

P.S. I have a beautiful new grandson named Ezra, born to Sol some weeks ago.

May 30

Dear Jesus,

I am very interested to hear of your clandestine visits to the Sisters who work in the town ports along the Sea of Galilee. I did not know so many of the Star lived and worked in secret along the western coast. Never having been to the sea — although you and I have both seen the amazing Nile River, do you remember? — I have often wondered what it must be like. You do an apt job of describing its beauty, my son, so gifted in words. Someday I hope to journey there. Sorry, though, I do not know a cure for your seasickness.

It was nice to hear that you and Juda have been together with Uncle Samuel at Galilee and that your brother has taught you more of his trade. He is a loner, our Juda. That stutter of his, I fear it stunted him socially. What a good brother you are. I'm sure he is lonely spending weeks in Galilee away from us. Does he have a girlfriend?

Joses is very serious about a young Nazarene girl, Ester. Do you remember her family? Of course you do. They are the only other carpenters in the village. Good people, though none of them as gifted in woodworking as James or Joses or your father, Joseph. Or you, my son. Anyway, they are sure to be betrothed or even married within the year. She is a pretty girl but only fourteen. I wish he had chosen someone more his age. Still, I like her, and Joses at twenty-two seems closer to sixteen. Young Ester has potential. Maybe she will care to work around here at Wellhouse. Maybe even learn to read and write. Who can say?

Simon is still bent on becoming a rabbi like his big brother and brother-in-law, Caleb. He is a very good reader. Not to mention an artist. You should see the images he has been drawing lately. He always was a scribbler, ever since he came to us and we first placed a stylus in his hand. I am enclosing one of his drawings for you. Such a busy boy, he has no time for girls.

Unlike his sister Anna and his brother James.

I worry about James tomcatting around the streets of Nazareth. Too handsome for his own good, that one. He thinks that I don't know he is out until all hours, but I hear him each night he comes in late. And the next day he is droopy-eyed and grumpy. I don't like the company he keeps; that Menachem the tailor's son is a wild one.

Anna is still Anna and Andrew. My newsgetter. A bit of the yenta in her, too. It's nice she isn't entirely a boy. She is still moony-eyed over the same girl here at Wellhouse. She spends much of her spare time at the orphanage.

Sol and the baby are doing well enough. I help out when I can. Four boys. What is Yahweh thinking? And this one has colic. What trials we women endure. Still, when he is not crying, Ezra is plump and beautiful. We all adore him. I think he is his father's favourite.

That's the news. You were expecting high drama? Wellhouse is thriving and too busy, what else is new? The Sisters send their love, especially Delilah, who, as you know, has a bit of a crush on you.

Love,
Mama

P.S. Very belated happy birthday greetings.
P.P.S. I, for my gift, received a very interesting birthday visitor.

June 10

Dear Jeremiah,

When are you coming back? I miss you. I miss us.

Love,
Mary (the other one)

June 14

Dear Elizabeth,

How are you, my cousin? We haven't spoken since the death of my mother. How many years ago now? Thirteen. I think it is time that we put this silliness behind us. Jesus and John are both grown men. That contest of wills between them is long over, so much desert sand in the wind. John, I'm sure, is a fine man with a mission. So is Jesus. He is now married nine years to Mary el Mejdel. We were sorry that you didn't come to the wedding. It doesn't matter that you didn't send a gift.

What I care about now is healing this rift between us. If you care to, that is. I always looked up to you. Our mothers had a particular bond.

I am sorry for my part that I called your John a vainglorious upstart.

And I forgive you for saying that Jesus was a spoiled, self-important prig.

Words can be so hurtful. I hope that these begin our healing.

Love,
Your cousin, Mary of Nazareth

July 3

Dear Martha and Lazarus,

Just a note to let you know that Mary and Jesus are bound for Bethany within the next three weeks. I didn't want them showing up on your doorstep without warning.

Hope you are well and that you will visit us. You are always welcome at Wellhouse.

Mary of Nazareth

August 11

Dear Rachel of Tyre,

I write you as a Sister of the Eastern Star. My name is Mary of Nazareth and I run a place of healing and an orphanage, called Wellhouse. We admit all who ask help of us. Perhaps you have heard of our work.

Or perhaps you have heard of me through our mutual acquaintance, Jezebel. She once mentioned you to me. I am sad to say that she has long since left this world. She was a good friend.

My son, Jesus of Nazareth, is also a healer. And a teacher. He's pretty good with wood and not a bad fisherman. He is travelling with his wife, Mary, to Tyre. They know no one there, so I am hoping that you can put the two of them up at your inn. There does need to be some secrecy about their time in Tyre. My son has ideas unpopular to some and much too popular an appeal. I'm sure you'll understand what I mean once you meet him. He will be travelling under the name of Benjamin. I turn to you in need and ask for your discretion.

Please send word via the messenger who brings you this scroll. Many thanks.

In sisterhood,
Mary of Nazareth

September 2

Dear Jesus,

We have had an epidemic in Nazareth! Six weeks ago it began. First the children, in alarming numbers. We watched, helpless, as they proceeded to shit themselves to death. Every child brought to us that first week died.

More came. Then the elderly. Gradually, young men and women in their prime.

All shitting. Not to mention puking and pissing. Shit everywhere. On our hands, our legs, in our hair. And everywhere, the stench. What misery! We retched until our tired muscles gave up and our noses surrendered to the smells.

Every single room in this place was full. There were few other patients at the time, thank Yahweh. We squeezed the children of the orphanage into a smaller room and set up extra bedding. What bedding there was.

By the end of the first day, every sheet, every piece of linen, every scrap of cloth had been sullied.

We heated great vats of water over open fires in the back. We strung drying lines across the garden. And washed. And boiled. And washed. And emptied. And refilled. And boiled. James and Joses offered every scrap of wood they could for the fire. When they ran out, they used good lumber or searched the scrub in the hills for bracken and deadwood. Simon fed the fire until he dropped asleep from exhaustion. Anna drew water from our well endlessly. She is so strong. They are all so strong.

Salome, Delilah and Sharon, our youngest Sisters, were responsible for the smallest and oldest. In shifts of three, Hagar, Eve,

Abigail, Bathsheba, Lilith and I tended the others. Naomi, Sol, and Sarah cared for the animals and toiled in the kitchen. Their gruel was the only thing our patients — those who survived, that is — could stomach. Hannah and Sophia were our tireless washerwomen.

Caleb, Joses and James hauled out the dead. A huge funeral pyre was built downwind of the town. I know, I know. Against the faith. Against the laws. But the only quick and sure force against contagion from the dead. Caleb saw the truth and did my bidding. He convinced the elders to nod their begrudging assent.

We barely had time or strength to feed ourselves. We slept sporadically, or when we could work no more. I am amazed and uplifted by the kindness we showed one another. This your incredible family pulled together throughout the crisis.

I remember James massaging my feet; Anna insisting that no one be admitted to my room until I had slept a full three hours. I saw Joses helping with the washing, alongside Sophia, trying to cheer her with a joke. One afternoon, Naomi and Sol made us a full supper and organized shifts so that each of us could sit down to a meal. Simon charmed us with his singing until he was hoarse. Lilith, having lived among the Romans, was relentless about our own cleanliness and sanitation; she ensured that our clothing and bedclothes were kept fresh to avoid infection. When time permitted or her charges were sleeping, Eve, my apprentice herbalist, helped me grind roots and make salve. And for my part, I tried to be cheerful and not to bark orders or whine. We all knew that one of us succumbing to despair would topple the whole.

I did my best to reassure the family and my Sisters that we would not become ill. But, in truth, Jesus, I could not be sure. I wonder at the risk I put us all at. I wonder what I might have done should this disease have spread like a plague amongst us, wiping out the extended family of Joseph and Mary. I have said many a prayer of thanks that none of us became ill.

And that's what twigged me. None of us did. Why not? And why the others? It seemed to point to only one thing: our well water is pure, untainted. Something had to be amiss with the water of Nazareth. And so I sent Joses to investigate, to speak with the village elders and priests. We learned that certain Nazarene families had been dumping and burying excrement and animal feces near the drainage to the village well. Shit leads to shit, Joses explained in his mother's plainest language. Have we learned nothing from the Romans about latrines and drainage ducts? When Juda returned, fish-laden, in the midst of the epidemic, he set to work assisting the village men and stonemasons — Anna among them, as the crisis waned — in building a proper aqueduct like those in bigger centres. Sharon and Sophia went amongst the village wives instructing them about boiling their water. And gradually the disease slowed its course. By week four, we received no additional sick.

But many died. Most of those who sickened, in fact. This is one of my great failures. I simply do not have the knowledge to fend off such an enemy. Despite the prayers of many, the death count rose. Of course, the weakest and smallest succumbed first. The human body can only take so much assault. Some merely gave up the fight — the illness exhausted them and they willed themselves to eternal sleep.

I have consulted and re-read many passages in Hippocrates and Aristotle. But while I find many diseases of a similar nature, I cannot pinpoint this malady. Do you know anything of it? What it is called? Where else it has struck? I hope that if you notice similar abuses of fresh water in your travels, you will urge and caution and teach, Jesus. I would not wish this illness on anyone. Even the Romans.

Sorrowfully, we did have one great loss amongst us. Sarah has died. Not of the disease but perhaps because of it. Her aged heart gave out one morning two weeks ago. She dropped dead as she stirred the soup, all alone in the kitchen. We found her with the spoon still in her determined hand. She and her cackling are much missed. I hope she is in heaven as she deserves after so many hard years of life. We held a hasty funeral; I couldn't get word to you soon enough. I know you will mourn her in your own place.

Slowly, things are returning to normal here at Wellhouse. We are tending the weed-filled garden, mending the goat-chewed fence. But I am numb with the numbers of dead. Did we need this scourge? So many are grieving in Nazareth. In my dreams, I am haunted by bewildered faces, fever-torn and blistered, babies squalling, the moans of the dying. And the unrelenting shit. Every colour and consistency. Do I need such nightmares at my age? I awake exhausted, defeated, unnerved.

I guess in time, this too will pass. Perhaps today I am just feeling old. At least I've found this moment to sit in the sun and write to you. I hope you and Mary el Mejdel are healthy in Tyre. I hope your work goes well. I miss you, my son.

Love,
Mama

October 24

Dear Jesus,

I write only hours after you and Mary have departed for Gamala. Already I miss you.

You are such a thoughtful boy for returning to be with your mama for Yom Kippur. Always I have much to atone for, but with you near, I drew from your strength.

Jesus, you asked me to whom and for what I prayed. We seldom pray together, so it is a fair question. But I know that you wonder sometimes what kind of godless woman I am, since I so often have words with or about Yahweh. Angry, bitter words. Words of resentment, disbelief, unbelief.

Still, I pray. For the soul of your father Joseph, for Bubeh and Zaydeh. For Sarah and other Sisters who have left us. For all who have died here at Wellhouse. For the families who grieve after the epidemic. For all the misfortunates of this sorry world.

And I pray for my own atonement. I have much to answer for. All the children slaughtered in your stead. For the great lie that I told at your conception.

Violence by my hand. Deaths I need not mention here; they are ever written in my lifestory.

Yes, my son, each year my list of things to atone for grows longer. I balk at my ineptitude as a mother and a woman and a human. I weep for my weaknesses and mistakes.

And if I am, if we are all weak and mistaken, then must not Yahweh, who made us in his image, also be fallible? Prone to error?

Imprecise judgement? Lapses of prudence?

I think so. And I try to forgive him. As he, presumably, forgives me.

You see, Jesus, faith for me is a difficult thing. An elusive, slippery thing. I suspect that my notion of Yahweh differs gravely from yours, from what you and the rabbinical brothers discuss and debate.

I'm not even sure Yahweh is a "he," Jesus. Who claims so but men? Who writes the stories? I am suspicious. I am even suspicious of the laws, while I try to respect and follow most of them. As you well know, I disdain the laws that prescribe and restrict women's actions, prohibit our participation in the synagogue, in the law, in letters and words. Laws that proclaim us unclean because we menstruate and lactate and conceive and give birth. Something stinks there. Something ungodlike, smelling of men. Old farting men.

Women of this world cry many tears. So my prayers are for them, for all victims of injustice. And for the pariahs, like you.

At the end of my prayers, I forgive myself. Or try to. But I find no absolution. Maybe it is the same for everyone. And that is why we turn to our great deity. Offer sacrifices and prayers. Forgive us our daily trespasses. Please. So we can get on with our lives. Sin again. Again. And again. Forgive us that we may sin.

I don't know. I am foolish. Although I prefer to think of myself as a wise woman. Herbology, not theology, is my craft. Still, I like these dialogues between us, Jesus. It is good to know that my thoughts and opinions matter to you. Thank you for asking.

Because of your visit, I am feeling better. My melancholia has lifted. Life and work will continue.

Love,
Mama

P.S. I didn't like the sound of that cough. Find an innkeeper, a woman who can cook up some chicken soup. I love Mary, but she cannot cook to save her soul. Eat your greens.

Hanukkah

Dearest Jesus,

Happy Hanukkah, my son. It is nice that you are spending the holiday with Mary's family, but I must admit that I miss you. And my nose was a little out of joint.

But we have had a wonderful Festival of Lights, filled with gifts and pleasures. On the night we lit the first lamp, the two families of Joses and Ester agreed to a spring marriage. For the second lamp, we offered Ester's family dowry gifts: a milk cow, laying hens and seven vats of aging wine (should be good for the wedding feast!). At the third lighting, Anna led us to the backyard to unveil the stone oven she has been making to supplement the smaller one we rely so heavily upon, and we ate the inaugural bread baked in the new oven by Naomi and Delilah. The women of Wellhouse performed a song written by Simon in praise of Mary, your mother, at the lighting of the fourth lamp. It made me weep, I tell you. Then we feasted on honey and sesame sweets made by Eve. For the fifth, we delighted in halvah to celebrate the appearance of Ezra's and the loss of Zachariah's first teeth. Sol's birthday fell on the sixth. The seventh saw the arrival of Mary with no tongue and her faithful bag of silver. On the final night, after we had feasted, while we danced together merrily in the garden, a visitor arrived. Your father, Jeremiah.

And so dear son, Hanukkah finds me the richest of women! Shalom!

Love,
Your Mama
(who feels much like a blushing girl)

February 18

Dear Jesus,

More good, if unexpected, news. Juda is to be married, to Dinah, a girl from the country of the Gadarenes. Her father, Jonah, a well-to-do fisherman, and I have just sealed the contract. He has made a gift of a fishing boat for Juda! Is this not wonderful? They will be married the same day as Joses and Ester, a double wedding! I am thrilled. You know I love a good wedding. I write in haste because the March 8th date is set and I want you and Mary to attend.

As well, we have our first Gentile Sister. Her name is Phoebe; she is thirteen and a good sight more sensible than many girls her age. She came to us shortly after my last letter to you. Pregnant. Of rape. By her father. So help me, I wish there was some way to prove this to the elders. But they are men, and side with men. Caleb is sympathetic but does not feel we would win this battle. Her father, a widower, is a respected Gentile merchant in the town. Well, I tell you this: he will never again have any business from us. He does not know that his daughter lives with us. Neither does he know she was pregnant. I heard that he searched for her for a brief time, but his interest seems to have waned. Small wonder, given his guilt. If indeed, he even has a conscience.

The abortive drugs worked swiftly. Phoebe is young and hale. She rebounded, then set to work and charmed her way into our hearts. She is adept with bone-setting, as I found when a young boy came to us with a broken leg from a farm accident. And she is strong at the sight of blood. Twice now she has assisted me in stitching up wounds. She has sure and nimble hands. She cooks! And does her tasks without complaint. She is quick to laugh. I am quite taken with her. Phoebe is a good fit for Wellhouse.

That is my news, son. Make your travel arrangements soon! Give my love to Mary, as always. I am glad to hear that she learns and grows with you and through your mutual work. It's gratifying to know that the orphanage and healing centre at Tyre continue. You are a wonderful son (and daughter). Peace be with you.

Much love,
Mama

P.S. I hear frightening things about Tyre. Like all port cities, it has a dangerous reputation. Keep your wits about you, Jesus. Keep a low profile. Stay in after dark.

March 27

Dear Jesus,

Well, the frenzy of the weddings has finally passed. True to his word, Jeremiah has purchased the land to the east of Wellhouse. All the boys, including Simon, are busy building extensions to our place of healing. New dwellings for the newlyweds. Juda is with us a few more days and then returns to Capernaum for his maiden voyage on his new boat, with his father-in-law Jonah and Uncle Sam.

It was a blessed wedding day, was it not? Caleb's graceful words. All my beautiful sons together in their finery. My beautiful daughters. My Sisters. Children of the orphanage. My beloved sisters and brothers, nephews, nieces, cousins, even my in-laws. And Jeremiah.

My heart warmed at the two of you talking together. Jeremiah told me that you spoke of Tyre and Sidon, two cities he knows well. Thank you, Jesus, for trying. I appreciate your civility towards him.

In addition to the great gift of my children's marriages and all our family together was the surprise gift of Izel. My long-lost and dear friend, she arrived shortly after you and Mary had left. You barely remember her. But I have wondered about her all these years. She learned of me and the weddings through the Sisters of the Eastern Star!

She has grown lovely and voluptuous with the years, after two husbands and now a new, young one. Izel, like a cat, lands on her feet. I admire her and learned much from her when you were a baby. She was an amazing helpmeet. I was sorry to see her depart so soon for Gaza. But now we will keep in touch. I will not lose her again.

I'm so grateful for the sumptuous feast, the plentiful wine. There was more than enough for all and for the many poor who came to our gate. A blessed day. A day when Yahweh smiled upon us. You cannot know, Jesus, how much it meant to me, to all of us, to have you and Mary present.

Much love,
Mama

P.S. Did you notice Simon's eyes light up whenever a certain pretty Gentile came near?

April 19

Dear Elizabeth,

I hope this letter finds you on the mend in En Kerem. Thank you for the kind gift of goosedown pillows that you sent with John for Juda and Dinah, Joses and Ester. We were all sorry to hear of your illness.

John has the look of your husband Zacharias. You must be so proud of your son. He is a serious young man, isn't he? His godly purpose is a tribute to you as a mother.

He and Jesus took a walk together past the town, the day after the weddings. I think they got along well and have much in common.

Please take care of yourself, Elizabeth. A chest ailment is a serious malady. Especially in one's senior years. I told John and now tell you that I have sent word to Leah, a Sister who dwells in En Kerem, to look in on you.

Love,
Mary

May 7

Dear Izel,

Thank you for your scroll. I am glad you have a trusted scribe in your grandson. I cannot believe I wrote that: grandson. Although we both have grandsons. To me you will always be young Izel, the girl who mothered me and taught me to be a mother when I was so far from mine.

Thank you again for making the long trek from Gaza to attend the weddings of my sons. I know that travelling is the Bedouin way, but such a long journey! I was much overjoyed to see you. I apologize again for my cousin John spilling your wine. He is — how shall I say — a rather graceless but earnest young man. I hope you were able to remove the stain from your shift.

As you heard and now have seen, Wellhouse is a place of some repute for healing. Each day I thank Joseph for his goodness and generosity in building our home. My life is very rich and full. And Joseph made it so. I still miss him.

Work is divided between ministering to the sick, caring for the recuperating, attending to the children. I also spend a good part of my time gathering and preparing herbs, dabbling with tinctures and mixtures, and reading. And observing nature. I learn from the birds which berries to avoid, what leaf is poisonous. From animals how one must carefully clean a wound. From trial and error which roots aid in stomach remedy. I watch nature grow and heal herself. From fire. From pestilence. And I think our bodies are not far from nature. She is a wonderful teacher. A holy teacher who shows me her miracles, if I am patient and watchful.

No, dear friend. I have not taken another husband, although I congratulate you on your latest. A handsome man. But your question was really a veiled inquiry about Jeremiah. The man with silvering hair who spent so much time at my side. Yes. He is the one. The father of my son, Jesus. And yes, my lover. That is all he has ever been or will be. He is married to another. And I am an adulteress. Many times over.

Jeremiah has been my sorrow and joy. For now I am content to be in his arms when I can. It is enough for this fallen woman. In love. I fall and fall again.

I close my letter, happy that you are again in my life. This afternoon I go to the hills to tend to the lepers. A colony of twenty-four. But I can do little except bring food and a little medicine. I am very fond of several of the women and one man, Bethesda, who was once a rabbi. We have words together about our God. He is quick with a joke, laughs at mine. Says he'll forgive my being a woman if I forgive his being a leper. I always leave with my heart lifted. And with thanks that I and mine are well.

Be well, Izel.

Love,
Mary of Nazareth

P.S. And yes, Jeremiah is a great lover, shame on you!

May 27

Dear Jesus, beloved son!

Just a short scroll to tell you my wonderful birthday news! Jeremiah is taking me to the Sea of Galilee! For a week-long respite from Wellhouse. I have never before had a vacation. At last I will see the beautiful waters you have so often told me about.

Be happy for your Mama, Jesus!

Love,
Mama

P.S. And did you receive the new pair of sandals in time for your birthday, my son?

June 5

Dear Jesus,

I am renewed and reinvigorated for my work! Who could know that the sea would so restore me? It is indeed lovely as you said, Jesus. So much water. One thinks there is no earth the other side. But there is.

We stayed at the Galilean Seaside Inn in a room with a beautiful view. We feasted on the fruits of the sea. We drank wine. Saluted life and love. Jeremiah and I.

Juda took us for several excursions on his boat. Once to fish. Although I was not much help, Jeremiah has hauled fishing nets in the past, and he was able to assist in pulling up the great mass of silver flashing bodies. Juda and he worked side by side for hours.

I am amazed at the sea's bounty. Her generosity. The sounds she makes at night. In the morning. Her many moods and songs. I am in awe of her power.

To her refrain I studied Jeremiah. That week was the most I have spent in constant company with him. I confess that though I have long loved him, I did not really know the man. Do I know him any better now?

He is quiet, was always a man of few words. When I was a girl, he did not really listen to me. Now I find that he takes great interest in what I say. About you. About Wellhouse. Our work. Jeremiah is not a man of great mirth, but he has a quiet smile, and smiles often. Or did that week with me. I don't think he is a thinker nor ever has been.

I resolved to ask him about his work, his means of making a living. "I know that you traded in narcotics, Jeremiah. Hashish. Opium."

"That is how I began. In jail and afterwards, my business … evolved."

"So there's more then to your trade?"

"Best that you not know, Mary."

"Is it so wicked, this work you do, Jeremiah?"

"Yes."

"What you do feeds what I do."

"That is a terrible thought."

"Why?"

"Weapons. I trade in weapons. I've made my fortune from death."

That is all he would say, Jesus. Now I am wracked with guilt that Wellhouse is funded by a weapons dealer. To whom does he sell? The Romans? The zealots? The Sicarii? Is he on the side of evil or righteousness? Whenever do weapons lead to righteousness? There are no holy wars! Damn it! When does war lead to peace? How do weapons heal?

I guess, in a perverse way, through funding Wellhouse.

But, as Jeremiah has said, as you have said, what a terrible means to fund good works. I have always known, as you have, that a paradox underlies Wellhouse. A bloody paradox, it seems.

I sought to bury the truth in the shifting desert sands. But at last, a wind has blown the truth into my face.

What can I do? Give up our work? Scale down? Or continue as I have, trying to thwart the ugliness behind the economics, put blood money to good use?

I know what you would have me do. Give up the money. Give up Jeremiah. For you, my son, the answer is simple.

But not so simple for your mother. I have asked for direction and guidance in this matter, believe me. Yahweh gives me no sign. Except the one in my heart that tells me I do right. Even though it grieves me to know, to cleanse the grains of sand from my eyes and really see how we are funded, have been funded all of these years. I am sickened as I write these words to you.

Nor is it simple to give up Jeremiah. In truth, I do not have him, Jesus. But for that week, a few days here and there. Many long absences over many long years. He is not mine. To have or to hold. I do not know why I cannot give him up. Again I looked to Yahweh. Again he was silent.

I am saddened to admit that my great love is a criminal. Yet that is not all there is to the man. I feel it when I am with him. A good core. A good spirit, even. Perhaps he is caught up in something bigger than he, a life from which he cannot extricate himself. Or believes he can't. Perhaps I merely make excuses for him.

Only this: I can tell him anything. And he listens. He hears. He knows me. Even without being with me, he knows me in a way that no other, except perhaps you, my son, knows. I do not want to relinquish that, give up that part of me I know through him. Through loving him.

You think I want it all. Maybe I am selfish. So be it.

Thank you for listening to my ramblings. You are always so compassionate when you write to me after one of my musing, confusing scrolls. Compassionate listening. You get that from your father.

Much love,
Your troubled Mama

August 16

Dear Izel,

Thank you for your very calming words in your last letter. I continue to work matters out in my mind. But it is helpful to have a friend provide a clear-headed list of all the good we do and need to keep doing at Wellhouse, no matter how it is funded. I am still unhappy knowing about Jeremiah's business dealings. Perhaps nothing is ever as easy or as innocent as it seems.

And I will also take your advice to try not to let his revelation ruin the memory of what was a beautiful, restful week. Or ruin what is between us, him and me.

I do not know that we will ever again take such a trip together. I find this being a lover to a married man complicated. I have read about other women of infamy who fell into beds with ease of conscience. Of course, these were wicked women, examples of what good Jewish girls should never become. But here I am.

And it's not the falling into bed that is hard. Too easy, in fact. And the bed itself, the love between us, has a force of its own beyond me. Illuminating. Cleansing. No, it is the making of the bed afterwards that I find difficult. The God-what-have-I-done the morning after.

Then I try to rationalize. Whom have we hurt? His wife. The other Mary. The rightful Mary. She doesn't even know about me, I reason. But how can she not? How could he make love to her as he does me? With such tenderness. Passion. Abandon. Then I worry that perhaps he does. And fret that he makes love to her at all. Ever. As if I have any right. And then I make comparisons. Between us as women. If I am beautiful as he says, his beloved as he insists, why does he stay with her? Why does he not put her away? Divorce her?

And then I am repulsed by my own thoughts. Where would she go with no children, no living family? To Wellhouse! What, am I crazy?

A great part of me respects Jeremiah for choosing to remain with her. It shows a kind of integrity. How could I live with myself if he foresook her for me?

Oh, it is too complicated. And painful.

Here is what I know. I love him. I desire him. Want to be with him, always. But I resign myself to whenever I can. As often as we can. As seldom as we must.

And this, despite the penalty if we are caught. (And we never will be!) Despite the law, men's or Yahweh's. And I'll thank Yahweh to keep his big schnoz out of my bedroom!!

Oy! That felt very good. Thank you for being my dear friend and Sister, even after our years apart. It is such a relief to write these words. I wonder what other women do with words they cannot utter for fear of beatings, or worse. Where do they put their words? Their secrets?

Thank you for sharing mine, Izel. I will honour yours.

Love,
Mary of Nazareth

September 20

Dear Jesus,

We have had an illustrious visitor. One Caiaphas, High Priest (or soon to be) of the temple in Jerusalem. He brought his only son,

Joshua, comatose on a litter. They came to Wellhouse when all the medics and physicians in the City of David had failed.

Lilith and Salome made up rooms for Caiaphas and his attendants. Abigail and Phoebe set about trying to lower Joshua's dangerously high temperature. We took him below to the wellspring and immersed him in the cool waters. I forced willow bark tea down his throat. By nightfall of the first day, the fever had broken.

Caiaphas was never far from me or the Sisters at work over Joshua, who was seriously dehydrated. Naomi and Hannah took turns putting spoonfuls of water into him. I asked Caiaphas a series of questions about this malady, which was no illness but a serious concussion from a fall down the priest's palace steps. The boy needed rest and stillness. Especially after the hot bumpy journey from Jerusalem.

At night, I heard Caiaphas praying for his son.

Five days passed. For five days we watched, patiently, as Joshua lay unmoving. Bathed him gently. Dribbled into him what water and gruel we could. Changed his bedclothes. And I talked to him. I spent hours talking to that boy.

Caiaphas was not so patient. For a priest, he was downright impatient. A pest! He made me nervous with all his pacing. Incessant questions about what we were doing and why. Finally, I shooed him out of the sickroom to the garden and insisted he stay there until I called him.

It wasn't long. That same hour, when I called Joshua's name loudly, his eyes fluttered. Then opened. I smiled at him. Then summoned Caiaphas, who wept with joy and relief. I left the two of them together.

We welcomed an exhausted but joyous Caiaphas to our table that evening. He did not join the men in conversation after supper, but instead sought me out in the garden.

"Mary, healer of Nazareth. I have much to thank you for."

"My work is my blessing and waking Joshua was thanks enough."

"How can I repay you?"

I shrugged.

"I am a rich man. I have gold and will send more to you."

"As you wish." Who am I to turn down money?

"When can Joshua and I leave for Jerusalem?"

"His mother no doubt grows sick with worry."

"His mother is dead three years."

Then I realized he'd been looking at me, in that way men have. He is about my age, a little older perhaps. Striking, you might call him. Severe. Not my type.

"You have many children, Mary?"

"Yes. Many. More and more each year." I told him about my family, my greater family of Wellhouse, the orphanage.

"You are a widow."

He was making me uneasy. "Yes."

"How do you pay for this place?"

"I have many sons. My husband left us well-provided for."

"I see." He paused. "You have not remarried."

"No. Joseph had no brother." And in that moment, in his look, I understood. There was condemnation that I was not someone's wife. But there was also hope. Invitation. Or desire for invitation from me.

"How unfortunate."

"I fare very well. I have my family."

"Yes." He smiled. "Family."

"And my work."

He nodded. "You do important work. Again and again, I thank you for curing my son."

"No more games on palace steps!"

"I assure you. There will be no more games."

His words bothered me, Jesus. There is something about the man I don't trust. He moves, he speaks with arrogance. So much surety of knowing.

I sent Anna-Andrew out to inquire of the village men about him. Caiaphas is indeed powerful. Second only to Annas, high priest of the temple in Jerusalem, and slated to be his successor very shortly. Men who have the ear of Herod and of Roman governors.

I shudder to think what he might have said or done had Joshua not recovered.

Not a word slipped about you and Mary. Or that I am a woman

of words and can read and write. I kept a modest tongue in my head, tried not to draw attention to myself.

However, Caiaphas paid me a great deal of attention. After another long seven days — and for once I did not work on the Sabbath — he, Joshua and the attendants prepared to leave. Caiaphas handed me the gold.

"I will return to Wellhouse."

"God grant you good health always, Caiaphas."

"I will return in health, Mary of Nazareth."

His eyes and his tone of voice were perfectly clear, Jesus.

Ah, my son. I do not like this turn of events. I do not like this Caiaphas. Let us hope his temple duties and his own family keep him far too occupied to give Mary of Nazareth another thought.

Love,
Mama

September 28

Dear John,

We are deeply saddened by the news of Elizabeth's death. I understand from Leah that your mother's health seemed to be improving, but deteriorated in those last few weeks. Her tired lungs and heart wore out, is the best way I can describe this malady. We see often in the elderly that a chest ailment can lead to death. I know none of this helps your grief.

Your mother and I repaired our rift of many years, although not in time for us to see one another again. So it gave me joy to see you at Juda's and Joses' recent weddings. Through you, the son John, Elizabeth and Zacharias live on.

Now Elizabeth is with Zacharias. Peace is theirs. Peace be also with you, cousin. May your life work also continue in peace. Please visit us at Wellhouse. You are family. You are welcome.

Love,
Mary of Nazareth

October 14

Dear Jesus,

Now that Rosh Hashanah and Yom Kippur are past, I find a moment to write to you.

It has been an unsettling autumn.

You know how Simon longs to be a rabbi. He has been studying ardently, and is such a good singer. He trains with Caleb, reads the Torah with devotion, praises Yahweh in his life, heart and mind.

Well, Malachi of the Pharisees now cites Leviticus and wags his finger at both Caleb and Simon for daring to offend Yahweh. A half-cripple should come to the altar? Become a rabbi? Read and teach the law? And this Malachi has the ear of the other Pharisees.

Hypocrites!

Some rumourmonger has also divulged the fact that Simon is bastard to a Gentile. A Roman, no less.

And his romance with our Gentile Sister, Phoebe, is the final straw.

With so many strikes against him, Simon's aspirations are daunted. He is an unhappy boy. His only solace is Phoebe. I try to cheer him by suggesting that they marry. This perks him up for a few minutes, but then he resumes his crestfallen attitude. Honestly, Jesus, I don't know what to do. Please write to him. Assure him that there is room for him in the work you do. That Yahweh has a purpose for him. My words fall on deaf ears.

James. A thorn in my side. Do I deserve such a tomcat for a son? He is worse than a goat. And he is getting a randy reputation, which he brings home to Wellhouse. Not to mention that I have twice had to give him a mixture of spikenard and sassafras for you-know-what! I never thought I'd stoop to matchmaking, but I must find a wife for him and quickly. Before he kills himself. Or gets killed.

Joses and Ester. Fighting like cats and dogs! All hours. Rousing us and our patients from our dreams and much-needed sleep. And the lovemaking make-up sessions afterwards! Barnyard sounds from their dwelling! I've had a talk with Joses about discretion. Now I must also speak to Ester. I throw up my hands at those two.

Dinah. My other new daughter-in-law. Nice girl, but whiny. All right already, so she misses Juda. So do we all. In fact, I can't wait for him to get home to cheer her up and get her out of my hair. I try to be patient. To find some meaningful way for her to occupy her time. She is queen of sniffles, that one.

Squabbling. Did I mention the squabbling between the Sisters? This past month has been especially bad. I am grateful that for the most part, the Sisters all respect and like one another. But sometimes! Like yesterday.

Naomi and Salome started arguing about the way Salome prepares the dough, for Yahweh's sake! Then Bathsheba chimes in on Salome's side. And Lilith has to get her two shekels worth in. Suddenly hair is pulled and claws are extended. Hagar, used to scrapping from her past nefarious trade, cannot resist digging in. Sophia tries to act as peacemaker in the fray and gets her face slapped for her efforts. Delilah attempts reason with her Sisters and sharp-tongued Lilith reduces her to tears. Sharon retaliates in Delilah's defense and Lilith then turns her venom upon her. Hagar leaps to Lilith's throat. Finally, Phoebe runs to my workroom. Eve and I have to abandon a delicate mixture we are working at to call a halt to this petty fighting. I find Hannah, who had just happened by with a basket of laundry, nursing a nasty scratch to her arm. Eve pulls Hagar and Lilith apart. Abigail, newly returned from market, applies salve to the catscratches and mutters annoyance. Then I impress upon everyone how important they are to me and to Wellhouse, soothe feelings, dry countless tears, facilitate reconciliations and apologies and an hour later return exhausted to my workroom where my mixture is ruined.

They are all suffering the curse. It is the only explanation I can think of.

Thank goodness Sukkot is upon us. We will have reason for a feast. We need to lighten up around here.

And I need to stop my kvetching already. I wish you and Mary a happy Sukkot.

Love,
Mama

P.S. Would it kill you to visit your mother?

November 15

Dear Jesus,

Terrible news! There is an anti-Roman uprising in Gamala. There are whispers of Roman atrocities. I am going to minister aid where I can. And to bear witness.

Love,
Mama

December 5

Dearest Son,

My heart is heavy. Preparations for Hanukkah seem wearisome. I am sickened by Yahweh's human creation.

I brought with me Anna-as-Andrew, able Abigail and Eve, who daily grows more adept at herbs and healing. We left shortly after Sabbath a fortnight ago. None of us were prepared for what we found.

Gamala was a nightmare.

When we arrived, widows, children, old people were wailing in the streets. Begging for alms. Their gardens, animal sheds, houses all razed by the Romans. Water poisoned with putrefying corpses of cattle and worse, dumped by the Romans. The stink of death and burning and human suffering everywhere. Flies. Vermin.

But nothing prepared us for the sight on the road out of Gamala towards Jerusalem.

Hundreds of posts. And nailed to crossbars the remains of men. Eyes pecked out. Rot and decay. The people told us that the Romans broke the legs of the victims to hasten death. Some were pierced with sword or lance. Bled to death. Others were gasping last breaths.

We had to leave them there, by Roman decree. None will redress these Roman atrocities!

I vomited until I had nothing left, until I burst a blood vessel in my eye.

Then, with the rest of the bedraggled survivors, I returned to Gamala to help them pick up the crumbs of life.

We gave away all the food we had. Ministered to the sick and malnourished. Lanced the boils. Applied balm to the wounds.

And that is all we were, really. Temporary balm. Our help was minimal. How can one begin to heal such grief? Such ugliness. Such sickness.

Many families, or what remained of families, left the city. Others persist doggedly on, rebuilding from the rubble.

Sorrowfully Anna, Abigail, Eve and I returned to Nazareth. Said prayers for the dead. More for the living.

I cannot bring myself to utter prayers for the Romans and their leaders who did this. Forgiveness and mercy are gall on my lips.

I will never forget. I will never forgive.

Love,
Mama

January 8

Dear Jesus,

As always it was a blessing to have you and Mary home. I marvel at the man you are, beloved son. So wise. Kind. Talented. That I should have such a son. Daily, I give thanks.

You are coming into your own, Jesus. There is a calm certainty about you. Not that I didn't see you riled to passion when we discussed your work. Or flashes of your temper at the mention of the Pharisees or the atrocities at Gamala. No. I mean there is a self-assurance that you are on the correct path. You step with confidence. And we are all reassured because of you. I wish you could always be with us.

Again, I want to say how humbled I was when you lit the final Hanukkah lamp and honoured me with your song. A song of praise for Wellhouse and the women who work here, a song of praise for your mother. I do not feel always worthy of praise. But it is nice to hear every once in a while. We all like to be appreciated. It was a beautiful song, Jesus.

Simon is feeling much better since you invited him to join you in your travels and teachings someday. There are many ways to serve Yahweh, he is finding.

It was heartwarming to watch you with your nephews and the children of Wellhouse. You know how to make children laugh. A wonderful gift. The children at the Tyre orphanage must miss you now that you and Mary are off to Sidon.

I have been thinking about our talk at the well. I know you don't understand me and my wayward ways. How can I be the mother you praise in song one night and the mother you argue with the next day? How can I be the mother of you and your brothers and sisters, the mother of Wellhouse, and such an impious Jew? I break the laws. I transgress. I fail. And I doubt.

That there is a great power and mystery in this world, I do not doubt. I see it in the healing body. I see it in the miracle of conception and birth. The breath of life. The solemnity and awe of death. In the patterns of nature around us. In the sun rising and setting. The moon and the stars returning to their places. The steady passing of seasons. The beauty of this world. I see it in our family. My rich relationships. I know there is a power greater than mine. Call it Yahweh, if you like.

I am filled with love and strength and peace when I consider this power. It is a light in my life. A candle in the dark, when I am alone. When I am uncertain or troubled, I go down to the well. I go out to the hills. I walk in the sun. Or under the stars. And breathe deeply. Drink deeply.

Yahweh, the Yahweh of the rabbis, baffles me. He is a man-god. A stern father. Forgetful. Inattentive. Capricious. Cruel. So like the hypocritical Pharisees. The angry father. The tyrannical husband. There is so little place for me and those I help in such a household.

But when I breathe or sing or dance or pray in my place, in my being, I feel a lightness, a lifting. I am alive and grateful to be so. To do this good work in my short life. My God calls me to make a small difference in my world. To raise up a family to be proud of. To love. Passionately. You. Mary. My children. Grandchildren. Sisters. The lost souls of this world. Those who have gone before like Joseph. Your father.

And Jeremiah. Your father.

My love is a benediction. My benediction is love.

Always know that I love you, Jesus.

Love,
Mama

February 27

Dear Jesus,

Caiaphas returned to Wellhouse. He complained of a back malady, but I knew he was feigning. We were polite and provided him with baths from our healing waters. The Sisters Salome and Delilah massaged his back many times over. My hope was that their youth and beauty would turn his eye from Mary, your mother. However, that was not so.

He found every possible occasion to stop me in my work and bend my ear. Seemingly about Wellhouse. My children. But in the end he came to the point.

"You should not be alone any longer, Mary."

I laughed. "I am hardly alone, surrounded by all you see here. I never have a moment to myself!"

"Still. It is not good for a woman to remain unmarried."

"I still mourn my husband, Caiaphas."

"The period for mourning has long passed."

"Nonetheless, I mourn. I do not want another husband."

The man stood still in thought. I'm sure I perplex him.

He took my chin in his hand. His touch was ungentle. "Mary of Nazareth. I am a patient man. But I am a man. You are a woman. A man and woman should be together. I will wait out this period of mourning. But my entreaties will not cease. I am a man who gets what he wants. Understand, Mary of Nazareth, I want you."

And then he crushed me to him and kissed me. My lips were bruised by his force.

Caiaphas left us abruptly that day. Tossed me another bag of gold from atop his camel. I caught it and his meaning.

I am very unsettled, Jesus.

Love,
Mama

March 24

Dear Jesus,

What marvellous Passover news you write to your Mama! Mary el Mejdel with child! After all these years! I am weeping as I write.

Now, I must be stern with both of you. Mary must return at once to Wellhouse. She must be indulged and coddled while she carries this child to term. And I am determined that she will. I know it will be difficult for you to be apart, but Mama knows what is best for a pregnant woman.

Make the journey from Sidon slowly and with great care. Ensure that Mary drinks frequently, eats and sleeps well. She carries precious cargo.

Thank you for this news, my son! And thank you for your words of reassurance about Caiaphas. You are right, of course. I do have choice and free will. I do not have to marry the man. I give my head a shake. It was the force of his words. I will plan what I must say to him when he next returns.

In the meantime, I take delight in the future. Yours and Mary's. It is a glorious spring!

Love,
Mama

P.S. And for Yahweh's sake, Jesus, pamper your wife!

May 7

Dear Jesus,

It is the month of our births, and Mary el Mejdel is resting quietly here at Wellhouse. At nearly three months along, she is coping. The Sisters and I pay her much attention. She misses you but is making herself useful in the orphanage. Mary has a gentle way with children.

I am expecting a visit from your father. I've not seen him but for a few brief days after Hanukkah. He does not know that he will shortly be a grandfather. I am eager to tell him.

No word from Caiaphas, thank Yahweh. May he disappear from the earth.

I send along a new robe, as the one you wore home lately looked so shabby. This is a garment made by many. Methuselah, the sheep, gave up his wool for the cause. Sol carded and spun it, wove it into soft fabric on her loom and dyed it with juice of eggplant. I fashioned it into a robe. Together, we send it to you with our love.

Love,
Mama

P.S. Happy birthday, Jesus.

May 14

Dear Izel,

I dash this scroll off to you, as Jeremiah arrives today and you can well imagine that I am anxious with preparations.

I call on your expertise as midwife. My daughter-in-law Mary el Mejdel is with child. She has never carried a child to term, but has been pregnant four times. We have her here at Wellhouse and are insisting that she rest and eat well. Yet she is lethargic and her colour is not good, I think. She is swollen in her legs and arms. Her face is puffy. Already, in her third month, she has labour pains. I have seen this before and know it is not a good sign. I have consulted my books and given her palmetto berries and yam and ginger. Do you know what else I might try? We need your advice.

Thank you, Izel. Please pay us a visit soon. I miss your dear face.

Love,
Mary of Nazareth

June 25

Dear Caiaphas,

No, now is not a good time to pay me a visit. My daughter-in-law is with child and having a difficult time. We need peace and quiet at Wellhouse and are not accepting visitors or minor cases. We also have had an infestation of lice, courtesy of the town drunk. I'm sure such conditions would not interest you. I am sorry that the pains in your legs persist. Perhaps a physician in Jerusalem can help you.

Best wishes,
Simon of Nazareth
for Mary of Nazareth

July 18

Dear Caiaphas,

Thank you for the gift of dates for Wellhouse. They are most delicious and will be put to good use. We thank you.

But no, this is not a good time for your visit. I suggest steam to relieve your chest congestion.

Hoping for your fast recovery,
Simon of Nazareth
for Mary of Nazareth

August 13

Dear Caiaphas,

We continue to monitor my daughter-in-law very carefully. She is in delicate health. The halls of Wellhouse must be silent. Even the children of the orphanage have been moved to adjoining buildings.

I am sorry for your boils. But the answer is no.

Simon of Nazareth
for Mary of Nazareth

September 12

Dear Jesus,

I cannot tell you how that man, Caiaphas, annoys me with his self-invitations to Wellhouse. And each response must be scribed by Simon to hide the fact that I read and write. The man is a plague! And I don't know how much longer I can fend him off.

Mary is now on complete bedrest. I know she misses you. Can you find a way to Nazareth during this month? A visit would help her spirits considerably and would ease your mother's burden. It's not easy to keep a pregnant and lonely woman happy. We have run out of Caiaphas' dates; Mary has such voracious cravings.

I don't mean to worry you, but I have sent for Izel to help us through these final weeks with Mary. Izel is somewhat of an expert, as I think I told you. Anyway, it will be nice to have an extra pair of hands around and the Sisterly support I know she will give me.

Jeremiah has come almost every other week to Wellhouse. He kibitzes with Mary el Mejdel and is overjoyed that he is to have a grandchild. Mary reciprocates and has grown quite fond of your father. He began to bring gifts for the baby, but I put the kibosh on that. Bad luck.

He knows nothing about that amorous hypochondriac, Caiaphas. I have enough to contend with these days. I don't need jealous men around Wellhouse.

Come home soon, Jesus. We need you.

Love,
Mama

October 30

Dear Jesus,

Soon after you left, Mary went into a deep sadness. She is crying in the other room as I write this. She says she knows the child in her womb is ill. That your leaving was the bad omen that sealed the infant's fate. Remember how she pleaded with you on your last night not to leave?

And truly, son. Did you have to go? Wellhouse is a safe haven for a short spell. Can your work not rest until the birth of your child? Is the treasure of Mary's womb not worth saving at least as much as healing the ills of others?

I confess I did not quite recognize you, Jesus, when I saw you. Too often, your talk strayed from healing to righting the wrongs of this world, to exacting vengeance upon the wicked and hypocritical. There is a hardness about your eyes, like that of the zealot. A strain about your mouth and a set of your chin that smacks of righteousness. Is this what happens when you lack the company of women?

Frankly, I was frightened. What has happened to your message of peace and hope? I know we are all moved to fury and revenge when we see the inequities of this uneven world. But Yahweh help us all, we come to our senses. May you come to yours.

How often have I cautioned you about your stubbornness. Your singleness of purpose. Your unyielding drive sometimes at the expense of others' feelings. And yes, what some call your arrogance. Your selfishness.

I am your mother, and I have the right to tell you that you were wrong to leave your wife in her troubled pregnancy. The world will still be hurting and wailing after the child is born. You can return to nursing it once Mary is nursing your child. You cannot save everyone, Jesus. Come home to those you can.

Love,
Mama

November 10

Dear Son,

In grief I write of the death of your daughter three days ago.

Mary el Mejdel went into full labour on the first morning of this week. It was not her time, but the baby would come.

I do not know how long the child had been dead in her womb. But there had been very little movement in the previous day or so.

She was born at noon. Perfect. Blue. And still. A relatively easy delivery because she was weeks before her time. Mary bled, but not alarmingly so. Rest assured that physically your wife is well.

We, all of us present, took turns with the baby. Izel washed her. Sol rubbed her soft skin with olive oil. I wrapped her in swaddling. Abigail held her and passed her to her mother. Mary was inconsolable. Finally, we had to wrest the baby from her arms. I gave Mary a sleeping draught.

The women and I prepared for the funeral.

We went down to the well. Lighted the candles. Burned the fragrant frankincense. Murmured our prayers. Sang songs of loss and grief. In the evening, Mary el Mejdel joined us. Keened with us. All the women of Wellhouse and our family, holding one another, rocking each other as if we were the infant, singing your daughter's spirit onwards to a better place where babies don't die or suffer. Olam Haba. Gan Eden. Where she will be safe. Where she will know that she is missed and loved by all of us here. Where she will not be blue but alight with health and happiness. Where she will not be still but ever alive.

So I hope. So I pray.

We buried her the next day. Caleb and Simon intoned and canted the ancient words. I offered my own silently. Everyone wept. Especially Mary. Especially Jeremiah. But I did not, cannot.

I am numb with loss.

And where are you, my son, in all of this? We await you in sorrow to receive you in love.

Mama

Part Seven

Theotokos

Today is my birthday.

Jeremiah sends money to tell me so. Otherwise I would no longer know or care about this or any anniversary of my birth. I have not seen his face in eighteen months.

I tire of these distances of time and space between us.

Eighteen months have passed since the stillbirth of my only granddaughter. Eighteen months Jesus and Mary el Mejdel have been home with us. Together we heal. Grief has been slow to pass. But we have found our ways. Mostly in simple things: walks in the hills, solace under the stars.

A little noshing here and there. I have put on weight these eighteen months.

Gradually tears give way to laughter.

But she is ever in our hearts.

Six months or so ago, Jesus resolved to go out into the world again. Not secretly, but openly. I do not have the mother's heart to discourage him. His work, like mine, is part of his healing. How can I dissuade him from his calling? Why would I?

Once a candle is lighted, we cannot hide it away, but must set it in the candle holder for all to see. I can only hope, Yahweh, that you do not snuff out his flame.

Times are dangerous. The Romans have stepped up persecutions of zealots. Of Jews. Caesar demands higher taxes. Despotic leaders are more jealous of power, Herod especially among them — just like his murderous father before him. Those who speak out against Rome are punished. Or worse. I can never forget Gamala.

Amongst our own people, there is much petty infighting. Rivalry for limited power. Arguments about the law that descend into divisiveness and bitter resentment. Sadducee against Pharisee. Rabbi against rabbi. Wealthy against poor.

These are desperate days. And my only begotten son wants to step into the middle of the fray.

What can a mother do? Only kiss his cheek and wish him well. He has a mission. To deliver people from despair and hopelessness. To empower them. To heal the sick and broken-hearted and defend the defenseless. To rail against Rome and all oppressors. He is a visionary. He is a fool.

And I, too, for raising him so. One foolish rebellious visionary begets another.

What do we achieve in this lifetime? Small footsteps forward. Minor cures only. The world goes on falling and failing, with or without us.

But I love my maverick first-born. Admire him. His bravery. His convictions. His integrity. His consuming passions. I rally behind him despite the odds. Yahweh, hear my prayer. Protect our wayward son. Spare him.

Late summer

Her mouth. Her wild hair. This is what I remember. They brought her writhing, screeching in the middle of the night. Roused us from our dreams. Pushed past Simon into the garden. By torchlight I barely recognized the daughter of a new family in town. But I saw the blood from where she'd bitten her lip.

Mary and I tried to hold her down, to secure her so she wouldn't do herself more harm. I sent Eve scurrying for a sleeping draught, but I had no idea how to administer it to this hellcat.

Jesus joined us. Sure. Calm. He stepped into the torchlight. Found the young woman's wild eye. Spoke soothingly into her ear — words I could not hear — even as she struggled and spat and shrieked. He touched her forehead gently.

Then above the din of her thrashing, her mad sobs, we heard, "Get thee from this woman, Satan, I command you."

And as if a spell were broken, the tempest in the woman stilled. She melted to the ground. Everything, everyone was silent. I could hear my own troubled heartbeat.

The family tried to pay us, but we would accept no money. They backed away from my son, bowing, scraping, ingratiating, fear and awe on their lips. They took their now-subdued daughter, tearful and grateful, through our gate, into the thick night.

I heard the word "Messiah," and the lock clicked into place.

Simon, Eve and Mary yawned off to bed.

Jesus ran a tired hand through his sleep-tossed hair.

"I'd like some tea. How about you, Mama?"

I looked at him. "How many times have you pulled that act?"

He shrugged. "A few, I guess."

Jesus padded behind me into the kitchen. I made tea. I knew he watched me. Waiting.

"Well, Mama?"

"Well. Well! Well, why don't you just fashion the noose for your own neck now?"

"You're overreacting, Mama ..."

"I am *not* overreacting, impetuous son of mine!"

"I helped her, Mama. I helped the family. You would have done no less."

"I would not have ... I would not ..."

"Yes, you would. Isn't that what you do? What we all do in this house? In this family? Help others? How is what I did any different from the fertility charm you gave Abraham, the money lender? You knew it was sham, but he believed, and your charm works on his belief. What about the love knot you gave the village goose girl last week? The sugar and water Hara the spice merchant's wife believes will cure her latest in a long list of complaints and ailments, all fictions in her mind? Your fiction cures hers. How is what I did to help that girl so different, Mama, answer me that?"

"It is different, Jesus, because I was not putting myself or you or anyone else in this family or this house in danger by playing the Messiah!"

He was silent, but his eyes were bright. Too bright. He faced me.

"What if I am the Messiah, Mama?"

"Don't be ridiculous."

"Answer me. How do you know I am not?"

"You are an impulsive show-off with an ego the size of the Sea of Galilee. That's what I know."

"If I say I am, if others say I am, then I am."

"Saying doesn't make a thing so. You know it and I know it."

"Nonsense, Mama. Saying makes it so. Especially saying aloud. Look what just happened with that girl. I commanded Satan from her, and Satan was gone."

"That was not Satan, but an ailment, a frailty of mind we both recognize."

"Do we? How do you know, Mama? How are you always so certain? If she and her family saw Satan, believed Satan, then she was Satan-possessed and my words chased him away."

"So the reasoning is that if you say, and they say, and everyone — except me, that is — says that you are the Messiah, then it follows that you are the Messiah."

"Yes."

"You are a meshuggener, not the Messiah."

"You are a stubborn old woman."

"Hmm. Well then my son, the Messiah. Why don't you go a step further, then? Why stop at Messiah? Why don't you say you are GOD, since saying a thing makes it so. Say it then: 'I am YHWH! JESUS IS GOD!'"

"That's not —"

"That's exactly where such thinking leads, Jesus. To grandiose notions. Power hunger. Glory hunger. A sickening of the soul. And a risk of your life. Your father would weep."

"Which one, Mama?"

"All three, Jesus." And I left him.

Fall

We had not really spoken again, Jesus and I, of the incident. Today necessity forced our lips at last.

They brought Jamal, wheezing the last of his breath. Once so lively and skittish, scampering over the hills with the other shepherds and goatherds, now a skeleton with barely enough strength to hold up his head to drink our hot ginger tea. His family had often come to us for herbs and medicine to help Jamal as he worsened these past six months. I told them his heart was faltering. That perhaps he was born with a sick heart. But parents who watch a child die before their eyes grow desperate. Like everyone in Nazareth, they had heard of the miraculous doings of my son. Now they wanted no part of my simple, inadequate woman's wisdom; they wanted the Messiah Himself.

I summoned Jesus to the sickroom where Jamal lay gasping. Then I assumed the corner where Jamal's family had relegated me. Jesus saw the gravity of the illness immediately. He turned frightened and sympathetic eyes on the anxious parents.

"Your son … is very sick."

"We know you can help him," Umut the baker bowed his head and began to pray.

Jesus touched the boy's forehead. Checked his eyes. His pulse. Looked at his colour. All as I have trained him to do. He squeezed Jamal's hand.

"You are very brave, Jamal."

The boy smiled weakly, slipping in and out of consciousness.

Umut's wife, Lily, appealed to my son. "Take this demon from him."

"This is no demon, Lily. The boy's heart is failing. He has hours left to him, a day, but no more. I am sorry. Take him home. Give him peace and comfort in his own home. I can do nothing for him."

"What?" Umut stopped his prayers, incredulous.

"We have money ..." Lily offered.

"I ... we don't want money. Your child is dying. I can offer little comfort ..."

"No!" Umut shook his fist at my son. "You," he pointed, "are the Messiah. You are the Chosen One. We have heard it told all about the village. We have ears. We have eyes. Some among us are saved. Why not our son? Why not Jamal? Why are we not worthy?" And he buried his face in his hands.

Jesus looked utterly bewildered.

"Please," Lily took his sleeve, "we are humble, simple people. Perhaps we have erred with Elohim. Not offered enough sacrifice. Sometimes Umut drinks too much." This last she whispered. "But we will mend our ways, if only ... if only you save Jamal."

"I can't save Jamal, but he will go to Gan Eden to be with —"

"I don't want him in paradise!" Lily's voice was shrill. "I want him alive with me, with us. I want him as he was before. Healthy. Alive. I want you to save him!"

"You don't understand … I am not what you think I am. What they say I am." Jesus backed away from her. "I … I am a carpenter. Sometimes a fisherman. A healer. But I cannot cure everyone. I cannot do it. I cannot. I am sorry. I cannot save Jamal."

Umut and Lily looked like dead people themselves. I stepped forward, quietly.

"We will help you bring him home."

Umut nodded.

Simon and Anna carried the stretcher out of the sickroom and out of Wellhouse. Lily and Umut did not look back as they left. I watched the dust settle from their passing feet before I turned to Jesus beside me.

"Humility is a hard lesson, Mama."

"Yes, Jesus. It is."

"I think I get it now."

"Good for you."

"But I am still determined to go out into the world and do my father's bidding."

"I never doubted it."

"You should never have told that story, Mama."

"You blame me?"

"No. But I wish I'd never heard it."

Me either, sweet Jesus.

Rosh Hashanah

We have had a pack of boys to dinner. Jesus has taken up lately with his cousin John, who calls himself the Baptist.

I am glad his mother is not living to see this. Elizabeth would be mortified. She and I were never close — that silly rivalry between mothers over their boys — but I wouldn't wish such a son on my late cousin.

John's hair and beard are unkempt. Indeed he is a very hairy man altogether, and he "girds his loins" — as he made frequent and rude mention at dinner — in animal fur. In truth, John smells. I kept my distance. Let the other women serve the meal.

I wish Jesus would likewise keep upwind of him. John is too wild for my tastes. Too ... too evangelical. Flaunting. Parading his appearance, his dunking of citizens in water, making wild gesticulations and utterances apparently sanctioned by Yahweh. He is very much the lead actor in his own tragedy.

The "Baptist" cannot keep his mouth shut. As if Jesus needs more example of that! His cousin is a bad influence on my only begotten son who has enough of his own unorthodox and dangerous opinions. John has lately taken to crying foul about the marriage of Herod Antipas to his niece, Herodias. Such unions happen and have since time immemorial. We have no business in others' bedrooms, not to mention that the Jews should keep their noses away from Caesar and his sycophants. We have enough trouble from Rome. And there are bigger battles to wage. Over wages, for instance! But John, outraged and odiferous, shouted and fumed throughout what should have been a peaceful dinner.

Along with Jesus and the "Baptist," Philip and Simon (not our Simon, Jesus calls this one Peter) barrelled in without washing their feet. Then the "sons of thunder" showed up: James (not ours either) and his brother John, sons of Zebedee. Neither spoke below a bellow the entire meal. All these fellows tracking in sand from the shores of Galilee with barely a nod of greeting to me or the other women of Wellhouse. Thank Yahweh they brought fish or we might not have satisfied their zealous appetites.

They drank wine enough, I can tell you.

Through most of the night.

As they argued and politicked and plotted against Rome on behalf of Israel.

Their manners set my teeth on edge. Salome and Mary spent all the next morning cleaning up after their revelry.

I noticed the thick heads and bleary eyes of Jesus' guests, but I didn't offer any cure to ease the pain. I say the headache cures the urge to drink.

I'm not sure I like these young men. They make me nervous with their talk of revolution. Nervous for my son and this family. Even more so because Simon and Anna-as-Andrew hung on their every subversive word.

Ah. When I face myself in the glass, I am afraid of my part in all of this. Harbouring young revolutionaries. Breaking bread with zealots. Housing insurrection. I feel those tremors underfoot again. And I watch Jesus step surely through the door, opened by his mother, into the tempest.

Yom Kippur

For our feast of atonement, I am feeding a multitude. Young men and boys. All with hearty appetites. Not merely for food, but for the words of my son.

There are twelve now. Others clamouring at the door to be let in.

I shudder to know that two of my own are amongst them, a third one hovering at the margin. Simon, as Jesus promised, has answered his rabbinic calling by joining his oldest brother's flock with the zeal of the disciple. This worries me. Now Anna also walks with Jesus as Andrew. No one but we know he is a she. What if Anna is discovered? Even James has surrendered his tomcat prowling and is sniffing around the edges of his brother's cause.

Jesus has made his selection. Twelve faithful. Or so he believes. In addition to Anna-Andrew and our Simon, Philip, Simon-Peter, and Zebedee's sons James and John, Jesus keeps company with a pasty-faced young tanner, Bartholomew; a naysayer named Thomas; Levi the tax collector; James, son of Alphaeus (whoever he is, some bigshot from Jerusalem); Thaddeus, a doctor (if only Anna ... but no ... none of my hopeless, maternal wishing); and a sullen young man named Judas Iscariot, who only lights up when Jesus is in his presence.

Secretly, this Judas is in love with Jesus. I told my son so. He laughed. But I know a great deal about men. And love. Judas loves the man he calls Master.

Myself? I don't like these boys' attitudes towards the women of Wellhouse (our Simon and Anna-Andrew are exceptions, of course). And some of the men oppose the women whom Jesus invites to his flock, begrudge their participation in Jesus' teaching. As though Joanna, wife of Chuza, Suzanna and our Phoebe are lesser beings, less important to Jesus' ministry. Most of all, the men resent Mary el Mejdel, Jesus' most beloved disciple. Especially that sourpuss Judas. Any sign of affection Jesus shows her is met with snorts of derision from that one. When Jesus kisses Mary's lips, I believe Judas wishes they were his own. I don't trust him. He is in a passion for Jesus, I swear to Yahweh.

Still, I pray for them all, even as we wear ourselves out feeding them. And I pray for all of us in these turgid, turbulent times. I pray for my misgivings, my misdeeds. For all I have lost. For all I am losing.

Sukkot

Joses has fallen behind with the orders in the carpentry shop. Everyone else, it seems, has taken to the road to spread the good word.

Then they reconvene at Wellhouse to eat and drink us dry.

Could that thick-as-a-rock Peter or that Janus-faced Judas pick up a hammer and nails and lend a hand? Would it kill the thunderclods James and John to schlep some wood? Would Mr. High and Mighty James-son-of-Alphaeus ever deign to help my James or Joses sons-of-Joseph the carpenter? Drop a few shekels into the pot to finance the larder? Does he know how much it costs to stuff his oversized gullet? Or does he think that money is heaven-sent?

How about if Levi the tax collector collected his own garbage and picked up after himself once in a while?

Do lazy Philip and pallid Bartholomew minister in their sleep? Because it seems, if left to themselves, they'd snore away the sunlit hours. Every morning it is Hagar's tedious task to rouse the two slackers.

On his last visit, I made John the Baptist lodge in the barn, such was his reek. Would it ever occur to him to take a shovel to the manure in the barnyard?

I am tired of Thomas sniggering at the women, especially at shy Delilah, whom he fancies but hasn't a clue how to woo. I doubt if he has a civil tongue in his head. She is too good for him, at any rate.

Why can't the lot of them follow my sons' and daughters' example and join in with the greater family of Wellhouse when they are here? Many hands make light work. Or didn't their mothers teach them anything?

To their credit, the Sisters of Wellhouse are infinitely patient with the disciples, as they're now called, much more patient than the mother of Jesus. I find it all a little much how these men carry on. Self-proclaimed teachers of my son's ideas. Healers. Ha!

Yes, yes. Thaddeus is a physician. I know. I know. I should be fawning all over the man. But he has a disease called arrogance that needs ministering. Never one to get his own hands soiled by consorting with the sick, he is always quick to give out unwanted advice — seldom good or useful — about how I should treat illnesses: from dyspepsia to heat rash to a pain in the tuckus. Which Thaddeus most certainly is. I say, physician, heal thyself!

And in the meantime the family of Joseph and the Sisters of Wellhouse continue their daily tasks for their daily bread. Which, despite the fabulous stories, does not drop like manna from the sky. Last time I checked, women were still doing the kneading and baking. Not to mention the washing and cleaning. How nice that we can accommodate men in their busy important work.

I am becoming resentful. And I told Jesus so.

"This is a house of healing. Not an inn."

"We are only staying a day or two at most. I thought you liked seeing Mary and me. Not to mention Anna and Simon ..."

"Of course, I love seeing you. That is not the point. These boys are eating us out of Wellhouse and home."

"We bring what we can. Philip brought fish ..."

"It's not enough, Jesus, and you know it. These men ought to be pitching in. Doing their share."

"I will talk to them."

"I doubt you will have much luck."

"Mama, they listen to me."

"Do they? When they like the message, perhaps. But do they listen to me in this my house? They do not. Least of all that moonsick Judas."

"I have spoken to Judas."

"Have you?"

"He knows that he cannot continue to challenge Mary. Or show disrespect to you or any woman who is of this house. Or by my side."

I raised a suspicious eyebrow. "How exactly has Judas challenged Mary?"

"He said ... he called her a whore."

I winced. Mary is not alone of her former profession in this house. I wondered what Judas might have said or intimated to Hagar or Naomi. What Lilith might do if she overheard. Which might not be such a bad thing, I allowed my wicked mind to hope.

"And Judas grumbled that she wasted money for the poor by anointing my head with oil."

"She is your wife and your beloved."

"I told him that also."

"Judas behaves so because he is in love with you, son. As I have said before." Jesus shook his head. He may be the light, but he does not clearly see. "They are all half in love with you."

"Mama ..."

"You should be wary of this cultist following."

"Anna and Simon are among them. James has all but ceased his ...

dalliances. The others are my brothers and sisters. The twelve do love me. Even Judas. But not as you suggest, Mama."

"All right, Jesus. I cannot make a believer of you. But I will give you my maternal warning. You dazzle them. And, yes, inspire them. They are drawn to you as moths to a lamp. I dread what will happen if the oil is used up." Or the flame is snuffed, and who might do the snuffing, I pondered in my heart. "If your ideas and your disobedience land you in serious trouble, where will these brothers be?"

"At my side, Mama. They will love one another and me as I have loved them. They would lay down their lives for me, their friend. As I would do for them."

"Yours is a fine example, my darling son. But not everyone is you. That is a sad and bitter truth."

"I find your distrust curious, Mama. You, who have trusted and taken in and aided misfits and lost souls all your life."

I thought of Jamin. Jake the pimp. Jeremiah. The Herods. And you, Yahweh. Yes, and me. Mary of Nazareth. We are all betrayers. We understand betrayal.

Jesus the great-hearted does not.

I fear a sword shall pierce us both.

Simchat Torah

John the Baptist is dead.

Little did I know that supper served to him in Wellhouse would be John's last.

And now I learn that his tangled head was served on a platter to Salome, daughter of Herodias.

What cruel ironies you fashion, Yahweh.

We grieve the loss of John. He was a young, fervent man who lived for you, Yahweh. A young man in the prime of his life. Why take such a man bent on saving your Chosen, Yahweh? Your mysteries confound me. But then, perhaps as I suspect there is no mystery at all. John got too close to power. His head was the price. And you looked down and did nothing. As usual.

Before he died, John baptized Jesus, of course. And added fuel to the messianic fire. Just what we need to further my son's cause and notoriety. The endorsement of a half-mad dead man. Cum martyr.

Jesus and I had words again. In the carpentry shop, where he should be spending more of his time, as far as I'm concerned.

I'm sure I am a gnat buzzing about his ear. But I am anxious about this open talk of hypocrisy. Criticisms levelled at the powerful. I agree, but I tremble. Jesus' crowds swell. As does the anger of the Pharisees, like the swelling of a gout-inflamed foot. I wring my hands and beg him not to do anything impulsive.

"Ours is a mission of peace, Mama."

"Is it, my son? Sometimes those friends of yours seem too eager for action."

"They follow my instructions, my example, Mama."

"So you have said. And so I hope."

"I understand. You don't approve of them."

"There is fervour in their eyes. A longing that looks like bloodlust, powerlust. I've seen it in your eyes, too."

"I know."

"That's not how I raised you to be."

"Ah, but Mama, I follow your example. You yourself instructed me in the fine art of subversion. How to undermine power. How to take matters into my own hands."

"Ayi! And now I beat my breast at the thought of just how I've mis-taught you."

"Mama!"

"Jesus!"

We stared at each other.

"Look. I can hear your voice ringing alarms in my head, Mama. I'm not hungry for power, but for justice."

"The two get confused. Especially with men who are zealous. Especially with talk of violence. Look what happened to John!"

"John is a martyr."

"John is dead. Who cares if he is a martyr? Your cousin and friend is dead."

Jesus looked down at the block of wood in his hand. "I miss him."

"As do I." Surprised, I realized I miss the son of Elizabeth, malodorous though he was. "His death is a warning, Jesus."

"I'm warned already, Mama. Still, my life is out in the world, not sequestered here."

We were talking in circles. But I couldn't keep my mouth from flapping like a common yenta. "That Judas is a schnook. And Simon-Peter —"

"Enough already! You're giving me a headache!" Jesus tried to laugh. "I'm aware of your opinions of my friends, Mama. But they have given up everything to be with me. To resist Rome. Through peaceful protest and solidarity."

"If you say so, son." I paused. "But I don't like the way they treat women — Mary, Sol, Phoebe, your female followers. The women of Wellhouse and the Star."

"I'm working on changing their attitudes. Not every Jewish boy has had the privilege of being raised by Mary of Nazareth."

The good humour returned to us both. A compliment always brings a smile, and my son knows only too well how to flatter his mother.

Jesus does not believe in the sword. In weapons. He is not Jeremiah. He is not a warmonger. He is peace. I can only hope that the boys who follow him will continue to be swayed by his finer judgement.

Jesus does believe in free will. I cannot tie him to this mother's apron strings. May he choose wisely.

Neither can I write the story of his life. Only hope that his stylus will not fail. That his story will not be short.

I admit it. I threw the apple. Deliberately.

I feel wicked as Eve in Eden.

And I am not sorry.

That Pharisee serpent, Micah, deserved that and more! Since the day he sought out Mary el Mejdel in Wellhouse, the man lives to torment and threaten me. Though bent from arthritis and age, Micah is still a viper who cannot keep his forked tongue silent.

I walked by the temple in the afternoon sun. Simply on my way to visit an elderly widow at the edge of Nazareth, which is where they put elderly widows when no one will have anything to do with them.

From the steps Micah shouted, "Woman! Know you that it is forbidden to labour on the Sabbath?" Then to those assembled about him on the stairs, "This woman harbours harlots!"

I turned sharp Mary eyes upon him. I am of an age where I grow more and more intolerant of intolerance. Perhaps it is the change of life. Hot flashes come with a vengeance. Perhaps it was the storm of anxiety in my heart over Jesus. Or perhaps I have just had enough.

Shielding my eyes from the sun's glare, I looked up at doddering Micah. Then looked past him. And saw. How the Nazareth synagogue fathers make their shekels. Just like the other priests, scribes, Pharisees, Sadducees in other towns and cities. There above Micah's head in the outer temple courtyard, a virtual bazaar of barterers. Sellers. Moneylenders. Gamblers. Wheelers and dealers. Traders and merchants doing a brisk and profitable business. Much silver crossing many palms. Instead of a sacred shrine our temple was a scurrilous souk. Open for business. Every Pharisee of our town licking his lips at every purchase. Pharisees have made our temple into a den of thieves.

Fuck their hypocrisy!

I took my shift in hand and mounted those ignominious three steps. Passed under Micah's accusatory nose. Behind his shrunken shoulders. I climbed up over him. Strode to the nearest table.

And taking it surely in these woman's hands, I turned it over. Upsetting the contents and their owner. He leapt to collect his spilled coins and souvenir trinkets scattered across the stones, berating me the while with curses. Others leapt into the fray, shaking fists. Crying foul. Birds and beasts for purchase in their cages, awaiting temple sacrifice, set to bleating, braying and screeching. A horrible bestial orchestra fit for Sheol.

"Is this what Adonai had in mind when he bid you build this monument to his might?" I shouted over the tumult at Micah. "Do you think that he prefers this show of disgrace to my healing on the Sabbath?"

I turned to another table, that of a moneylender. "Before the temple of your God," I cried, "I curse your commerce!" And I tossed that one over, too.

I'd made my way through three or four and was setting a cageful of doves free when Anna-Andrew rushed towards me.

"Mama!" she hissed. "Get out of here!"

By then I'd caused quite a ripple. Other neighbours and acquaintances were busy at table tossing, it seemed. Obediah the beggar upturned the apple cart and took off with a hatful for his supper. One bright red orb rolled towards me.

I picked it up, though Anna-Andrew was doing her best to steer me away from the temple turmoil. Pulling free of her grasp, I took quick and steady aim. And hurled it at the now-befuddled Micah.

Mary of Nazareth is quite a good shot, I don't mind saying.

The apple hit Micah squarely on the side of his head. It knocked him over.

May it knock some sense into him.

I don't care that he's an old man. He's a nasty old man. May he have an earthquake in his skull.

Anna and I stole away. No one knows who threw the fruit at the old man.

Except you and me, Yahweh.

And we're not telling.

November 17

My dear Mary of Nazareth,

I will be travelling to your town before Hanukkah to seek your expertise about an inflammation I have been suffering. It is my hope that your grief is now past and that I will find you and yours well.

Caiaphas

P.S. I have heard some talk of your son. Jesus, is it?

I shudder at this latest from this priest who kisses like a tyrant. I try to remember that he is a holy man, but his postscript makes me nauseous.

Three weeks before Hanukkah

"I have heard that he champions the weak. That he preaches mercy and compassion. That we must turn the other cheek and love our enemies. That he receives sinners and eats with them."

"He is my son, Caiaphas."

"I have heard that he teaches on the Sabbath."

I thought of the apple and smiled. "There are those who need to hear his words every day of the week, just as there are ills to cure, mouths to feed, injustice to fight every day of the week."

"He is not a favourite of the Pharisees."

"No."

"Nor the Sadducees."

"No, I suppose not."

"In fact, I've heard that he says uncomplimentary words about us."

"All true."

"The words? Or that he says them?"

I stifled a chuckle. "Eve tells me the inflammation is better today. Our herbs are working their charm on you."

"Don't bedevil me with your charms, Mary of Nazareth. Don't think you can abort my purpose with riddles and woman's meandering from the point. I tell you these things about your boy out of concern for you. He must curb his tongue. Or trouble will follow."

"He's a man, not a boy. I can't stop him. Nor would I."

"I see the rod was spared such a child."

"You see very little, Caiaphas." You see as far as your nose and your own power permit. But I did not speak this last aloud.

"I see an attractive widow before me. One who should have a man in her life, but who has a willful, foolhardy boy, instead. A son I can protect."

"Protect?"

"From the wrath of the Sadducees and from the fist of Rome."

The doves cooed softly in the leaves above our heads.

"And your price?"

"I ask for little. Only that you permit me to visit you here in Nazareth. That you receive me as ... your visitor. Consider seriously my offer of marriage."

"And my son?"

"Will be safe, if he stops purporting to be the Messiah."

"The people call him that."

Caiaphas stepped closer to me. Took a wisp of my hair in his thick fingers.

"You should teach him the art of reticence, Mary of Nazareth."

I pulled away abruptly. "Why should I? It was never my way." And I left him sulking and sunning in the garden.

Jesus and Mary are travelling the shores of the Jordan River. Best they are not here to witness the manipulations of this man.

Today I send hasty word to Jeremiah, despite his two-year absence from my life. I can think of no one else to turn to. I wish, more than ever, that he and I were husband and wife so I could send this Caiaphas packing home to Jerusalem without false hope.

I have written a script. Like the great dramas of Scythopolis. Worthy of the pen of the tragedian Ezekiel. I have conceived a grand part for Jeremiah. I pray that he learns his lines quickly and well.

For I fear that if I openly rebuke Caiaphas, he will turn his power against my son.

Yet the thought of yielding to him brings bile to my mouth.

So a drama is all I can think of to put this Caiaphas off. Another conception. Another story. Another lie.

Hanukkah — Fifth Night

My heart is light as down.

Jeremiah arrived with a show. Oh, he was masterful! A retinue of servants, Mary with no tongue among them. Well-dressed and resplendent, Jeremiah burst in as my stage directions prompted. All of our patients took notice, Caiaphas among them.

"Joseph of Arimathea, come to fix my betrothal."

Before the gathered of Wellhouse he presented me with the wealthiest dowry I have ever seen or heard tell of. This was Jeremiah's embellishment of my script; I had suggested only a modest bride price. Perfumes of Arabia, silks spun far in the East, gold and silver coins in finely carven chests, intoxicating spices, a young camel. It was overwhelming.

And that golem, Caiaphas, was gape-mouthed.

"Mary of Nazareth, widow of Joseph the Carpenter. I offer these dowry gifts at the lighting of the first lamp of Hanukkah to seal my commitment to you. If you will have me."

Jeremiah-Joseph shimmered in his silk robes. His silver beard and hair gleamed in the candlelight. He dazzled me. Just as he did all those years ago. My heart longed to be his only Mary.

I recited my lines. "It would be an honour, Joseph of Arimathea, to be your wife. I accept your bride price."

"All here bear witness to this agreement?"

My Sisters, family, Wellhouse residents nodded or murmured their assent. On cue, Simon stepped forward to embrace "Joseph."

Delilah and Hannah prepared to lead Jeremiah and members of his retinue to spare quarters.

"I look forward to supper." And Jeremiah kissed my cheek.

Our scene finished, I looked for the missing Caiaphas, who was already packing to leave.

"Why did you not tell me of this man, this suitor?" Caiaphas' voice sounded squeezed.

"I could not presume that he would consider me worthy to be his wife."

"But you are not a stupid woman, Mary of Nazareth. You must have had an idea."

"An idea, yes."

"And you told me nothing. How long ... how long has this man been in your life?"

"He has been a family friend for many years. He knew my husband. Recently, Joseph of Arimathea's wife died." Although of course, Mary, Jeremiah's wife, still lives. "We ... reconnected you might say."

"I see." Caiaphas drew himself up to his full height, towering and glowering over me. His passion nearly choked him. "I am not an easy loser, Mary of Nazareth. I am ever grateful that you saved Joshua, and that you have cured my ailments on occasion. But do not think that I doubt I have been tricked. Do not think you are immune to me."

Caiaphas shoved me against the wall, crushing me with the weight of his body, of his words, of his mouth on mine. He fumbled with my garments, wrenching them above my waist, fingering me with his brute hands. I tried to break free, cry out, bite his lip. For the second time in my life, I was trapped by the force of a man. Terror beat at my breast.

Bathsheba beat at the door. She pushed it open. Immediately, Caiaphas fell away from me. I reassembled my clothes.

"What are you doing to Mary?" she demanded.

"Nothing. Get out."

"No. You, Caiaphas." My voice shook, but my resolve did not. "You, get out! From this house of healing. From my home. From my life!"

"Woman, I leave." He hoisted his pack over his shoulder. "Remember this day as you know I will. Be warned. The next time your son, your Jesus, steps within the walls of Jerusalem will be his last. Caiaphas has spoken." And he left.

The Sisters ministered to me. Jeremiah took me to his arms and to bed. Days have passed and the horror has subsided to a bad dream. Each dawn lifts my spirit. Each dawn, Jeremiah-Joseph shows no sign of leaving. I have prepared a room for him. Washed the curtains and linens. Rearranged the few pieces of furniture. Brought lilies to scent the air.

Tonight we light the fifth Hanukkah lamp together.

I know he will leave. But he intends to divide his time between his lives and wives. This he has promised me. Though I will never marry him in the eyes of Yahweh and the law, yet I will embrace him as mine, if not every night, many nights. It is a pledge we have made, each to the other. We will never again be long apart while we live.

Mary can have Jeremiah of Capernaum; Mary of Nazareth will have Joseph of Arimathea.

No more secrets in Wellhouse. The Sisters tiptoe past our room discreetly. My children, who have long known that I know this man, look the other way. I only wait to tell Jesus on his visit home next week.

We are free of Caiaphas.

Hanukkah — Eighth Night

The Feast of Lights draws to a close. My love slumbers. We have made love and love. The scent of love fills this room. The touch of love is everywhere upon my body.

I write at the window under the full winter moon.

My life is full as that moon.

For Hanukkah, my family and my Sisters were together. What greater blessing could there be at Mary's laden table? Beautiful Sol, Caleb, and my grandsons growing tall as bulrushes. Joses and Ester with Ira, my sweet newborn grandson. Juda, home from the Sea of Galilee, beside an attentive Dinah. Simon and Anna, back from their teaching in Sepphoris, seated beside handsome James, just returned from Tiberius. To my left, my beloved Jeremiah. At my right, Jesus and a radiant Mary el Mejdel. Izel beaming across the table at me. My Hanukkah guest and gift of a friend.

Phoebe served the figs, lingering long by Simon's place, while Bathsheba sweetly sang a familiar folksong. We all joined in the chorus. Spontaneously, Abigail, Hannah and Delilah began to dance as Lilith drummed. Soon all the women of Wellhouse were circling together. I held fast to Naomi's right hand and Eve's left. Laughter pealed as the pace quickened to Lilith's rumbling drum. Salome broke away in a singular dance and I followed her lead, twirling over to Jeremiah as once I had all those years ago.

Our song and our dancing ended. We collapsed on cushions, fanning our selves, jubilant from our exertion. Then the great family of Wellhouse were treated to a beautiful recitation by Sophia, talented in words, a poem of her own creation.

Purple night deepened to black. Our menorah lamps burned low. Wine cups emptied. With the last of the sweets consumed, the children were carried off to bed.

Silently, Jeremiah took my hand and I led him to our chamber. In the quiet, he slipped my clothes from my body and slipped into me. I shiver to recall. I shiver now again with desire.

So I will leave this stylus. This scroll. These words. And I will waken him.Together we will rise again. Our love a resurrection. Let him drink, let him taste Mary and be reborn in me.

Alleluia.

Purim

Since the Festival of Lights I have seen and heard my only begotten son speak to the multitudes three times. I understand why he so moves the populace. He brings tears to these mother's eyes. Could he make his mother prouder?

Jesus is an orator. A spinner of tales. A wise young man. His voice can be humble and gentle one minute, as he accounts for the children and the meek of this world. In the next, it shakes with wrath for the cruelties of the Romans, the greed of the Sadducees. His tone is waspish when he talks of the Pharisees, the scribes, the lawyers. Then he is weeping, we are all weeping, for the great beauty of this world, the possibility that is the human spirit, the human will to do better, to do good. Laced through it all is his love for the divine. The sacred. For you, Yahweh.

The family of Joseph and the Sisters of Wellhouse arrive early to get good seats on the hills beyond town. Soon other pilgrims traipse up the rise. Then others. By the appointed hour of Jesus' talk, people carpet the scrubby slope, straining their ears and shading their eyes to better hear and see the Messiah.

His beginning is a sigh. The spirit of one man becomes the collective sigh of all of us on the hill. Then the sigh becomes breeze, carried up and above our heads. A prayer on the wind. The wind that travels throughout all of Judea and this land that was to be for your Chosen, Yahweh. A whirling, swirling tempest of hope and longing, borne of grief and suffering, circling above that river of milk and honey up into your heaven, up to your ears. Cycling and swivelling back down again to rest upon the breeze-tossed hair of my son. Jesus.

He tells us about the mighty who will fall. The sick who will be made well. He begs for compassion for the poor, the meek, the grief-stricken. The hungry, the thirsty, the persecuted. He praises the pure of heart, the merciful, the peacemakers. He promises a better time to come. Asks us to forgive wrongdoers, those who hurt us. To set an example for each other. He chides us for our material desires, our covetousness, our needless, useless worries. Urges instead that we think beyond our petty selves, that we give alms, that we help the unfortunates of this world. He asks us not to judge or be hypocrites in our lives or our prayers. That we treat our neighbours as we would hope to be treated. With grace. With kindness.

Jesus' words hover above our heads as he finishes.

Then someone calls out, "Blessed is the womb that carried you, and the breast that nursed you."

"Indeed," my son responds, "blessed is she. Blessed are women."

A man yells, "Every day I thank God that I was not born a woman."

And Jesus replies, "You are wrong, friend. And your ignorance wrongs both women and God. Ignorance is a slave; knowledge is freedom. Women are great in knowledge. In woman grows the fruit of truth. If we are joined to her truth, there will be fulfillment."

"Where is your mother? Your family? Your father?"

"My father is in Olam Haba. My mother?" Jesus scans the crowd. He sees me and smiles. "My mother and my brothers and sisters are those who hear the divine word and live it."

He is such a nice boy. What can I say?

Part Eight

Lacrimosa

They say many things about that day. They tell tales about the weather. About the signs. About what you said. Many untruths. Many stupid things.

Ah, my son, my son.

Eight months grieving have not removed your face from my dreams.

They took you down from that wretched cross. Mary said I spat upon the Roman guard who tried to drag away your body. Said I cursed him. The men backed away, reviled. I do not remember. I only remember cradling you in my arms, on my lap, as I did all those years ago when you were a babe. Your eyes were dead. I closed them and wept and rocked. I wept for your father and your father and your father. I wept for myself. I wept for the world. I wept for the two other dead whose mothers were not there to weep for them. I wept for all mothers. I wept for Mary el Mejdel. I wept for loss of you.

Ah, my son, my son. My young and beautiful man. What were you thinking? I know. That you could change the world. That you could change their minds. That you could change them.

You should be here now with me, with Mary. She is great with your child and great with grief. We miss you so.

Somehow we got away, all of us, with you from that place of skulls.

Then we bathed and anointed your body. Mother and wife. You the infant. We washed away the shit and piss of your suffering. Removed that horrible crown of lies. Cleansed the still weeping wounds. Kissed your cold lips. We wrapped you in swaddling, we two. Only then did the others carry you to the tomb. We women walked behind as always, our work being done.

The last time I saw you alive and well, you were jesting as you raided the larder again. And the wine cellar. That was the night we prepared a great feast for your repast with the boys in the Garden of Gethsemene. Do you remember? Mary and Mary cooking. You teasing. Snitching bites. I made you leave the kitchen before you got hair in the matzah dough. Now all I have is a dead clipping of that hair. I saw the sadness around your eyes even then. Why could you not stop and save yourself?

My son, I have been very angry at you. I have cursed you for what you've done to this mother's heart. I have beat my pillow many nights wishing it were your face. I have screamed. Ripped my hair. Torn my flesh.

But I have done now. I have turned my rage elsewhere. I will never stop being angry. But no longer at you, my beautiful son.

Peter came to the house last month. I threw him out. None of those boys, not a one, defended you. I have done with them. They go about talking miracles and visions since your death. Reciting your final words. Writing it all down like big important men. Claim they have pieces of your shroud, of your cross.

Cowards. Liars.

There are no pieces of your cross; Mary and I set it aflame. Nothing left but ash.

As for your shroud, it lies with you still. Intact. Not a thread missing.

I know.

Oh, there was much ado about your empty tomb.

Fools.

If they could see farther than their stupid noses.

Did they really think I would leave you to them? Those vultures?

But there is much to be gained for the Movement if they treat your disappearance as a miracle. The Movement. If you could hear and see what is being said and done in your name …

The Movement claims you are the Son of God. They evoke the names of angels. Speak in hushed tones of your resurrection, your ascension. It all smacks of power-and-glory hunger.

I don't know whether to laugh or vomit.

Mary and I visit your sepulchre when we can. Jeremiah, too. I hope you are at peace.

I look for ways to go on. I bury myself in my lifework. The Eastern Star has been a great comfort. Our circle of women, as ever, surround me with love and solace. Just yesterday Sol, Mary and I delivered a baby boy. It was a difficult birth. The mother was very brave. When he was at last released and squawling healthily, we three midwives looked at one another beholding the possibility that is life.

Very soon we will behold another new life in your own child. I will be again grandmother and midwife. Mary's time grows near. Her pregnancy has been a trial. For so many reasons. But she is well. We dare to think her baby will live. Together, we will raise a fatherless child. Still, the thought of meeting your son or daughter gives me a kind of peace. Joy.

I have had several such moments. And I must admit that I begin to smile, even to laugh. I try not to think I am betraying you. That in daring happiness, I forget you. Absurd. But that is a mother's heart. I know you want me to laugh. We laughed together a great deal, you and I.

You were never an easy son. That Messiah stuff went to your head. But you were a good son. A good man. A very good man.

Ah, my son, my son. So much was wasted. For what?

My bitterness again. I hate so many for what they did to you. For what Judas did.

Judas. The birds pecked at his corpse until there was nothing left but the silver that fell from his pockets.

Herod? Suffering badly of gout. Pilate? A mysterious ailment. He is covered with painful pustules, head to toe. Caiaphas died of asphyxiation in his own cold bed. Curious.

The Pharisees and the Sadducees are doddering idiots who will die like their fathers before them. And they will be replaced by other idiots. Other tyrants equally intolerant.

And what of Yahweh? By all reports he is doing well. He doesn't say much to me, Mary, his disavowed handmaiden. He didn't intervene on your behalf. After all you did in his name. God is an ingrate.

Of course, I bear much guilt in all of this. It was I who began the lie thirty-some years ago. Your death is my penance.

Your final word reft my heart.

"Mary?"

And I, at last, could do nothing. Neither will, nor write death away.

My son, my son.

Jesus.

Loss of you will never from my heart.

PART NINE

Sophia

The journey frightens me. If I were fourteen and stupid, I would be excited. Stupidity is liberating. But I am very far from fourteen. My hair is white. And I am very far from stupid.

And Ephesus is very far from Nazareth.

My feet are not what they used to be. I must take medicine for my many aches. My eyesight is dimming. And this old lady's bladder. Such a bother.

But these are excuses. I don't want to go. I don't. I want to stay here comfortably in my old age. With my family. My grandchildren.

And I am afraid.

I am afraid that I will never see their beautiful faces or Nazareth again. That I will never walk the cool halls of Wellhouse, or bathe and pray in her waters.

I am afraid I will die in that foreign place.

I am afraid of death.

Yahweh knows why. Old people are supposed to be used to the idea already. Supposed to be getting ready. Ha! Not Mary of Nazareth. She is not ready to die.

And I guess that is why I make this journey, after all. I'm not dead. I'm very much alive, despite some of the shortcomings of my body. Still vital.

Maybe I'll meet a man. Take a lover. Some young, foolish gull. Never thought of that.

Yes, I'm alive. And spitting mad! At that self-proclaimed maven Saul. Paul. Whatever he calls himself. Spokesman of the Movement! I need to teach that boy a thing or two. He is attributing all sorts of things to Jesus.

Yes, yes. Some things I can understand. Admit to. Nod at. I can even respect his admiration of my son. I can tolerate much of what he says about the goodness, the godness, that lived in Jesus.

But!

I do not and cannot and will not tolerate what he has been saying in my son's name about women. About those, like Anna, who love others of the same sex. About sex. The man is a freak!

I also must set him straight about that Son of Yahweh stuff. If I can, that is. Paul doesn't much like to listen. Except to himself. Or when heavenly voices blast.

He certainly hasn't listened or responded to a single letter I've written to him. Me, the mother of the man he professes to know so well! For a reputedly prolific letter-writer, Paul is a lousy correspondent.

Neither did he speak with me when he, Peter and James met with the apostles at their fancy council in Jerusalem. Didn't have time for Jesus' most beloved disciple, Mary, or his mother. Dismissed what we had to say. Bid us be quiet in the temple. Cover our heads.

So the girls and I need to get to Ephesus and give Paul a good finger-wagging. And we intend to stay put until he listens. Stops clamouring like a cymbal, clanging like a gong, long enough to hear what we have to say about Jesus, his charity, love, agape.

The girls. Mary el Mejdel, now past her prime of life. Phoebe, wife of my Simon. And the light of my life, my granddaughter, Priscilla. Jesus' only child. Now a young woman.

She has the look of her father. The eyes. The smile. There is some of her mother in her, too. And a little too much of her grandmother. But then again, maybe it is her father I see. Jesus. My son in the daughter.

Or maybe it is all the wishful thinking of an old woman.

I cannot believe that he is dead so long. His unborn infant now a grown woman. Where are those years? I turned my face away, then looked up, and they were gone.

Oh, I know the years were busy. With living on after Jesus. With helping Mary el Mejdel to term and through a difficult delivery: we almost lost her. Then with child-rearing. Simon and Phoebe's marriage. Sol's children. Caleb's long illness and recovery. The birth of Joses' children: Thomas, Elizabeth, and Jacob. Juda's sons, Mark, Isaac, and Seth after Ira. Anna's wanderings and heartbreaks, her finally settling down with Beth here in Wellhouse.

Women. The mortar of my life. My Sisters of Wellhouse, coming, going. Women of the Eastern Star. Ordinary women who needed midwives. Desperate women who needed abortions. Injured women whose limbs needed healing. Broken women whose lives needed mending. And their children lost, suffering, abandoned, damaged, dying, cold, hungry, empty. Women giving love. Much love and much giving. And as always at Wellhouse, work and reward. Life and death.

My little sister, Deborah, died last year. I still shake my head in wonder. One shouldn't outlive one's younger sibling. Yet I endure. Now Sam, Ruth, Joanna and I remain of the house of Anna and Joachim. I miss Deborah and wish I could talk with her still. I will miss her family while I am in Ephesus.

I will miss them all.

I will miss my life. This good life. In this good place.

My town. My people. My hills. My bearings. My place. My life. My livelihood.

Despite so much pain and loss. Because of pain and loss, too, this has been a good life.

I roll up the scroll. Will I open another? Take up the stylus again in the city of Ephesus in the shadow of the Temple of Artemis? I wonder about that goddess. So reviled by the Jews and the Movement. What are they all so afraid of? Her many breasts? I'm told she has hundreds, but men have always loved breasts. So why should they fear a multitude? Perhaps they are afraid they will drown in her milk, in her mother power. What do I know? I look forward to looking on her face, even if she is a graven image. I like the idea of a she-god. Yahweh, you should take a wife. Maybe you would soften towards us, your children. Israel could use a mother, these days.

Jesus' death did nothing to still the talk of rebellion. The open hatred between and within factions. The surging hatred of Rome.

My son was no hatemonger.

He would have been better alive than dead. I can't see what good is going to come from this Movement in his name. Already there have been persecutions of his followers. My instinct tells me that more atrocities will be committed. In the name of Christ. Whoever he is. I shudder to think.

So the Christians have their Christ. And the Jews keep longing for the Messiah. And the Romans have a pantheon of gods to assure them that they are divinely chosen to oppress and rule Israel.

And I? I have this sweet-smelling grass on which I rest my bony bottom. These flowers and herbs that render medicines. The beautiful hills around our town. In quiet times like this I steal away and remember the beauty of the Sea of Galilee. Her power. Her abundance. The song of her waves. And I feel the sun warming the creases of my face. The wind playing at my ear. I breathe, and I feel a song rise to my throat. A prayer I offer to the day. Another day I get to live. To watch the goats and young shepherd kicking up to the crest of the hill. The children at play in the village, or my garden, or my daughter's home. To hear the voice of Simon singing in the dusk or Priscilla laughing. To remember my beloved friends and family. Joseph. Mama and Papa. Bubeh and Zaydeh. Izel. Jez. Jeremiah. Jesus, my beautiful, lost son.

I feel your presence, sometimes look up expecting to see you sitting across from me, anticipating your embrace. After all these years, the lack of you still makes me weep with abandon and grief. When the tears stop, sometimes a warmth steals across my heart and into my bones. I like to think it is your warmth, never gone. Never extinguished. An eternal flame. You are not gone. Your spirit lives in me. In Mary. In the many lives you touched. In your precious child. In this air I breathe.

That is when I am strong. Those days when I believe.

But there are many when I don't. When I stare into the abyss of this life and the end of it and see only the utter uselessness of your dying so young. When I think that your body has mouldered away to dust, where I, too, shall soon return. My life, though longer, will it have more or less meaning than did yours? In five generations will my great-great-great-grandchildren even remember my name? Who I was? Who I am?

I write these things so that, maybe, they will. So that maybe this story of my life will not be forgotten. I will seal my words in a jar. I have so many scrolls similarly stored deep in Wellhouse. Scrolls about birth and death. About killing a man. Rescuing a woman. Saving a son. Watching him die. Maybe someday daughters of my granddaughter will read, laugh at my follies, learn from my terrible mistakes. Maybe they will recognize themselves in my youth, in my spirit, and think well of Mary of Nazareth. Maybe, by then, they will be free to write and think and act, and they, too, will have marvelous stories of their own to tell. To remember. To keep alive the spirit of woman and of being a woman in a man's world.

A man's world. It is a marvel that so many years I have worked my woman's work in a man's world. So many incarnations. Healer. Teacher. Mother. Wife. Lover.

Jeremiah. His name still rises quick to my lips. I lift my face to the evening stars and wish him goodnight, wherever he is, wherever his spirit resides. If it does.

It was hard after Jesus. It is hard to lose a child and carry on loving. So much attention must be given just to keep breathing through the pain. But we managed. Somehow. He in his quiet way. I in my busy way. We made a great deal of love, and not much of talk. Jeremiah, my balm between the bedlinen. As we started, we ended.

He died at home with Mary. The other one. The wife. Mary with no tongue brought the silent news. I had only to look in her face to know.

I do not know where he is buried. I do not know if his wife still lives. Mary with no tongue never came to Wellhouse again.

I do know that one grief becomes another becomes another until they all well up into one great aching of love and loss and nostalgia and wishing for another hour together. Another five minutes. Another thirty seconds to say what we didn't say. What we should have. What we forgot to say. Or to just hold onto each other, to hold onto what we love and never, never let go.

Growing old is lonely. No one told me that. Not Mama. Not Bubeh. Not Joseph. Not even Jeremiah. You miss everyone so.

What moment would I seize upon if I could freeze time? The day of Jesus' marriage? A moment at the Sea of Galilee? The second I first loved Jeremiah?

But if we stopped time? There would be no Priscilla dancing along the curve of the road, coming to find me this very moment. There wouldn't be this leap in my heart at the thought of her and me, her mother and Phoebe going off on a grand adventure together.

Maybe I do have time for another story, even at this late hour in my life.

It is time to let this ink dry. Collect my wits and the rest of my herbs. Get home to packing. Put this scroll safely away.

One last thing ...

Yahweh. I have known many blessings. Much love. Love surrounds me. Buoys me. Drives me onward. Love is the best theme of my life. Thank you for this love.

I don't understand you, Yahweh. I don't believe in you. But I forgive you.

More Fine Fiction from Sumach Press ...

• River Reel
A Novel by Bonnie Laing

• Revising Romance
A Novel by Melanie Dugan

• Roads Unravelling
Short Stories by Kathy-Diane Leveille

• Gifts: Poems for Parents
Edited by Rhea Tregebov

• Outskirts:
Women Writing from Small Places
Edited by Emily Schultz

• Aurat Durbar:
Writings by Women of South Asian Origin
Edited by Fauzia Rafiq

• Cast a Long Shadow
A Novel by Leena Lander

• The Middle Children
Short Fiction by Rayda Jacobs

• Penny Maybe
A Novel by Kathleen Martin

• The Other Side
A Novel by Cynthia Holz

• The Y Chromosome
Speculative Fiction by Leona Gom

• Grizzly Lies
A Mystery Novel by Eileen Coughlan

• Just Murder
A Mystery Novel by Jan Rehner
Winner of the 2004 Arthur Ellis Award
for Best First Crime Novel

• Hating gladys
A Suspense Novel by Leona Gom

• Masterpiece of Deception
An Art Mystery by Judy Lester

• Freeze Frame
Mystery Fiction by Leona Gom

Find out more at www.sumachpress.com